HIS FROZEN HEART
A ROCKY POINT WEDDING BOOK ONE

VANIA RHEAULT

✽ Created with Vellum

ABOUT THE BOOK

Mitch has given up on love . . . until he meets her.

Burned in a horrific accident, he never believed he could find a woman who would see past his scars.

But she makes him face more than just his fears of a broken heart. Is he brave enough to do what it takes to keep her love?

Callie hides her secrets . . . she's afraid if Mitch discovers them, he won't want her.

When their relationship turns too hot to handle, she'll have to decide if it's time to fight fire with fire, or if it's time to walk away before she gets burned.

CHAPTER ONE

"**Y**ou're here!"

Callie Carter tugged her suitcase into the Rocky Point Resort's lobby as Marnie Zimmerman, the bride-to-be and Callie's best friend, shrieked across the room making several people stare, a little old lady grin, and Callie laugh.

"I told you I would be, but my dad didn't make it easy," Callie said, easing her suitcase to a stop in front of the registration desk and setting her purse on the counter next to a display of resort brochures.

Marnie frowned and shoved her fists onto her ample hips. "You deserve a break. You work too hard."

"No one knows that better than me. I had the time coming, and there wasn't anything he could do about it."

Her father didn't believe in taking a break. Horace "Ace" Carter didn't believe in downtime. Rest. Taking care of her emotional health, her physical health. He believed in getting the job done, no matter the cost. And for the past eight years, she had. But rubber bands, stretched too tightly, eventually snap, and she was almost there.

"I'll make sure you have fun . . ." Marnie said, linking

her arm through hers while the front desk agent ran her credit card and handed her a small stack of papers.

"Here's your key, Miss Carter," the agent—her nametag read Sophia—said, giving her an honest-to-goodness key attached to a maroon keychain that had the gold Rocky Point Resort logo stamped into the plastic. "You're in room 231, next door to Marnie and James."

". . . Starting tonight," Marnie finished.

She untangled her arm from Marnie's and pulled her suitcase behind her. She'd left a few dresses hanging in her car, but she'd go back for those later. "What's tonight?"

"I planned a get-to-know-you dinner. Jared's picking up Leah in Marengo, and she'll be here later this afternoon. I can't wait for you to meet her. Hell, I can't wait to meet her!"

"You're positively giddy," she said, laughing. She stopped at the base of the set of stairs that would take them to the second floor. Purse hanging from the crook of her elbow, she hugged Marnie. "I'm happy for you."

Marnie hugged her back so hard her spine cracked. "I *am* happy, and I'm happy you could be here."

"I wouldn't have missed it."

She was honored Marnie asked her to be a bridesmaid, and she hadn't thought for a second about saying no.

Standing outside Callie's door, Marnie said, "I know you want time for yourself after that long drive. Take a nap, order a bottle of champagne, whatever you want. We're meeting downstairs for dinner, and I'll introduce you to everyone then. I'm so excited!"

Marnie's platinum blonde hair shimmered in the fluorescent lights, her pin curls, red lipstick, and clear skin giving her a Marilyn Monroe glow. She even had the curves to go with it, and she'd always envied Marnie her softness.

Callie worked out seven days a week, three-hundred and sixty-five days a year. She had to. It was part of her job. Speaking of . . . she might be on vacation, but she still needed to work out. "You said the resort has a fitness center?"

"Yep," Marnie said. "It's downstairs by the pool. It's not as big as the set up in your basement, but it will work."

"Thanks. I'll see you tonight, then."

"Sounds good. I'm so glad you're here!" Marnie hugged her again and hurried down the hallway.

Smiling, she shook her head.

She let herself into her room and shoved her suitcase into the closet. The room smelled like any hotel room she'd ever stayed in: air freshener and recycled air.

A huge gift basket sat on a table tucked under the window that overlooked a thick swatch of trees. A brochure the resort supplied said there were woods to the west, the lake to the north, ski slopes on the east side of the building, and the town of Rocky Point to the south. She leaned against the table and skimmed the brochure. The resort offered quite a few amenities. Maybe she'd try her hand at skiing while she was here.

In the bathroom, she washed her face and dried her skin with a bleached white hand towel. She hung it back on the bar and frowned at the water pooling at the bottom of the bowl. "That's great," she muttered.

She needed a working sink. If all the pipes were connected, the bathtub might be affected too, and she wanted to be able to shower in the morning. Or tonight after dinner.

Using the phone on the nightstand, she called the front desk. "I need maintenance." It wasn't that late in the day, and she hoped someone would be able to come by her room soon. "My sink's plugged and won't drain."

She recognized Sophia's voice. "We'll have Mitch up there right away."

"Thank you."

She should've asked to be transferred to room service. Marnie's suggestion she order a bottle of champagne sounded better and better, but she didn't bother calling back.

Even though she was on vacation, she shouldn't drink too much. Her father told her she needed to be in control at all times. What if someone needed her? He always had an example at the ready of a time when he'd been able to help someone.

Service was a calling, and, unfortunately, it wasn't room service.

Ace Carter spoke of their occupation as if they were ministers or missionaries.

He expected her to behave as such.

Someone knocked on her door, and she pushed the heavy thoughts away. This was supposed to be a vacation, and it wouldn't feel like one if all she did was worry about her job and what her dad thought of her. She'd fought hard for the time and won, and she needed to make the best of it.

She opened the door expecting an older man, balding, wearing a t-shirt and stained overalls carrying a battered red toolbox, and she blinked in surprise at the man only a few years older than her standing in the hallway.

Her gaze traveled from his dark brown hair to his green eyes, over his strong nose to his chapped lips. Slim but strong with the way he carried an enormous toolbox, that was, actually, red.

He shifted slightly, and asked, "Did you need maintenance?"

She flinched and hid a gasp behind her hand.

The skin on the right side of his face was a mottled different shades of pink, shiny smooth in places, puckered in others.

Through the crackling of heat in her ears, her mind whispered, *fire*.

Mitch was used to the stares, the stunned silences, the pity and the sneers. He'd become numb to it, and he ignored her widened eyes and the shocked gasp when she saw the right side of his face. The scar started at the top of his hairline and rippled down his temple and cheek, across his jaw, and into the neckline of his work t-shirt. It spread farther than that, but besides doctors and nurses, few had seen it, and Mitch intended to keep it that way.

"Maintenance?" he asked again.

She moved her hand away from her mouth. "Y-yes. The sink in the bathroom won't drain."

"I'll take a look."

She didn't step aside and he reached out to nudge her away from the door, but she shrank back.

So, she was going to be like that. When he'd taken the job, the manager of the resort, Desiree Arnold, told him not to put himself into situations that could cause trouble for either the guest or himself. If he felt the need to have someone with him while he did repairs, then that's the way it would be. Desiree hadn't brought up his scars at all, but he didn't need her to point out the obvious. He looked a hell of a lot scarier with his scars than he'd look without them.

"Would you like me to call Sophia at the front desk and ask her to sit with you while I fix your sink? Or would you like to go to the bar and have a drink while you wait? It'd be on the house." He carried vouchers in his toolbox to offer guests who weren't comfortable being alone with him. A free drink to encourage them to wait elsewhere so he could work in peace.

No one turned down free drinks, and her refusal surprised him.

"No, it's fine. I'm sorry. You took me off guard."

"I usually do that to people," he said mildly, stepping into her room. Before he shut the door, he asked, "Are you sure?"

The question brought him back to the last time he'd tried to make love to a woman. She'd been adamant she could handle his scars.

It turned out she couldn't, and he'd never tried again.

She nodded. "I'm fine. I, ah, washed my face, and the water didn't go down."

"Sounds like an easy fix." He'd spent the past seven years as the resort's maintenance man, drawing on his own experiences helping his dad fix things around their house. Desiree, who'd been in an unexpected jam when the previous maintenance man suffered a heart attack, hired him on the spot, making it clear it was probationary.

But there hadn't been anything in the resort he couldn't repair. His three-month tryout ended with a pay increase and a small room furnished with a bed and barebones kitchenette. He wasn't required to stay there, but Desiree liked having on-site maintenance twenty-four/seven and he didn't have anything else to do.

Last month Desiree told him that several of his old classmates would be trickling in for Marnie Zimmerman's wedding and they'd be filling the resort for two weeks' worth of wedding events. At the time he wondered why she bothered to say anything. It wasn't like he'd never worked with a full resort before. Desiree and her sales manager hustled to keep the rooms full all year round.

It was only after, while he thought about their conversation over a tuna sandwich, that he realized what she'd been getting at.

He didn't recognize this one, though. She hadn't graduated from Rocky Point. He would've remembered.

The sink was a normal hotel sink, bright lights fastened to the wall above the mirror, and the vanity was next to the toilet which was across from the tub and shower. He hunkered down on the floor with his toolbox and removed the extra toilet paper, a box of Kleenex, and a hairdryer from the cabinet to reach the pipes.

He hadn't brought a bucket, and he shoved the wastebasket under the pipe to catch the water as he removed it.

The brunette had disappeared and he worked in silence.

The culprit of the clog was a wad of hair and a delicate diamond ring.

Satisfied that fixed the problem, he cleaned up. Dirty water filled the wastebasket forcing him to take it with him. He couldn't empty it in her bathtub or sink. Desiree hired only the best housekeepers, and Sophia said this woman hadn't been in her room long. If she would've gone to the bar he could have dumped the water and cleaned up after himself, but he wouldn't do it now.

"I'll have housekeeping bring you another wastebasket for the bathroom. I'm sorry I had to use this one."

She laid on the king-sized bed staring at the ceiling. "Did you find out what was clogging the sink?"

"Yeah." Free of dirt and hair, the ring sparkled, a platinum setting showcasing the modest diamond. "Did you lose a ring?"

"No. Can I see it?"

He shrugged. He didn't know why not. He'd only take it to the registration desk where they would research the history of the room and ask if anyone lost a ring recently. If they couldn't find anyone who had, the ring would sit in the safe as part of their lost and found.

She rolled off the bed, and without the slightest hesitation, held out her hand. He dropped the ring into her palm.

Sliding the ring on and admiring the sparkle, she said, "I would be freaked out if I lost something like this."

"I wouldn't buy something like this," he said. He caught the bitterness in his tone and pursed his lips.

Startled, her gaze met his. "You don't want to get married?"

He wiggled the ring off her finger, his skin brushing hers.

The way she looked at him, like she didn't see the scars, not once she moved past her initial reaction, made him think that maybe one day he could find a woman who could see beyond his injury.

He scoffed.

Yeah, when pigs flew.

"I learned a long time ago women want Mr. Perfect, and I have never been, nor will I ever be, that kind of man. Have a good afternoon, miss, and enjoy your stay."

Outside her room, he dropped his toolbox on the floor with a loud clatter and hugged the wastebasket stinking of dirty water close to his chest.

Closing his eyes, he tried to forget about hers.

"I'm off the clock," Desiree said before Mitch could even step inside her office.

"You're never off the clock."

She smiled, red lipstick coating her lush lips. Her eyes, so brown they appeared black, matched her skin and made the white blouse she wore pop in contrast. "Neither are you."

He lifted a shoulder. "Nothing to report," he said, beginning a basic rundown of his day. She said she didn't need this, but as the years went on, they'd settled into a comfortable routine.

He slouched in a chair in front of her desk. "A plugged-up sink with a ring that went to lost and found. One of the dryers in housekeeping is starting to lose heat, but I don't have the part. I ordered it earlier. Hopefully it will come before Carmen has to stop using it altogether."

"How's the pool? Marnie Zimmerman asked if it could be closed off one night for her wedding guests. I hate doing it because it puts the other guests at a disadvantage. I'm making her pay a rental fee, and she'll only have it to herself for two hours. If the pool's having issues, can you check into it before Monday?" She tapped her pen against her blotter.

"It's been fine, but I'll check over the pumps and pH levels again." He did that every day, but Desiree had her own responsibilities and didn't look over his shoulder.

He paused. If he asked, she'd never let him live it down, but all afternoon he thought of the brunette who had actually looked into his eyes while he spoke to her about the lost ring.

"What?" Her shrewd gaze zeroed in on his. "You want to ask me something."

He rubbed his fingers over the slippery scar tissue along his neck. "I feel sorry for your kid. You know everything." He weighed his options. Ask, and open himself up to teasing, or not ask, and not know. What the hell. "The woman in 231. Who is she?"

She smiled in delight. "You like her."

"She didn't look at me like I was a freak show. It's a first," he muttered. "I want to, ah . . ." He didn't know what he wanted past her name. Ask her out on a date? Yeah, right.

"No one thinks that," she said as her fingernails clicked against her computer's keyboard. "I'm looking up our reservations. Here she is, Callista Carter. The scan of her driver's license says she lives in Decatur. She's part of the wedding. Her room's blocked out under the code we gave Marnie's discount."

"Thanks." He stood. "Anything else?"

She shook her head. "Nope. Heading home soon."

"See you in the morning. Have a good night."

"You too."

Mitch ambled to his room that was located in the back of the resort near the pool and electrical room. His sleeping room doubled as his office and a large desk took up a quarter of the small space.

For everyone else, the weight of the day would slip off about now. The workday done, time to relax. Not for Mitch. This was the part of the day where he felt out of sorts, lonely, and tense with feelings he couldn't describe. He didn't have plans. He didn't date. He didn't have friends besides Desiree, though they didn't hang out in a social capacity, and Ivy, a bartender in the lounge. Every once in a while he'd grab lunch with one of them in the dining room. Sometimes Desiree had ideas and plans to go over with him or Ivy wanted a change of scenery from his room or the kitchen.

No, evenings meant eating dinner alone, watching TV, and going to bed early. Sometimes he sat in the lounge and people-watched while he sipped on a beer. Or he talked to Ivy, if she had time. Desiree said she didn't mind if he kept it to a minimum, and he'd taken to doing it maybe twice a week.

He'd do it tonight and keep an eye out for her. The brunette. Callista.

While he sat near the fireplace and watched the fire burn.

Callie dressed for Marnie's meet and greet in a green dress overlaid with black velvet flowers. Spaghetti straps rested on her shoulders, but they weren't what kept her dress in place. No, that honor belonged to her 36Cs. No matter how much she worked out, she could never lose weight in her boobs. She tolerated the teasing— after all, she did work in a male-dominated occupation—but deep down, she was proud of her girls and the way they filled out her clothes.

A little cleavage never hurt anyone.

A small patch of skin on her left arm glistened pink under the lights and matched the maintenance man's scar that covered the right side of his face.

It never ceased to amaze her how something so beautiful could be so deadly.

She rarely thought about her scar, and swatting away the thought after the brief glance at her arm, she grabbed her purse and headed toward the room Marnie reserved for dinner.

Tonight she'd meet everyone in the wedding party, Marnie's parents, whom she had a few times already when they visited their daughter in Decatur, and she'd see James, Marnie's fiancé. Meet *his* parents. She'd heard about Autumn, one of the other bridesmaids, and Leah, the woman Marnie worked with. Maybe she'd make some friends, though it wouldn't do her much good. She didn't have time to hang out.

She passed groups of people in the hallways, children wearing their swimsuits and racing in the direction of the pool. A couple wore thick winter clothing, and she heard them chattering excitedly about a moonlit cross-country ski run.

That sounds like fun, she thought as she followed the gold engraved plaques attached to the walls, guiding guests to where they needed to go. Maybe she would ski, too. She'd looked over Marnie's schedule of events and she'd have plenty of time to herself.

Voices floated to her before she reached the room and warily, she peered around the doorjamb.

"There you are!" Marnie said, racing across the carpet and grabbing her arm. "Did you have a nice afternoon?"

She opened her mouth to answer, but Marnie said, "Wait! Drink first."

Numerous times she'd teased Marnie about her love of Prosecco. *Was every day a celebration?* she'd ask, groaning. *Of course*, Marnie would always reply, *I woke up, didn't I?*

Nothing had ever gone wrong for Marnie Zimmerman, as far as Callie could tell. Good job, hot, rich fiancé. Parents who supported her no matter what she wanted to do. Popular in high school, if the pompoms Marnie kept as a souvenir were any indication.

But she couldn't begrudge Marnie a thing because she was so freaking nice.

Holding their glasses, they settled at an empty table. A server started setting out breadbaskets.

"Tell me what you did this afternoon." Marnie's gaze darted around the room.

"You don't have to babysit me," she said. "You can mingle."

Marnie poked her. "I'm mingling with you. You're always at work, and I've been looking forward to this. I'm going to make sure we have a blast!"

"Thank you for asking me to be a bridesmaid." Callie squeezed her arm.

Her excited expression softened. "There's no one else I would have asked."

"Tell me who everyone is," Callie said, then sipped her champagne. It wasn't any wonder why Marnie loved it. The wine fizzed, and after a couple of sips, so did her blood.

"You know James," Marnie began, pointing a red-tipped finger across the room at two men hunched over a cell phone. "That's Jared Hollister, he's James's friend from high school. They're watching the Viking's game, but pretty soon I'm going to tell them to knock it off. I can't believe my dad isn't over there. You know my parents. Leah's in the corner, hiding. I feel bad. I haven't been able to talk to her much. But do you see Jared? He keeps looking at her like no one's going to notice." Marnie giggled. "Autumn isn't here yet, but neither is Cole. Those two are a match made in heaven, you mark my words. They're going to cover my wedding for the newspaper's blog. There's Logan, talking to James's parents. You've met him too, right?"

She nodded. James and Logan clerked at the same law firm after they graduated, and a few years ago, they opened their own practice. She met him when he and James stopped by Marnie's place.

"He's not happy being home," Marnie whispered.

"Why?"

"He doesn't get along with his family and he didn't want to come back to Rocky Point. It's a big favor to James that he's here."

"That's too bad." It *was* too bad when people didn't get along with their families.

It wasn't that she didn't get along with hers, but she could be honest with herself, at least, and admit that a break from her father was welcome.

At her insistence, Marnie left her to sit alone while she played hostess, but she didn't mind. Marnie's mother came over and sat with her, and when the waitstaff served dinner, Callie's table companions included her in their conversation about winter activities.

Ice fishing didn't sound appealing, but she'd give anything a try. She hadn't had a vacation in forever and she'd take every opportunity to have a good time.

Everyone was eating dessert and sipping coffee, but she was debating heading back to her room to soak in a bubble bath when a slim woman wearing a navy cocktail dress slid into the seat next to her. "Callie. I'm sorry I haven't been able to get to you until now. I'm Autumn Bennett. Nice to meet you."

The blonde held out her hand, and Callie shook it firmly. She'd never been a woman to do a wimpy handhold in lieu of a good handshake. Her father said it made women appear weak, and over time, she'd come to enjoy the slight surprise from people in response to her strength.

Autumn didn't ruffle, only wiggled an iPad out of her purse that had a detachable keyboard. "I write for the *Rocky Point Daily Journal*. You won't mind if I interview you for the blog, will you?"

"No," she said. "Marnie warned me you'd want to ask me a few things."

Laughing, Autumn asked, "Warned? I'm hardly that bad. But I *am* nosey. I'm a reporter. I wouldn't be good at my job if I wasn't."

She tilted her head in agreement. "What do you want to know?"

Autumn opened a document that contained a list of numbered questions. "I'll ask you what I'm asking everyone else. This part of the blog series is about getting to know Marnie's wedding party."

"Who's going to interview you? Marnie said you're a bridesmaid as well?"

She parted her lips, then stopped. "Well, I guess I can interview myself."

Callie *tsked*. "That's no fun. You should let Marnie do it."

"That's a great idea! Okay, let's get started. I don't want to take up too much of your time. How do you know Marnie?"

"We share a wall of a townhouse complex in Decatur. So, I guess you can say we're neighbors. We got to talking one day when we were both doing yard work, and before I knew it, we were friends."

Autumn smiled. "Marnie's like that. She could make friends with a tree stump."

"Yeah, she could." She sipped her coffee.

"What do you do for a living?"

"I'm a firefighter."

Autumn widened her eyes in surprise. "That's right. I remember Marnie saying something about that. Wow. That sounds dangerous."

"We see fewer fires than you might think. I've been involved in only a handful in my time at the department, but they were bad ones. A lot of it is training, keeping in shape, checking smoke alarms, that kind of thing. Maintaining the trucks. I'm not that far up the chain of command, but I like where I'm at." Even if her father gave her a hard time about it.

"That's really interesting," Autumn said, tapping away on the keyboard, documenting her answers. "Did you grow up in Decatur?"

"Yeah. I'm a Minnesota girl through and through."

"Me too," Autumn said, focused on the screen. "I met Marnie in elementary school. We grew up in Rocky Point, so did Jared, Logan, and James."

"It seems like a nice little town."

"It is. Did Marnie say you drove here?"

"Yeah. It was pretty. I've never been this far north before."

"Take time to explore, there's lots to do here. The high school hockey team is playing in a big game tomorrow night. You should go."

"What would I do at a hockey game?" she asked, resisting the urge to curl her lip. She liked sports fine, didn't have a problem with football, hockey, like that, but that didn't mean she enjoyed going.

"Watch it?" Autumn laughed, packing her iPad in her bag. "Sit with me? Marnie and James are going."

Callie jerked a shoulder. "I guess so. Is it a wedding party thing?" She'd have to go if it was a wedding party thing.

Autumn read her straight through. "Yes, it's a wedding party thing."

She resisted the urge to sigh and said, "Okay. I'll see you then."

"Have a nice night. Oh, there's Cole, chatting with James. I'll send him over to take your picture for the blog. You don't mind, do you?"

"No, it's okay. Have a nice night."

Autumn threw a quick smile over her shoulder and scurried across the room.

Cole snapped her picture, a couple of different poses, and afterward, mentally drained and ready to go, she found her purse laying under the table. Escaping the meet and greet took longer than she thought it would, people wanting to introduce themselves and chat, but changing her mind about going to her room, she decided to walk around the resort. Explore, like Autumn suggested.

She hadn't taken the time to look in at the pool or check out the fitness center, which should have been the first thing she did. She couldn't skip her daily workouts, especially if she was going to keep eating the way she had tonight. The steak was fabulous and the chocolate cake was named accurately on the menu: Sinfully Sweet Seven Layer Chocolate Cake.

If she didn't work that off, it would stick to her ass in ten seconds flat.

She toed off her heels and walked the hallways, passing by guests on the way to their rooms. The pool was about to close for the night, but the lights sparkled against the water and the pungent scent of chlorine wafted to her nose through the door.

The workout center was right next to it, and though the lights were on, it was empty. The room wasn't that big, but it provided all the usual equipment: treadmills, ellipticals, exercise bikes, and weights. A large flat screen TV was attached to one wall, but nothing was playing. It would suit her for the next two weeks.

For a little town like Rocky Point, the Rocky Point Resort was a luxurious oasis in a frozen tundra. *Had that been ad copy on the brochure?* She huffed a laugh. She wanted to visit the salon, and maybe she and the other girls could have a spa day.

She walked through the lobby where the front desk agent working swing shift sat texting on her phone.

Shoving it quickly under the counter as Callie shuffled by, she asked, her cheeks blushing with embarrassment, "May I help you?"

"No, that's okay. I'm going to check out the lounge."

"It closes at two AM," she said, and Callie nodded.

"Thanks. I'll keep that in mind."

She found the bar, a large inviting space all wood and glass, dimly lit except for a large fireplace along one wall, the fire crackling bright and hot. A bartender wearing a black vest and white shirt, her hair pulled back in a long, messy brown ponytail, wiped glasses using a bright white cloth.

The maintenance man who fixed her drain brooded in front of the fire and looked as if he didn't want to be disturbed.

He suddenly lifted his head, and his eyes met hers. Undecided, she stood there until he beckoned her over.

Fatigue shadowed his face, and something else.

Something very familiar to her own features whenever she looked into a mirror.

Sadness.

It was like he'd conjured her out his dreams, and as if by magic, she stood in front of him, her hair brushed back and secured with a barrette, silver earrings dangling from her ears, and her dress, God, her dress, green and clinging, her legs a mile long showcased in a skirt so short it left nothing, and everything, to his imagination.

"You look like you want to be alone," she said, though she dropped her shoes and sank into the chair next to his.

"Sometimes a person can have his fill," he said, lifting a beer bottle to his lips.

"And sometimes it feels like it's never enough," she said.

"That's true, too."

Ivy hovered and he wanted to shoo her away, but she had a job to do and he kept his mouth shut. She asked Callista, "Can I get you something to drink?"

"Umm . . ."

"If you don't want to drink, that's okay," he said, setting his bottle aside. "I've been nursing mine all night."

"It's not that I have anything against it, but, I think I'm okay, thank you."

"Coffee, then?" Ivy asked.

"That sounds good, Ivy, thanks," he cut in, taking the decision out of Callista's hands. If she declined coffee too, then it wouldn't give her any reason to stay . . . and he wanted her to stay.

"Are you enjoying your visit?" he asked, trying to sound casual.

If Desiree ever caught him willingly participating in a conversation, she'd never let him hear the end of it. He was a loner, and everyone knew it. Unapproachable. Unfriendly.

Always scowling, always had a black cloud hanging over his head, with an appearance to match his grouchy demeanor.

He'd called her over, for God's sake, to talk.

This woman from Decatur who could look him in the eyes.

"So far," she said, crossing her legs and letting her purse fall to the floor near her shoes. "I'm in town for a wedding."

"Marnie and James's," he said, rising to help Ivy with the coffee tray. She didn't need it, but resort folk stuck together and she'd had it as bad as he had over the years. "Thanks."

"No problem, Mitch," she said, giving him a shy smile.

He might have asked her out, but she'd had her heart broken in high school and hadn't gotten over the asshole who hurt her. Combine that with trouble at home, and he knew when a woman said, "Hands off," even if she didn't say it out loud.

The asshole in question was in town for the wedding. He'd keep his eye on Ivy and make sure she wasn't hurt again.

"Mitch?" Callista asked, reaching out for the mug he offered her. "That fits you."

"I'm named after my grandfather on my Dad's side," he said. "Mitchell Sinclair." Hands full holding a mug and the carafe, he couldn't reach out to shake her hand, but he wanted to. Wanted to touch her.

"It's nice to meet you. I'm—"

"Callista Carter." She narrowed her eyes and he realized his mistake. "I mean, I asked about you because—"

Callista picked her things up off the floor and stood in an angry huff. "Because you're a creeper. You pegged me as a woman alone at the resort and wanted to—"

"Talk because you're the first person I've met since the accident who looked at me like I wasn't part of a freak show."

The words rushed out of him. If he let her leave in a haze of fury, not only would she never speak to him again, but she might complain to Desiree. Worrying about that made him feel like a jerk, too, because he didn't want to make Callista uncomfortable, but he sure as hell didn't want to lose his job. He didn't know what he'd do in town if he couldn't work at the resort. He'd be fucked. No one else would hire him. Not with the way he looked. Not with the things he'd done.

She sagged. "I'm sorry, that was uncalled for. I should know better because . . ." She dropped her shoes and purse onto the carpet near the chair and sat on the edge of the cushion. She picked up an empty mug and looked into the cup.

He tensed, waiting for the truth. She was only being nice, she was only being polite because he worked at the resort. She only wanted to stay on his good side in case something else broke in her room and she needed it fixed.

She met his eyes. "I know what fire can do, and I'm . . . used to seeing . . . injuries . . ."

"That's not true. You see the people underneath," he said, holding the carafe to fill her mug. If she wanted to stay.

She held out the sturdy white mug that had the Rocky Point Resort's logo on the front, and he breathed a silent prayer of thanks. Steadying his right hand, the scar pulling tight over his knuckles, he poured.

"Thanks. For both. It can't be easy for you."

He poured his own mug of coffee, leaving room for cream. He offered her the half and half, and she nodded, allowing him to fill her mug to the brim, the white swirling into the black.

"Who said life was easy, Callista?" He said her name again because he liked the sound of it, how it brought to mind starry summer nights and the wind chimes his mother hung on the porch.

"You can call me Callie," she said. "You're right. It's not. But it looks . . . pretty bad."

"It is what it is."

"Yeah."

They sipped their coffees in front of the crackling fire. He absorbed the pain and fury the flames represented in his life. It fueled him, the misery, reminded him that every day of hell was what he deserved.

"I need to go," he said, breaking the silence, slamming his mug on the table near the tray.

Startled, Callie bobbled her mug and coffee sloshed over the side and dripped down her leg. "What? Why?"

"I just do." He couldn't let himself get used to this. Callie might be the only person in the entire world who could see past his scars, but she didn't know the story behind them, and once she did, she'd never talk to him again.

"Do you want to go to the hockey game with me tomorrow night?" she asked, clutching the mug.

"Freak shows don't go to hockey games," he snarled, his heart snagging as her face crumpled. "I'm sorry I bothered you. I won't do it again."

He strode out of the lounge shaking his head at Ivy as he passed by the bar.

He looked back at Callie who sat in her chair, gripping her mug, staring into the flames.

Fire had started this whole goddamned nightmare.

The nightmare that was, and forever would be, his life.

CHAPTER TWO

Callie drooped in her chair, her hands wrapped around her mug.

The hardships of burn victims weren't new to her. Victims had long roads to recovery. Skin grafts, infection, physical therapy, and that was only the physical part of it. Some burn victims never emotionally moved past their injuries or the trauma that caused them. Maybe Mitch was one of those people.

"His life hasn't been easy." Ivy appeared like a ghost, and Callie's skin prickled. She picked up Mitch's mug and placed the creamer on the tray.

"What happened to him?"

Ivy looked down at his mug that was still half full. "That's not my story to share, but I'm sure you'll find out about it soon enough. There are plenty of people who would be happy to gossip about Mitch and what a worthless human being he is."

"Why does he stay here if people feel like that about him?" she asked, appalled.

"People are cruel. Everywhere. Do you think he'd get away from the looks and gossip moving to a different city?"

"Maybe not, but he'd have more of a life living in a place where people didn't have such closed minds."

Ivy sighed. "He's okay here, at the resort. Let him be." She paused. "He likes you. He's never spoken with a stranger before, not by choice. I'd hate to see him hurt."

She searched Ivy's face for jealousy but found only compassion for a man who had turned from a coworker into a friend.

"If you respect his privacy, you'll wait until he tells you instead of listening to the garbage people will say."

"All right," Callie said, but he probably wouldn't try to talk to her again. She'd been around fire long enough to know that living with scars was secondary to how a person became injured in the first place. It was obvious talking to her brought it all back.

Besides, she was hardly in a place to help Mitch deal with that kind of trauma. It would be best if she kept her distance for the rest of her time in Rocky Point.

Ivy picked up the tray and shifted on her feet. "I'm not warning you off . . . I'd like to see Mitch with someone but . . . he's . . ." she trailed off.

She snagged her shoes, shoving her fingers through the tops, and grabbed her purse off the carpet, looping the strap over her arm. "It's okay. I understand what you're saying. He's safe at the resort. He has friends here who accept him. I won't disrupt that."

"I want him . . ."

Touching Ivy's arm, she said, "You want him happy. You want him to be able to live a normal life. I'm sure you mean well and that he appreciates it, but he knows it won't happen. Especially if he stays in Rocky Point."

"I know."

"You look like you're not feeling well. Are you okay?" she asked, concerned.

Ivy blew out a shaky breath, her skin pale. "One of the girls called in sick and I'm working a double to fill in. I'll be going home soon."

"Okay. Be careful driving. Goodnight."

"Goodnight."

Exhausted as well, she padded to her room. Because of Mitch, she'd stayed up past her bedtime and she wouldn't even be able to sleep in. She wanted to keep up with her workout schedule or the first week after her vacation would be a bear.

In her room, she washed her makeup off and brushed her teeth.

The water slid easily down the drain.

She dropped into bed and tossed and turned, tortured by vivid dreams of fire and green eyes staring at her through the flames.

Before the sun came up, Mitch began his circuit in the resort's fitness room. If he'd been stronger, maybe things wouldn't have turned out like they had. He'd heard about people developing super-human strength in times of crisis. Lifting cars off people or being able to run long distances quickly to find help.

That hadn't happened to him. He hadn't frozen in fear because he remembered through the smoke and shock he'd been brave, but he'd grown tired of fighting and there hadn't been anything more he could do.

His brain had shut down and the paramedics found him sitting on the shoulder of the road, the fire's heat melting the snow around them, rocking back and forth mumbling words they couldn't understand. He hadn't felt the pain from his burns. Only the pain of failure and the sharp shrieks of misery and death slashing like an axe through his skull.

He hadn't been able to save them.

He started on the treadmill, shuffling until the blood started pumping through his veins. He was a mile in when the door of the fitness center squeaked open and Callie stepped into the room wearing shorts, an exercise bra, and a bright neon pink tank top. Face free of makeup, her hair fastened into a high ponytail, shadows rested under her eyes and strain pulled at her mouth.

She looked like she'd gotten about as much sleep as he had.

Close to none.

He regretted how he treated her last night. How he'd stormed off after the simple invitation.

"You can use the one next to me," he said, hoping to break the ice.

She stood uncertainly near a treadmill two away from him. "I don't want to bother you," she said stiffly, her shoulders tight, twisting her hands together.

"It's fine."

Her workout clothes revealed as much as her dress, and as she programmed the treadmill, he took a moment to appreciate her toned arms, flat stomach, and strong legs.

"Do you workout to look good, or to be healthy?"

Callie started the treadmill at an incline, and he grimaced at his paltry level one. He could do better.

"Both, I guess, and for work. What about you?"

"For work." It wasn't exactly a lie. He stood on his feet ten to twelve hours a day and he lifted heavy things more than occasionally. In the summer he mowed the resort's grass, and in the winter he blew snow. Overall, his job was easier if he stayed in shape. "And I help my parents around their house."

"They live in town?" she asked, already working up a sweat.

"Yeah. I grew up here. Went to the high school." He raised his incline two levels and picked up speed. His calves started to protest, but he couldn't let Callie overtake him. Plus, the challenge would do him good. Mix things up. They weren't in competition.

Nope.

"You know Marnie, then."

"I know Marnie, and James, and Jared, but I didn't hang out with them in school. They were popular."

Callie flicked a glance at him, and she eyed his treadmill's display. She pushed buttons on hers. Higher. Faster.

He wanted to do the same, but he had a sinking suspicion she was in better shape than he was.

"You weren't?" she asked.

"I was a good-looking guy, but no, I wasn't popular. Only a middle-class citizen." He tried to joke, but his melancholy tone buried the forced joviality.

One of the small things he lost in the fire. His looks. But other people lost more that day and he rarely thought about it.

That was a lie.

He thought about it every time he looked in the mirror.

"I find that hard to believe," she huffed, pushing the Up arrow on the treadmill.

Okay. He couldn't look weak.

He could handle the speed, but holy shit, he'd never be

able to match her incline. His heart slammed against his ribs and sweat poured down his face. He already reached his limit, but he bumped up the speed and his feet pounded against the tread.

Callie, on the other hand, sounded as light as a deer prancing on a cloud, her feet keeping perfect pace.

He bet she could run all day and not need a break.

The stamina she had . . .

How strong her legs were . . .

His cock twitched, and thankful he wore baggy shorts, he focused on the run.

"What? That I wasn't popular or that I was good looking?" He didn't dare look at her. One wrong move at this speed, and the tread would spit him across the room. He'd land on his ass in a heap of hurt and embarrassment.

"That you weren't popular. You have that charisma popular people have."

"Oh? I thought I was a bitter bastard now."

"You try to be, but I can see through you."

He believed her, and it scared the shit out of him.

A heavy silence fell over the workout room, the whir of their treadmills the only sound.

Callie looked at his display and bumped up her speed. She grinned, a dimple flicking in her cheek, catching him off-guard.

She was playing with him, and it did a funny thing to his heart.

Grasping the rails to keep from hurting himself, he grinned, knowing the right side of his face didn't work right, his smile turning into a sneer.

She didn't seem to mind, only moving her gaze between the display on his machine and his eyes, laughing when he increased his speed. They pounded the tread, laughing between gasps of breath.

"I can't anymore," she finally panted, slamming her hand on the Stop button.

Gratefully, he did the same.

They dropped to the hardwood floor.

Sweat glistened on her face, pleasure sparkling in her light brown eyes.

He stopped laughing and swallowed.

God, she was gorgeous, and more, she looked at him like he was a normal man, a guy she met to work out with. A man she'd ask to breakfast after a shower, only, she tried that already and he'd ripped into her for being friendly.

He cleared his throat and resisted wiping the sweat off her forehead that was close to dripping into her eyes.

"I'm sorry about last night," he said. "I didn't mean to lose my temper."

She shrugged and stood.

He was afraid she was going to leave, but she only grabbed a hand towel off the fresh stack near the water fountain and dried her face.

"It's fine. I mean, you hurt my feelings, but Ivy explained you've had a tough time and that it was better to leave you alone."

Dammit. He hadn't considered Ivy would defend him, but of course she would. More than friends but less than lovers, they were soldiers, wounded in different wars. She had his back and he had hers.

Callie handed him a towel.

"Thanks."

"You're welcome."

"We're not together."

Inspecting a weight bench, she said, "I didn't get the feeling you were, but she was clear enough."

She changed the weights and sat, preparing to do bench presses.

"Do you want me to spot you?" he asked, rising to his feet. His legs trembled.

He'd pay for the run, but he didn't mind. He hadn't had that much fun in a long time.

"That'd be great."

They worked out in silence for another hour, and at seven-thirty, he set the weights down. "I need to get ready for work."

"Can you give me ten more minutes? Hold my feet while I do my sit-ups?"

"Sure. Kicking it old school?" he asked.

"I like doing them this way." She tossed her towel aside, pulled out a black rubber mat, and dropped to her butt.

He knelt on the mat, and she scooted near him. He caught a whiff of her scent. Sweat, and something sweet, like honey.

She finished—he lost count after fifty—and sat next to him, breathing deeply through her nose, her eyes closed, her arms resting on her knees.

That's when he noticed the burn.

Brushing his fingers over the patch of bright pink skin, he asked, "What happened?"

Her eyes flew open, startled, but didn't pull away.

He feathered his fingers over her soft skin.

She swallowed. "Marnie called me in a panic. She had a grease fire in her kitchen, but no fire extinguisher. I got too close when I put it out. I knew better, but Marnie distracted me. She was hyperventilating, and I tried to calm her down and put the fire out at the same time. That didn't work very well."

"Why didn't you call the fire department?"

She frowned. "Why? I was right there. There was no reason to."

He grabbed her arm. "This is the reason. You were hurt."

"You've never gotten hurt on the job?" She raised her eyebrows.

Giving in, he skimmed his fingers along her jaw. Perspiration dampened her skin. If he kissed her there, she would taste of salt and something he couldn't have.

"Yeah, I have, but that's different. I was at work. Why did Marnie call you?"

"Because we're neighbors. Because we're friends and she knew I'd know what to do."

"At your expense."

She reached out, her hand trembling, and lightly trailed her fingertips down the side of his right arm.

He wore a muscle shirt, confident he'd be the only person working out this early in the morning. In all the years he'd worked out in the resort, he'd been wrong once.

Her touch . . . it hurt, and made his nerves flicker and itch, flare in a pain that would never heal. Another man would enjoy Callie's touch, and he would too, anywhere else.

Scar tissue was different, and he gritted his teeth against the sensation that felt like worms writhing beneath his skin. Eating at him underneath the surface.

He needed all his strength to not jerk away.

"And yours," she whispered.

"Did Ivy tell you what happened?"

She shook her head. "No. She said it was your story to tell."

His stomach heaved. "Can you . . . stop?"

She yanked her hand away. "I'm sorry."

Staring at the floor, he muttered, "I'm not a normal man, Callie."

She wrapped her arms around him and pressed her lips to the scar tissue near his ear. "No, you're better." She sprang to her feet and stormed out of the fitness room.

He sat, stunned.

His skin burned.

Fuck.

In angry strokes he washed his hair, let the hot water sluice down his body.

Better than normal.

He *wanted* to be an everyday Joe. Go to work, come home to a chubby wife and a couple of kids.

Go to the bar to have a drink with friends.

Average. Boring.

Better than that.

Fuck her. Who did she think she was, planting ideas in his head? Ideas and thoughts and things he'd never have. Not only because of the scarring, but because that wasn't what his life was like anymore.

And it would never be any different.

He dressed and was sitting in Desiree's office with a cup of coffee in his hand by nine.

"You seem tired this morning." She sipped coffee out of a black mug that had "Queen" written in elegant pink script on the front. Her bright red lipstick stained the top of the Q. "Is everything all right?"

He paused.

Desiree wasn't his friend, not like Ivy, but she had eyes and ears around the resort, and if he didn't tell her, she'd find out anyway.

"I used the fitness center this morning."

She tilted her head, black tendrils that escaped her updo framing her face. "You do that every morning."

"Yeah, and I'm usually alone. This morning Callista came in, and . . ."

"And?"

"I don't know." He raked a hand through his hair. He needed a haircut but hated going into town. Even for something as simple and as basic as that.

"What do you mean, you don't know? Did your brain leave your head when she walked in?"

"No." Usually he enjoyed Desiree's sass. She spoke to him as easily as she spoke to anyone, and he found comfort in that.

"Then what?"

"She talked to me."

She opened her mouth to make some glib quip, but her eyes softened and she leaned forward against her desk. "Honey, then maybe you need to talk back. You're not destined to be alone, no matter what you might think."

"She doesn't know the story."

"And you think it will change her mind about you?"

"Everyone else did."

She frowned. "That's not true, and you know it. The town is divided, yes, but you don't side with the people who understand. You side with the people who blame you because you blame yourself. What are you scared of? Her blaming you or *not* blaming you?"

"She sees me." That was the whole of it.

Desiree hooted. "And that scares the shit right out of you because no one bothers to look anymore. Get out of my face and let me do my job."

He stood, taking his coffee with him. He wouldn't find any sympathy here. In fact, if he told her more, he wouldn't be surprised if she hunted Callie down and gave her a lungful of encouragement.

"And Mitch?"

"Yeah?"

"I don't mind if you get something going with this woman. We don't have any policies regarding staff fraternizing with other staff or guests, though Lord knows Stacy and I have gone around and around about it. Human Resources can be a pain in the ass, but she sometimes has a point, too. Callista Carter is a guest, a guest of a couple who is bringing in a substantial payday having their wedding reception here, and her comfort is the resort's top priority. If she starts to . . ." She sighed. "Just be careful."

"I got it."

The last thing he wanted was to lose his job. He rarely needed to go into town, having everything he needed here. He didn't want his bubble popped because he went after something he couldn't have.

In the hallway outside Desiree's office, he let a pit of disappointment settle in his stomach. It wasn't her seeing past his scars that made him want her.

His attraction was all male. The accident hadn't taken that away from him.

His cell phone rang, and he answered the front desk's call.

"One of 231's outlets isn't working. Are you on a job? Can you go look at it?"

231? That was Callie's room.

He sighed in resignation.

He'd stay away from her. As soon as he finished fixing her dead outlet.

Fuck.

Callie wasn't usually so bold when it came to men, at least, not in her personal life.

She demanded respect at the station house, and because of who her father was, she was given it ten-fold.

It also helped she'd earned a reputation as a competent firefighter through hard work, determination, and a fearlessness required to run into a burning building.

To risk her life to save another.

She'd never had a problem dealing with her male counterparts in the department, but having two brothers and a hard-assed father constantly keeping an eye on her, she didn't date much. No one was brave enough to take on her family.

While she washed the sweat off in a hot shower, she wondered what her family would think of Mitch.

She squeezed the water out her hair in efficient twists and wrapped a towel around her body. Grabbing her cell phone, she guessed she had ten to fifteen minutes of talk time with her brother if he wasn't busy. She selected the number of the in-patient facility her brother checked himself into to dry out, and the woman who answered the phone put her on hold.

Brandon didn't have access to his cell, and family members were encouraged to write letters. In the few weeks Brandon had been there, she'd only managed one letter and a "thinking of you" card.

"Hey, Callie," he said, answering the call. "To what do I owe the pleasure?"

She sagged onto the bed in relief. This man was the brother she missed. His voice sounded clear and cheerful.

"Hi! I'm in Rocky Point for Marnie's wedding, and I thought I'd call and see how you were doing."

"Good. Same shit, different day. Therapy, therapy, therapy. Movie tonight, and the mobile library is coming by later. I have the new James Patterson on hold."

"You sound good," she said, her voice soft.

"I feel good. But . . . Dad . . ."

"He can't make you do anything you don't want to do," she said, gripping her phone.

"Yes, he can. You know he can. He makes you, doesn't he?"

She opened her mouth to say it was different for her, but it wasn't. Ace was as hard on her as he was on his sons, only, she hadn't been dealing with it for as long as they had. Her cracks were only just beginning to show.

Her damp hair trickled water down her back, and she shivered.

Instead of answering, she said, "I met someone."

"Whatever you do, don't introduce him to Dad. If he's not a firefighter or a cop, he's not good enough. Ace won't have anything to do with him."

"That's what I was afraid of."

"I gotta go. We're having breakfast in a minute, and I'm on KP duty. I hope it works out, Callie, I really do. Don't let

Dad take him away from you. He's done enough to all of us, even if Zach can't see it."

Zach was their older brother and the spitting image of their father, in more ways than one.

Without saying goodbye, Brandon hung up, and her phone beeped.

At least he sounded better. Clearheaded. Strong. A positive step up from the beaten-down barely functioning alcoholic he'd been before he went to rehab.

Away from their dad, Brandon could figure who he was beyond a firefighter and Ace Carter's son. He'd tried to find himself at the bottom of a bottle, but that had only made things worse.

Therapy was a better option, though he'd resisted at first. After a few days, he realized therapy was a chance to be heard because God forbid Ace Carter listen to something he didn't want to hear.

In the bathroom, she put on a robe and brushed the snarls out of her hair. She was meeting Marnie for breakfast and she'd dry it and curl it a little. Look like she made an effort. She didn't have plans after that, except going to the hockey game later tonight, and maybe she'd poke around town or try some skiing. Maybe she'd take a nap. She was on vacation and she might as well take full advantage.

She clicked the hairdryer on. It didn't do anything and she frowned. She clicked it off and back on, then off, and back on. She unplugged it, plugged it back in, and tried to turn it on again.

Finally, she set it on the sink.

Dammit.

She pressed the tiny button in the middle of the outlet to reset it, then turned the hairdryer on, but that still didn't do anything.

She sighed. She needed the outlet near the sink. If she was only staying overnight, or for a couple of days, she'd make do with the outlet near the desk across the room, but she had several events to attend for the wedding and the dead outlet would be a major inconvenience in the next two weeks.

Though she didn't want to bother Mitch, she called the front desk.

The woman who answered said she'd send maintenance to her room as quickly as possible.

She wanted to see him again. She liked his company. The serious way he had about him. Intense, but in a good way, though he still had some little boy inside him. She'd glimpsed it when they were racing on the treadmills.

The right side of his mouth didn't respond when he smiled, but his eyes sparkled when she made him laugh.

She wanted to see that again.

The sparkle.

Someone knocked on her door, and Mitch stood on the other side holding his massive toolbox and a clean trash bin. No one replaced hers, and he remembered.

"Hey," she said, stepping aside to let him in.

He stared at her for a long, hard minute, his gaze traveling from her wet hair, down to the cleavage her robe exposed, to her bare legs glistening with the body lotion she applied after her shower.

He cleared his throat and mumbled, "You should get dressed before I do my job."

She hadn't given one thought to changing, and she realized her mistake when his neck stained red in embarrassment.

Suddenly, his behavior annoyed her and she bit back a retort.

He was hardly a monk. Surely he'd seen a woman's bits and pieces, and more than that.

She didn't know how old he was, but she could make a fairly accurate guess since he'd gone to school with Marnie, and Marnie was six years older than her thirty years. No one made it to their thirties without having sex.

He was attracted to her, and she wanted to prove it. What she'd do with the knowledge, well, she'd figure it out once she had it. Maybe she could talk him into a date.

A kiss.

Maybe more.

She wanted more.

Whatever that consisted of.

Especially whatever that consisted of.

He worked with his hands, his fingers and palms calloused from manual labor.

What would they feel like against her skin?

"I'm okay," she said, but she clutched the lapels of the robe closer to her throat. "I'm covered more than I was in the workout center this morning." Hiding a smirk of victory because he couldn't deny it, she turned and flipped the bathroom light on. "It's the outlet here. It won't work. I'm meeting Marnie for breakfast soon and I need to dry my hair."

He had no choice but to follow her to the vanity.

She secured her robe's sash around her waist and hoisted herself onto the counter near the basin to watch him work.

She crossed her legs.

He pretended not to notice, and she smothered a laugh.

Without saying a word, he chose a Phillips screwdriver out of his toolbox sitting on the floor and started to loosen the little white screws holding the plastic cover in place.

He'd showered, and the fresh, pure scent of Irish Spring permeated the air around them.

He wore crisp, clean work jeans and a green flannel shirt that had the Rocky Point logo embroidered over the left pocket.

"Are you sore?" she asked, uncrossing and crossing her legs.

She'd never considered herself a vixen or a hussy—her father wouldn't let her be one in any case—and flirting was a new feeling.

His hands stilled. "Sore?"

"The workout this morning?"

"Oh. No. Probably tomorrow. You're, ah, in pretty good shape." He took the white plastic frame off the wall and began to inspect the wiring. "This all looks fine. Did you try flipping the switch?"

Switch?

Shit.

Her cheeks flamed. "What switch?"

CHAPTER THREE

Mitch would have laughed if he wasn't so turned on . . . and if he wasn't so annoyed she put him through all of this when she hadn't tried the switch to give the outlet juice.

She looked smarter than that.

He narrowed his eyes.

He flipped the switch that was right next to the light switch, plugged the hairdryer in, and slide the power button up.

The hairdryer whirred and blew out hot air in seconds.

Silently, he turned the hairdryer off, unplugged it, and secured the plastic frame back to the wall. He finished and dropped the screwdriver in his toolbox, the sharp sound accentuating his annoyance. "Is there anything else?"

She sat on the vanity, her fingers twisted in her lap. When she looked at him, tears filled her eyes, and his heart plummeted to the floor.

"I'm sorry," she whispered. "I really had no idea. You must think I asked you to come to my room to, to make fun of you or something."

"I don't think that." He stepped between her knees and cradled her face in his hands. Her brown eyes glittered in the light shining over the mirror. She didn't have a speck of makeup on her face and her skin glowed. He ran his fingers through her damp strands and the scent of honey he'd enjoyed earlier wafted to his nose. "But I think you want more from me than I can give you."

"How do you know?" She sniffled, smoothing her hands over his chest. "Will you . . . will you give me a hug?"

"A hug?" he echoed. He hadn't read her wrong. Despite the accident, he could still read a woman, and she'd been flirting plain as day. He'd enjoyed it, too. It'd been a long time since a woman felt comfortable enough to let her guard down to tease him.

She rested her cheek against his shirt. "Just a hug."

It wouldn't only be a hug, but he wrapped his arms around her, and she nestled into his embrace.

Desiree's warning rang in his ears, but he kissed the top of her head. They could be friends at least. He needed more friends.

He'd never kissed Ivy, his brain taunted him, and he told himself to shut up.

She looked up, her lips parted, her breath coming out in little gasps that stiffened his cock. It'd been too long since he felt a connection to someone, and the way she met his eyes, not once moving her gaze to the right side of his face, he only wanted her more.

Lowering his head, he met her lips, and she wrapped her arms around his neck.

Soft, her breasts pushed against his chest, and her legs hugged his hips as she clung to him.

She brushed her lips over his cheek, his good cheek, the

cheek that could feel all the sensations, and down his neck where she nibbled at his skin.

He couldn't help himself, and he traced his fingers down her throat and into her robe where he rubbed the pad of his thumb over her nipple.

She jerked, and immediately he withdrew. "I'm sorry, that was too much," he said, trying to step away, but she held on, not letting him go.

"No. I wanted . . . I mean, it was a surprise, but not . . . I liked it. Do it again," she said, and covered his mouth with hers.

He didn't let himself touch her again, and after another minute of her breathless assault on his mouth, he untangled himself and stepped back.

Disappointment clouded her eyes, and he cupped her cheek in his rough palm. "I'm new to this, Callie, and you need to be patient. Can we . . . can we spend some time together? Slow?" The words felt like a big gob of peanut butter in his mouth, and he tried to talk around it, force the words out. "Maybe a date?"

"Will you go to the hockey game tonight?" she asked.

A high school hockey game wasn't slow and it wouldn't turn out well, but she didn't understand his life, the way he had to live, and if she could see it for herself and tell him to fuck off before he became too attached, the less it would hurt in the long run. "Okay."

He wanted her smile to be worth it, wanted her happiness to be worth it, but his survival and his parents' safety were the only things that could matter and he knew they wouldn't be worth it at all.

Near ten o'clock Callie wrapped a bulky cardigan around herself as she walked down the hallway to the dining room to meet Marnie.

Mitch left her room after nuzzling her mouth with his one more time. Had he wanted more, she would have given it to him, no question. There was something about him that made her want to give him everything she had. She hadn't been this carried away by a man in a long time and she enjoyed the rush, but she could understand the wisdom in taking it slow.

Enjoy the rush, but also enjoy the anticipation.

Her stomach growled in response to the scent of pancakes and butter, and she sat in a chair next to Marnie who was talking to James's mother. "I spoke with Desiree, and there's absolutely no rooms available for Auntie Ruth," she said. "Good morning, Callie."

"Morning. Good morning, Mrs. Fox," she said, helping herself to a carafe of coffee.

"Call me Linda, dear," she said, lifting a mug of coffee to her lips. "Two weeks will be very long with this 'Mr.' and 'Mrs.' business."

"Thanks." She'd met James's parents a few times at Marnie's, and she liked them very much. It seemed Marnie would have no problems getting along with her new in-laws.

Linda sighed. "I told that woman she'd regret it. My sister-in-law has never been the brightest bulb on the Christmas tree."

She smothered a smile. "What's happening?"

"James's aunt decided to come to the wedding after all,

but she wants to fly to Rocky Point sooner rather than later, to party with us. There's no room at the inn, or stable either, though that's where she belongs. No disrespect to Jesus," Marnie said.

"James will find her something, though it should be Roy's job," Linda said, poking her husband's shoulder.

"I'll figure it out," Roy muttered. "We're talking about something important here."

Linda scowled. "Rehashing last night's football game isn't important."

"It's a helluva lot more interesting than wedding stuff, right, son?"

James heaved a sigh. "You know I can't agree with you, Dad. Marnie's sitting right here."

Marnie glared, then laughed. "Damn straight."

Giggling, Callie loaded her plate at the breakfast buffet and settled in her seat. Starving after her workout, she attacked her bacon and eggs. "Where's everyone else?"

Marnie counted off on her fingers. "Leah's in her room, sleeping in, the poor thing. She's going into town with Jared later. She didn't bring anything warm to wear, the crazy girl. Logan's at his cabin . . . he rented a cabin instead of staying in the resort. Jared's at work, I think, or he'd planned on going in today. Autumn's at work, too, and you're here. That's everyone."

"You're lopsided," she said, pausing with her fork halfway to her mouth.

"What?" Marnie clutched at her breasts. "My right has always been a little—"

"No!" She laughed. "Your bridal party. You're lopsided. How come?"

"Oh, nothing terrible. I wanted three friends, and James only has two good ones, good enough to ask to stand up with him. At the rehearsal we'll figure out the best way for you all to walk down the aisle, since pairing up isn't going to work."

"I can walk by myself. I don't mind."

"We'll think of something. He was going to ask his cousin, Brady, Auntie Ruth's son, but—"

"He's in prison again," James cut in. "It's why Aunt Ruth didn't want to come in the first place. She's embarrassed."

"She got over it quick enough," Linda muttered.

"She should be used to it by now. If it's not one thing with him, it's another. Anyway, we'll get it straightened out. I'm not worried. Did you have a good time last night?" Marnie asked her.

"Yeah. Your mom kept me company, and I met Autumn. She interviewed me for her blog. Cole's hot." The cameraman who'd taken her picture for Autumn's blog post was very good-looking, but she sensed a current between him and Autumn.

"Yeah, he is. He was the class clown in high school. Honey, you could always ask Cole," Marnie said to James. "You guys used to be friends."

James was already shaking his head. "We lost touch for a while there. It'd feel weird."

"He and Autumn could walk together. We don't have a ring bearer, either. Cole's son would be perfect. He's adorable."

"Better decide," Linda said, pushing her plate away. "Cole and Ty would need tuxes ASAP."

"Grabbing Ty a tux would be easier than finding a dress for a flower girl, and Briar's too old to be in the wedding."

"Briar? That's a pretty name," Callie said.

"Jared's daughter. She's sixteen. I tried to think of a way to include her, but there wasn't one."

"Everyone has kids."

"Leah doesn't. Jared and his ex-wife married young. Rita's a really close friend of mine, but she couldn't make it. When are you going to find someone and start popping out babies?"

She suppressed feelings of want when she thought about children. The few men she'd dated hadn't appreciated her choice of occupation. The odd hours, the level of commitment, the danger. Her dad and brothers added a second layer, assessing them as potential threats, ah, husbands.

"Not anytime soon. You know, because of my job."

"Don't wait too long," Marnie said, rubbing her stomach, "and feel like I do. The longer you wait, the tougher it is."

"It will work out, babe," James said, rubbing Marnie's back. "The important thing is we found each other, finally."

Marnie kissed his cheek. "Yeah." She turned back to Callie. "Going to the game with us tonight? Jared's the manager of the sports arena. He'll be there keeping an eye on things. Autumn's going to do a write up for the blog, and Cole will be there filming for the new's sports segment. Leah might go. It'll be fun."

"I'm going, and I asked Mitch to go, too."

Marnie blinked. "Who?"

James elbowed her. "Mitch Sinclair. You haven't seen him skulking around the resort with his toolbox?"

"Oh!" Marnie blew out a breath. "*Oh.*"

She stiffened. "He hardly skulks. Good word, though."

"He skulks. I didn't mean anything by it except he never talks to anyone, and when he does, he looks like he's in pain." James winced. "That's not what I meant. How did you convince him to go to a game? Last I heard, he didn't do anything with anybody."

"I had to have maintenance come to my room a couple of times, and we met when he fixed my sink drain yesterday. He's a little unsteady, but who wouldn't be?"

Marnie frowned. "Do I need to talk to Desiree? You're paying a crapton of money and the least they could do is make sure your room's okay."

Waving her off, she said, "It's fine. This morning was my fault. But, I've spoken to him a couple of times, and . . ."

"And?"

James pushed away from the table. "And?" he teased his fiancée. "You have to ask? He was fixing more than something in her room. I'm going into town with Mom and Dad. Do you need anything?"

Marnie flicked a smile at James and then narrowed her eyes at Callie. "No, I think I'm okay. If I change my mind, we'll be in town for the game tonight."

"Okay. See ya later," James said, throwing his napkin onto the table. He gave Marnie a smacking kiss on her lips. "Be a good girl."

"We'll see you later, dear," Linda said, patting Marnie's hand. "Lovely to see you again, Callie."

"You, too."

She poured more coffee into her mug and waited while Marnie remained silent until James and his parents walked out of earshot.

"Spill it."

"I don't know what you mean."

"Like hell you don't. Tell me about Mitch."

She set her mug aside and pushed the cold eggs around her plate with her fork. "I met him yesterday. My sink wouldn't drain, and he unclogged it. I knew right away what happened to him. I mean, I know burns when I see them, and he seemed . . . taken aback when I wasn't—"

"Grossed out?" Marnie asked.

She pursed her lips.

"Okay, that sounds bad," Marnie said, "but he's used to being stared at. He has to be. I remember Mom talking about what happened, and Rocky Point hasn't given him much . . ."

"Support?"

"I guess you could say that."

"What happened? Last night I looked around after dinner and went to the lounge. I met Ivy, but she wouldn't tell me. I guess they're pretty close friends."

Jealousy flared bright and hot. He wouldn't be kissing her if he had Ivy, would he?

Ivy would be a better match for Mitch than she would be. Ivy seemed to be more in Mitch's league. More suited somehow. Like they had more in common.

"I don't know about Mitch and Ivy. I'm out of the loop when it comes to town gossip. You have a thing for him, huh?"

"We kissed in my bathroom, after he looked at my outlet."

Marnie smiled. "Is that what you're calling it now?"

Her mouth dropped open. "No! God." She buried her face in her hands. "No. My *real* outlet. Near the sink."

"I know, I'm teasing you. Look, I know you want to know, and it's not a secret. He used to be a school bus driver. About seven years ago, he was on his morning route to pick up kids south of here, who lived in the rural areas. There isn't much between us and Marengo, and those kids don't have a closer school to go to. It was wintertime, and the highways . . . everyone said they should've had a snow day, but the school district kept school in session. It had been a hard winter already and parents were giving the school pushback because they canceled so many times."

She waited impatiently. She knew this was going to be bad, and wanted, no, *needed,* to hear the rest.

Marnie paused, thinking back, and Callie pictured Mitch as a bus driver. It brought a smile to her lips. He'd be good with kids.

"The driver of a semi-truck was supposed to be headed to Rocky Point to make a delivery but had gotten turned around. He was going too fast, it was storming, and the roads hadn't been cleared. Mitch was at a bus stop and the semi smashed into them. The bus caught fire. Mitch thought he managed to get all the kids off, but there were two little girls, sisters . . . They didn't make it."

Pressing a hand to her mouth, she stifled a moan. "How did he, how was he . . .?"

Marnie shook her head. "When the police questioned him, he said he didn't see them. He could hear them screaming and tried to go back."

"He's a hero."

"Not to the girls' parents, not to the rest of that family, or their friends. Most of the town wanted Mitch to leave and never come back, but he held his ground. His parents live here and he didn't want to leave them. The accident gave poor Ruby Sinclair a heart attack, and while Mitch was trying to heal, he was worried about his mom. It was a bad time."

"That's terrible," she whispered.

"Yeah, it is. People can be assholes. But, according to my mom, he hasn't been in a relationship since then. He's very protective of his job here, and his parents. He may not be emotionally ready, even after all this time, to be with someone."

"Are you warning me off him?" Callie would take Marnie's opinion seriously because Marnie knew the situation and she didn't.

"No. If anyone in the whole world is right for Mitch, it's be you."

She squeezed Marnie's hand. "Thank you for that."

Marnie sipped her coffee and patted her lips with a cloth napkin leaving a trace of lipstick behind. "I'm going to poke my head in and say hi to Leah, then head to my room. I told James I'd do a little digging for Auntie Ruth and maybe nap before the game tonight. Did you want to come with me to see Leah?"

"No. I don't want to be a crappy bridesmaid, but I thought I'd go to town."

"You're going to dig up stuff on Mitch."

Her mouth quirked. "Maybe."

"Go see Autumn at the newspaper. You'll be killing two birds with one stone."

"How's that?"

"She can help you get the information you need, and you won't be being a crappy bridesmaid."

"Thank you for understanding."

"I'm marrying my best friend. It took us a while to circle around to each other, but we made it. I'm ecstatically happy, and I want everyone I know to be the same. But please be careful. Take it slow, all right?"

"I think you and Mitch are on the same page," she admitted. "This morning I would've let him do more than look at my outlet if he would've wanted to."

"You are strong, compassionate, caring, and gorgeous. If you want him in your bed, you'll get him there."

"I know, just give him time to *want* to be there."

"So there're no regrets the next morning." Marnie winked in that sassy way she'd always found so charming. "See you later."

"See you later."

She sat at the empty table and sipped her lukewarm coffee.

She looked forward to seeing Mitch tonight. To tell him she knew what happened and it didn't change the way she felt.

How did she feel?

Like she wanted to hold him in her arms and protect him from the world.

It didn't Callie take long to find the newspaper's office building. Marnie said that a few years ago they moved into an empty department store. It made finding the building easy. The signage still stood alongside the highway, the bright red faded to a sickening pink.

A receptionist sat behind a large desk, typing on a computer wearing a headset attached to a phone system.

She couldn't imagine what kind of news a little town like Rocky Point would have to report day after day, but the receptionist looked busy, and she stood in front of the desk until the redheaded woman looked her way.

"I'm looking for Autumn Bennett," Callie said.

"Do you have an appointment?"

"No. I'm sorry."

The receptionist smiled. "No problem. I think Autumn's around here somewhere. Let me ping her cell phone." She typed something into her computer. "It'll be a moment until I can find out if she's in the building. Help yourself to a cup of coffee."

She'd drank enough at the resort and didn't want any more, and she ambled around the lobby instead. Framed front pages decorated the walls, and she read the headlines to give herself something to do.

"Callie! Hey!" Autumn greeted her, hurrying into the lobby. "How are you?"

"Good. I was hoping I could talk to you, if you're not busy."

"Is it Marnie? Does she need help?"

"No, but, umm . . ." Callie glanced at the receptionist and then back at Autumn.

Autumn got the hint. "We can talk in my cubby, come on."

Callie followed her through the bullpen to the back of the building, Autumn's heels clicking against the tile. "Sorry about that. Not much stock in the Lifestyle's department, if you know what I mean. Out of sight, out of mind."

"It's no problem."

Gesturing to a chair, Autumn said, "What can I do for you? Wedding stuff?"

"No. Not really. I had breakfast with Marnie this morning, and we were talking about Mitch. She said you might have some information about that."

"Mitch Sinclair and the fire," Autumn said, tapping a pen on top of a notebook.

"Yeah."

"That was a sad time. Are you sure you want to dig through it?"

"I like Mitch. I want to know what happened."

"Okay. I'll have to bring you back to the research

department. All the older articles are on microfiche. The Marengo paper picked it up. Decatur did, too. You didn't hear about it?"

"Maybe, but seven years ago I was only twenty-three and trying to find my footing in the fire department after I graduated from the academy."

Autumn shot her a look, her eyes wide. "I didn't know you were younger than us. You look older." She blushed. "Sorry. No woman wants to hear that."

She jerked her shoulder. "It's no big deal. Firefighting's tough. I'd be surprised if it *didn't* show on my face."

"Is that why you're interested? Because of the fire?"

This time it was Callie who blushed. "No. Like I said, I like Mitch."

"Oh, you *like* him, like him," Autumn said over her shoulder as she led Callie even farther back into the building. "I didn't realize."

"I didn't either, until this morning. I asked him to the hockey game, and he said he'd go."

Autumn barked out a laugh. "Well, he likes to you, too, to agree to something like that. Mitch rarely goes into to town. And to a hockey game? Forget it. It might be too much, too soon. I'll be right back."

She stumbled over her boots and righted herself before Autumn saw her. Too much too soon. That couldn't be possible. The accident was seven years go. Everyone had to reenter the world at some point. Hadn't Mitch by now?

Autumn disappeared and a few minutes later and came back carrying a box of film. "If I remember correctly, we reported on it heavily for a couple of days, but after that, news came in more sporadically. Bits and pieces of Mitch's recovery, his mother's. Did Marnie tell you about his mom's heart attack?"

She nodded.

"I think there was an update about the semi-truck driver. I don't remember what happened to him. But all in all, it disappeared rather quickly." Autumn rushed to add, "As far as news stories go. Of course, Mitch is still dealing with it after all this time, but his daily struggles aren't news. That sounds callous, but it's just the way it is."

"I get it. Thanks for helping me."

"It's not a problem. I hope you find what you're looking for," Autumn said, settling her in front of a machine. "The anniversary of the accident is coming up. It happened right before Christmas break, which didn't help Mitch's cause at all. Come find me when you're done. I need to get back to work, but SueEllen's around. If you need help, flag her down." Autumn pointed to a curvy woman who had short black hair and a snake tattoo circling down her arm. She carried a teetering stack of files. "She's our odds and ends person. There's nothing she doesn't know."

"Thanks."

The film flew too fast to read as she adjusted the speed, but barely five minutes had gone by when she hit what looked to be the first and biggest story of the fire.

SAINT OR SINNER the headline read, and at that, her hands shook in anger.

Like he'd had a choice letting those girls burn.

Under the headline was a large black and white photo of a burned-out bus.

The hollowed skeleton of the school bus didn't surprise her. She'd come across burned vehicles a time or two. What did were the tears that clogged her throat. Mitch had been in that fire, had sacrificed himself to save the lives of small children in his care.

It's what she did, every time she went to work, and

while she felt proud of Mitch for doing what he did, there was a part of her that mourned what he lost.

Her father didn't understand that. Didn't understand that every time she ran into a burning building she lost a little of herself. A little piece of her mental health. A little piece of what made her human.

Maybe until that moment she hadn't realized it herself because she'd never gotten hurt, not physically, not the way Mitch had.

She began to read.

In a horrific accident no one in Rocky Point could have predicted, the community lost two of its own yesterday morning when a semi-truck collided with a school bus.

The bus, driven by Mitchell Sinclair, 29, resident of Rocky Point and high school graduate, burst into flames. When questioned, Sinclair stated he was halfway through his route, but the number of children, though few, proved to be too many for Sinclair to safely remove from the bus.

She scoffed. The reporter made it sound like Mitch didn't have it in him to rescue anyone, and the fact that he had rescued most of the kids had been pure luck.

Two children lost their lives that cold, snowy morning. Their names are being withheld at this time to respect the family's privacy.

Sinclair suffered third-degree burns and is currently being treated at a medical facility in Decatur, Minnesota. No other information is available about his condition at this time.

The article went on to explain the history of the Rocky Point, the school system, weather, and how the accident was the most tragic the citizens of Rocky Point had seen in decades.

She zipped the microfiche along and stopped at the date two days after the accident.

BUS DRIVER'S MOTHER HAS HEART ATTACK, blared the headline, and her heart thrummed in pain. Anything that hurt Mitch was going to hurt her too, and she held her breath while she read.

Ruby Sinclair, 59, was admitted into Good Samaritan Hospital late last night after having a heart attack. Emergency services were called to their residence at 1116 Elmwood Drive, at 10:14 pm. Her husband, Charles "Chip" Sinclair, made the call. Authorities were also summoned to the scene to investigate what appeared to be violent vandalism targeting their son, Mitchell Sinclair. Ruby Sinclair discovered a scarecrow hanging from a tree in their front yard when she took their dog outside that evening.

The blurred photograph of the scarecrow dangling from the bare tree accompanied the article.

Ruby Sinclair's condition was not released by hospital staff and no further information is available at this time.

She couldn't imagine how Mitch had felt trying to recover and worrying about his mom on top of it.

She didn't come across any of the conflict Marnie or Autumn mentioned until three days later when the little girls' identities were released.

PARENTS MOURN LOST DAUGHTERS

The two girls who lost their lives in the bussing accident on Wednesday morning were identified as Crystal Ward, 8, and Allyson Ward, 10. Parents are Karen and John Ward. The funeral will be held at Our Savior's Church on Benton Blvd, Saturday morning at 10 am. In lieu of monetary gifts, the couple asks that donations be given to Angels on Earth, an organization that assists parents with funeral expenses who have lost a child.

Sources say the parents of the girls are doing as well as can be expected. A family member who asked to remain anonymous had this to say: "We hope Mitch Sinclair burns in hell for the pain he's caused our family. He was in charge of those kids. Their lives were his responsibility. He deserves everything he gets."

Harsh words, but a sentiment that has, unfortunately, been repeated since the accident. We can only hope time heals all wounds.

She didn't want to read anymore. She was afraid of what she'd find. Mitch's mother must have been okay or Marnie and Autumn would have told her otherwise.

The accident had taken place seven years ago, but reading those articles made it feel like last week. It wasn't fair to Mitch that he was still hiding because of something that wasn't his fault. He deserved his own life and going to the hockey game would do him good. She knew it.

Callie waved at SueEllen, told her she was done using the microfiche machine, and found Autumn in her cubby.

"Did you find what you were looking for?" Autumn asked.

"I can't believe how this town treated him," she said, plopping into the spare chair in front of Autumn's desk. "And his poor mother."

"It was a nasty time," Autumn said, closing a file on her laptop. "The girls' funeral was packed. The school brought in grief counselors to talk to the kids. The holiday bonfire the town hosts every Christmas turned into a memorial and prayer service. Something like that in a bigger city like Decatur, it would have been a blip on the radar and something else would have taken its place practically the next day. The fire and Crystal's and Allyson's deaths were the only things people talked about until early April when a family of four broke through the ice in their pickup truck and drowned. It was a long winter for the Sinclairs. All of them."

"It's time Mitch stopped hiding from the people in town. It was seven years ago."

"Is that what he wants, Callie?" Autumn asked, swiveling in her chair. "Mitch isn't a cause to take up. He's a person, who has feelings."

"He said he'd go to the game tonight. I'll be with him," she said, stubbornness lifting her chin.

"You won't be enough. I'll help, if I can, and so will the rest of us. Sit with us, okay?"

"Thanks. I appreciate that. I'll let you get back to work."

"See you tonight."

She pushed down the wiggle in her stomach. Mitch wasn't a cause, she agreed with Autumn on that. He was a person, and the time had come for him to be treated like one.

CHAPTER FOUR

"Are you sure this is a good idea?" Ivy asked, sitting in the recliner in the corner of his room.

Mitch buttoned his shirt. It looked the same as his work shirt but without the Rocky Point logo stitched above the pocket. "This is the worst idea I've ever had, but it's Callie."

"She's not one of us. She doesn't understand."

"Yeah. I know." Ivy didn't mean one of us, as in a Rocky Point resident, she meant one of us as in, "We're outcasts and Callie isn't."

"She'll get the hint soon enough. All I have to do is walk into the arena. It's not like I don't go through this all the time. She just needs to see it."

Grocery store, hardware store, it was all the same.

"She seems nice. I talked to her a little after you stormed out of the lounge. What made you change your mind? I heard you tell her no."

"I kissed her, and she let me."

She scoffed. "This is about sex? I thought you were better than that."

"It's not about sex."

She narrowed her eyes.

"Well, it kind of is," he said. Ivy was his best friend, okay, fine, his only friend, and there was no point in lying to her. "You remember Yvonne? I thought we had something, until she wanted . . . and she couldn't . . ." He cleared his throat against the catch. The memory still hurt.

"She wasn't good enough for you," she said.

"I think you have that backward." He looped his belt through his jeans.

"She wasn't good enough for you, and I'm having serious doubts about Callie, too. If she knew you, she wouldn't ask you to do this."

"She *doesn't* know me, and that's the point. After tonight she will, and she'll scoot her cute little ass off into the sunset like Yvonne did. Get it over with."

"Why do you keep trying?"

"What, and give up like you?" he asked, but he instantly regretted it.

The pinched look on Ivy's face became more pronounced, lines digging into her forehead and bracketing her mouth. "I didn't give up. I have other obligations."

"How are you, anyway? With Logan back in town?"

"We haven't spoken, and that's fine by me."

He read her face. It was anything but fine. "You two will run into each other eventually."

"My break's over," she said, hopping off the recliner. "I hope things go okay tonight. I'll find you before my shift tomorrow."

"How many days in a row have you worked now?"

She jerked her shoulder. "I don't know. I lost count after thirty."

"You need a day off or you're going to get sick. And how does Desiree let you get away with that? Stacy should be up her ass about it. It's against the law or something to work that many hours."

"I fill in where I need to fill in, and Desiree knows it. I need the money. Don't you dare say anything or I'll be screwed."

"I won't say anything."

"Good. Talk to you later."

She stepped into the hallway and closed the door behind her, leaving him alone to finish dressing for the game. He told Callie he'd stop by her room to pick her up, and they would drive together.

Because of the accident, it'd been a long time since he attended a Polar Bears game, but time hadn't helped the memories fade. The other day he picked something up for his dad at the hardware store, and Greg Larson could barely look him in the eye to hand him his receipt.

It amazed him how long someone could hold a grudge, but it was more than a grudge and he couldn't forget that. Two little girls had lost their lives because of his carelessness, and that deserved more than a cold shoulder.

Dressed to sit in the frigid temperatures, he trudged down the hallway and up the stairs to Callie's room.

The way she looked when she opened the door made him think tonight would be almost worth it. Just to spend time with her.

Almost.

"You look pretty," he said.

Callie stood in her doorway dressed in snow boots, jeans, a black parka that had faux silver fur around the hood, and a black and silver pompom hat. She held black mittens in her hands.

"Thanks." She chewed on her bottom lip and didn't

speak as he led her to his truck parked in the staff parking lot located behind the resort.

"Did you change your mind?" he asked, resigned. Of course she would. She'd had time to think about it. She'd had time for her friends to tell her this was a bad idea and now she was looking for a way out without looking like a bitch.

It relieved him, in a way, that he could go back to his room and pretend none of this ever happened.

He opened the truck's passenger side door and waited to hear her excuses.

She climbed in and twisted, facing him. "No. I'm . . . nervous. I haven't been on a date in a long time."

He huffed out a laugh, angry that he was happy she hadn't changed her mind after all. "You and me both, kid."

"I'm hardly a kid," she said after he settled behind the wheel.

He looked at her out of the corners of his eyes. "You're friends with Marnie. I assumed you're the same age as the rest of us."

"I'm younger than she is. I turned thirty this year, but Autumn said I look older. I work a lot. I guess that's where she got it from."

He drove down the steep hill, his tires easily finding traction in the snow. "What do you do for fun?"

"Nothing much. Sleep. I hang out with Marnie sometimes, if she's not with James. My family keeps me busy, but my dad and I don't get along that well. I don't like seeing him if I don't have to." He stopped at a red light and she looked out her window. "Do you like living at the resort?"

"It comes in handy, no pun intended. It helps me save. No mortgage or rent or anything like that."

"That's nice."

"Yeah, it's not bad."

The conversation felt awkward, yet familiar, soothing. Strangers attempting to get to know each other. First date jitters made him feel normal and he took comfort in that. That he could do normal things like normal people.

Until they went inside.

He idled in the arena's full parking lot. The building's lights glowed, and a stream of people moved toward the doors.

He turned the truck off, and they sat in silence. He searched for the courage to warn her, and finally he said, his voice raspy, "I don't know how it's going to go in there."

She unbuckled her seatbelt and leaned toward him. "It will be all right." She kissed his cheek.

That's what he'd rather do. Stay in his truck and make out like teenagers.

"I hope so. Can I get your door?"

"Sure." She smiled at him and shoved her hands into her mittens.

He opened her door but resisted kissing her, even though her sitting on the seat made them eye-level. With his hands around her waist, he helped her jump out of the cab. They walked across the lot, the snow crunching under their boots, and he held her mittened hand.

"Everyone will be here," she said, and he focused on her voice to calm the blood rushing through his veins. "Marnie and James. Leah. Autumn said she'd be here. I visited her today, to see where she worked."

He'd never stepped foot inside the newspaper's offices. After the accident, reporters from all over the state called him, begging to interview him, and he had to change his number three times before they finally left him alone.

"Did you manage breakfast with Marnie?" he asked.

They shuffled inside the arena with the throng of people. He lowered his head and pulled his hat down.

"Yeah. James and his parents were there. Leah skipped breakfast."

"Who's that again?" he asked. People were looking at him, brief glances out of the corners of their eyes or flat-out staring. Either Callie didn't see it or she was ignoring it because she kept right on talking as if nothing was happening.

"One of Marnie's bridesmaids. I told her she was lopsided. James has Jared and Logan as groomsmen, and Marnie asked me, Leah, and Autumn. She didn't act like it bothered her, though."

"She'll figure it out," he said, staring at his boots. "Did you want something to eat or drink?"

Hostility swept through the lobby where it opened into the concession area, and it mingled with the scent of burnt popcorn, hot dogs, and the crisp smell of cold air clinging to the jackets of the people streaming in from outside.

"No. I'm fine, let's go find a place to sit."

He held her hand and guided her toward the stairs that would bring them down to the ice. In the stairwell, a woman stopped in front of them and glared. "What are *you* doing here?"

He turned away and kept going, urging Callie to do the same.

"Where do you want to sit?" he asked as they stood near the rink. The players warmed up, shooting pucks back and forth or zigzagging along the sides. Cheerleaders did their thing, skating from one side of the ice to the other, ensuring everyone in the crowd could watch their routines. One player patted a cheerleader's butt, and she shook her pompoms at him, laughing.

It'd be nice to feel so carefree.

"Let's go up," Callie said, waving to the top of the bleachers. "It'll be impossible to find anyone here. This place is packed."

"It's the biggest game of the year," he said. Like he knew what he was talking about.

The crowd started chanting, "Pol-ar *Bears!* Pol-ar *Bears!*" while they stomped their feet.

On the way up, a man stepped in front of them. "Takes a lot of nerve to show your face here," he said, his nose an inch away from Mitch's.

It took all of his willpower not to flinch.

It's what he came here for. To show Callie what his life was like when he attempted to live with any kind of normalcy.

"We want to watch the game, same as anybody," she said, gripping his arm.

The man stepped back, surprised someone was defending him, until he saw who it was. "Got a woman to do your dirty work. Like a coward." He moved past him, his shoulder slamming into Mitch's, and he leaned against the handrail to find his balance on the narrow stairway.

"What an asshole," Callie said, raising her voice over the pop music the cheerleaders were skating to. "Let's sit here."

"I don't need you to fight my battles for me," he said, sitting on the wooden bleacher. An older couple glared at them and slid farther down the bench, giving him and Callie more space than they needed.

"I'm not. I'm sticking up for a friend."

"It's not going to earn you any favors."

"I don't care about them. I care about you." She brushed her mitten over the scarring on his cheek.

"Oh, you do?"

She blushed. "Yeah. I do."

"You're using me for my maintenance skills," he teased, trying his best to ignore the aggressive looks two people sitting in front of them were shooting over their shoulders. Their toddler caught sight of his face and began to cry, her big blue eyes full of tears and fear.

"I have to admit, I liked watching you work this morning."

"You *did* ask me to your room when you didn't need me." He forced joviality into his voice, but he was becoming more and more agitated. Couldn't she see how people were acting around them? Couldn't she feel the hate swirling around the arena like an angry storm?

She wrapped her arms around his and whispered into his ear, "Maybe."

A large group stomped up the stairs and chose to sit on the bleacher behind him and Callie. They settled in, and one of them kneed him between his shoulder blades, knocking him forward. He resisted the urge to turn around. It could have been an accident and he didn't want to call attention to himself.

The game started then, and people stopped staring at him to sing the national anthem and watch the hockey players fight over the tiny black puck.

He relaxed enough to enjoy the first period, though the hostility around them hadn't dissipated.

When the period ended, several people scooted off the benches to head up to the concessions or use the bathrooms. "Do want something to eat? Or a drink?" he asked, hoping she would say no. He didn't want to leave the safe haven the bench had turned into, but he wouldn't send her upstairs to the concessions counter alone. Too much of a gentleman, he'd have to brave the crowds and the lines if she wanted popcorn or a soda.

"No, but I wish I could find everyone, at least to say hi. Marnie and Autumn told me this was a bad idea, but it's been—"

"Mitch Sinclair?"

An older man wearing a blue security jacket interrupted her, and Mitch stiffened. "Yeah?"

"We've had some complaints." His eyes glinted hard behind black-framed glasses and his lips were stiff. "You're making a lot of people uncomfortable, and I'm going to have to ask you to leave."

"He has a right to be here," Callie said, leaning around him. "We're on a date."

"Is that right?" he asked, sneering. "And who are you?"

Mitch knew him from somewhere, the man's name just out of reach, but he couldn't place him. Maybe from church a long time ago. Or the pharmacy at the drugstore.

"I'm Callie Carter. I'm one of Marnie Zimmerman's bridesmaids."

"Miss Carter. You're not from around here. I don't suppose you know what happened—"

"I know what happened," she snapped, and he put a hand on her knee. "It was a long time ago, and he deserves a life."

"I'm not one to take sides," the man said, his eyes narrowing, obviously lying. He'd chosen sides a long time ago. "But those little girls died in that fire, and some would argue that Sinclair doesn't deserve what you say he does."

He wasn't going to sit and listen to Callie argue with arena security. If he didn't belong, he didn't belong, and he was tired of pretending that all the belligerent behavior going on around them didn't trample his spirit. "It's okay,

Callie. It's nothing less than what I expected. You can stay, if you want. I'm going to take off."

"I'll go with you."

Shame burned as he hurried to the nearest exit. He didn't care if he had to walk around the building to his truck. He wanted out as quickly as possible.

Callie had to trot to keep up with him, but he didn't slow down.

Humiliated, frustrated, and dejected, he slammed out the door but held it open for her, and she burst into the parking lot. "It's not right."

He leaned against the wall, resting his head against the cold brick. "It went better than I thought it would."

"It still sucks," she said, stepping between his legs and wrapping her arms around his waist.

"Come on. Let's go back to the resort."

She sighed. "Okay."

He drove through town, the roads empty. Everyone was either hiding from the cold or at the game.

Even the resort seemed quieter than usual, and he parked behind the massive building next to Ivy's car.

"Why don't you go inside? I'm going to take a walk and cool off."

He preferred being outside, alone. He didn't mind his own company, and the isolation comforted him.

"No. I'll stay with you, if you don't mind."

Anger scratched at the back of his throat. "I don't need a goddamned babysitter. I'm not going to hurt myself because a bunch of assholes don't want me around. I'm used to it, Callie. I'm used to being the town loser. It's fine. Go inside."

"Why can't I stay with you?"

"Why? So you can get tired of me later? So one day

you'll realize that how people treat me will rub off on you? No thanks."

He took two furious strides toward the lake. He needed the wide-open expanse of nothing. He needed the silence, the stars.

But he turned around to Callie's hunched shoulders, her hands shoved into the pockets of her parka.

He swore. She'd only been trying to be nice. "Callie?"

She looked over her shoulder. At least she wasn't crying. He didn't want to make her cry.

"If you want to walk, come on."

"Are you sure?"

"Yeah."

She brightened. "Okay."

"Why do you want to be around me so much?" He followed the trail packed down by snowmobiles and ATVs to the water. Empty docks lined the shore, and snow hid the sandy beach.

A light wind blew, chilly fingers poking down his neck and under his jacket.

Little dots of light moved across the ice, hearty souls braving the cold to take a late-night ride. He didn't own his own snowmobile or ATV, but the resort had purchased a few several years back and while he wasn't a mechanic, he did ride them on occasion and made sure nothing was wrong with them.

"Why do you want to be around me?" she replied, grabbing his hand the best she could with her mittens on.

"Who says I do?"

He'd missed this. The back and forth between a man and a woman. The teasing, light-hearted camaraderie people found when they enjoyed spending time together.

"You did. When you said you'd go to the hockey game with me. Marnie and Autumn warned me, but I didn't listen. I'm sorry."

He squeezed her hand. "It's okay. Sometimes you have to try."

He sat at the end of the dock, letting his feet dangle. The snow and ice would numb his ass, but he didn't mind. Being outside in the cool air made him feel better than going back to his room and sulking. Or going to Callie's room and making love to her, which is what he really wanted to do.

"You told that security asshole you knew what happened, but you're still here."

"It's what I did this morning. Marnie told me the story, and she suggested I talk to Autumn."

"*That's* what you were doing at the newspaper offices," he said. "Looking me up. I should've known you'd do it sooner or later."

"I didn't do it to hurt you. I wanted to know what happened."

"Well, now you do."

He stared across the frozen water.

Callie tucked herself into his side and he wrapped his arm around her, though he knew he should pull away. But he couldn't keep doing that either because if he did it too many times, she'd think he didn't want to be with her.

And he did.

Too much.

"I'm sorry about your mom. Is she okay now?"

"She's fine. You read an article about that, too, huh?" Every minute of his life during that time had been put under a microscope. Background checks, how he'd behaved in school. How his parents had raised him. What church congregation he'd belonged to. Everyone had been looking for a reason to blame him for the deaths of those little girls.

"Yeah. They said she had a heart attack. It sounded terrible."

"I wasn't coherent around that time. It took me a while to surface . . . to care about what was going on around me."

"Because of the pain."

He did push her away then, stood angrily to his feet, and turned his back on her. "Because of the pain? No. Because two little girls lost their lives that morning. I will never forget them, ever. I hear their screams in my head every waking minute. Do you know what that's like? Of all the stupid things to say. *Because of the pain.* You have no fucking idea what you're talking about."

Callie definitely said the wrong thing, and Mitch had every right to be angry. She hadn't forgotten about the two girls, but she'd learned to numb herself over the loss of life.

A dog, a cat.

An old woman who died of smoke inhalation before Callie found her.

A child hidden under the bed in fear.

The father who ran back inside his burning house to rescue his trapped wife leaving a toddler orphaned.

The young woman who wasted time trying to save photo albums and didn't make it out.

She wasn't callous or unfeeling, but she had to lock part

of herself away or she'd end up like her brother, in rehab, trying to drink away her fear and pain.

"I know you did your best and it wasn't your fault those girls died."

"My best wasn't good enough."

"That's true for a lot of people. It's true for me."

"Tell that to their parents. Tell that to their grieving mother and father who sued me and the school for damages."

"It was an accident, and you were hurt, too."

"No one cares, Callie."

"I do." She tugged on the rough material of his jacket, asking him look at her. "I do."

He rested his cheek on the top of her head. "I'm sorry for yelling at you."

"I deserved it. I said the wrong thing. I didn't mean you cared more about yourself, but you must have been in excruciating pain. Give yourself credit for getting through that, at least."

"They don't give you much choice," he murmured. "I was on suicide watch for a long time."

"Did you think about it?"

"Yeah, but not in an obvious way. I didn't want to eat, I barely slept unless the pain medication knocked me out. I wasn't interested in anything outside my four walls at the hospital."

"Loneliness would have killed you then."

"If it weren't for my parents. I saw a therapist for a while . . . she said my mom's heart attack gave me something to live for. I needed to take care of myself to take care of her. She's right, I guess. I forced myself to follow doctor's orders. I needed them to release me as quickly as possible. I needed to see her."

"You're a good man."

"No, I'm not."

"Yeah, you are. Will you kiss me?" she asked, tilting her head. She wanted him to kiss her under the stars. Wanted him to feel the compassion and understanding that had been building up inside her from the minute security at the arena asked them to leave.

He touched his lips to hers, warm and soft. He kept his face clean-shaven, and his smooth skin rubbed against hers.

Sighing, he leaned away.

"Do you want to go ice fishing tomorrow?" she asked.

"I can't. I visit my parents on Saturday mornings, but after you're done, maybe we can meet up. There's a guest checking into one of the cabins and Desiree asked me to double check that the hot tub's fixed. I'll show you where I watch the deer."

"That would be nice. Walk me back to the resort?"

"Sure."

She grasped his hand. She didn't want him standing out here alone.

At her door, she reached onto her tiptoes and kissed him again. She wanted to feel his hands on her and she wished he'd come inside her room, but he said, "Goodnight, Callie," and she let him go. He made plans to see her tomorrow, and after the night they'd had tonight, she felt fortunate he wanted anything more to do with her at all.

He'd wanted to follow her into her room. The invitation had been clear in her eyes and he'd been close to saying yes. Very close.

How long had it been since he'd made love to a woman? Before the accident. Too long to be without companionship, too long to go without pillow talk. That had always been his favorite part. Lying in bed, cuddling, chatting in whispers, after a round of amazing sex. Of course, the last woman he'd done that with married someone else and drove a minivan full of kids now.

He undressed and tossed and turned on the lumpy mattress. He wasn't going to be able to fall asleep, and exhausted, he slid out of bed and made a cup of coffee in his tiny kitchenette.

He sat at the small table wedged into the corner of his room and flipped through the pages of a scrapbook. It'd break his mother's heart to know he'd kept the articles written about him. Callie must have been at the newspaper's offices for hours if she looked through all the articles about the accident. There were so many.

During his recovery, finding them had been easy. There wasn't any lack of people who wanted to shove what he'd done in his face. Hate mail had stuffed his mailbox.

Sipping his coffee, he skimmed the articles. Though his scars and pain caused by nerve damage stayed with him every second and he thought about those girls every waking moment, it seemed a lifetime ago since the fire. Slowly, painstakingly, he'd built a small life for himself. He'd found a job he liked and people stopped harassing his mom and dad. For the most part, they left him alone, too. Out of sight, out of mind.

Callie's presence dragged it all back front and center.

He wondered if she'd noticed not one person said one kind thing at the game. Not one person approached them and said they were happy he was getting out and about again.

Mitch dumped the last of his coffee down the drain and flung himself into bed, disgusted and annoyed.

Callie's compassionate brown eyes started this stupid way of thinking. He'd never get his life back. He didn't *want* his life back. He'd sentenced himself to life in prison, on his terms, to make up for the lives those little girls lost because of him.

He liked his life.

Small, closed in.

This was what he wanted.

It was what he wanted, but he fell asleep wishing he could wrap Callie's hair around his fingers as he slid into her and bury his face in her neck while she murmured into his ear.

After eating a light breakfast he asked one of the housekeepers to bring to his room, Mitch strode out to his truck wearing his work clothes.

His mother usually had chores for him to do. Not many in the winter months, but he kept their driveway clear of snow and their roof, too. He always wasted a couple of hours tinkering in the garage with his dad, taking apart the vacuum cleaner or replacing the spark plugs in the snow-blower, then talked to his mom in the kitchen while she made lunch.

They constantly worried about him, though they never said anything. His mother had been relieved he'd gotten the job at the resort, and they'd fallen into an uneasy, but for the most part comfortable, way of life.

Red paint screamed at him over the length of the

parking lot, and he swore under his breath, his angry exclamations turning white in the frosty air.

Someone had taken a can of spray paint to his truck. Even from this distance, Mitch could read STAY AWAY on the driver's side.

Seemed like more than memories were going to come back and bite him in the ass.

Dammit.

MURDERER sprayed in capital letters took up the entire passenger side, and FUCK OFF on his tailgate would greet anyone behind him.

He had no other way into town unless he asked Blaine to drop him off in the resort's shuttle, and his parents would wonder why in the hell he'd do that. Better to show them and explain. Rumors spread fast, and he wanted them to hear everything that was happening from him first.

Taking the back roads, he passed only a few people, one old man giving him a crusty eye as they passed each other, but he had to park on the street and there would be no hiding the filthy words from his parents' neighbors.

His father, holding a paint brush and a can of white paint, looked guiltily over his shoulder. He never could hide his emotions.

Mitch stiffened and climbed out of his truck. "They got you too, huh?" he called.

Chip Sinclair used his shoulder to push his wire-rimmed glasses up his nose. "I was hoping to get rid of it before you got here."

"Doesn't matter," Mitch said, taking the brush. "They did it to me, too."

"I'm sorry, son," Chip said, letting the brush go without a fight.

"Nothing to be sorry for." He finished swiping the

white paint over the black words. His father had done enough he couldn't read what was sprayed there, but he assumed it matched his truck. "How's Mom? Did she see?"

"No. I found it when I took Luna out for her morning constitutional."

"Can't you say the dog had to piss?" he asked, as angry as he was amused.

"Luna's a lady. She doesn't piss, she tinkles," his father said, laughing. "Come on. It's too early to eat lunch, but your ma wants to see that you're okay."

"I thought you said she didn't see this," he said, pointing the brush at the house.

"She didn't, but she's got ears. Billie Jean called her last night."

Billie Jean had lived next to them since Mitch was six years old. An old busybody, she kept his mom company drinking iced tea on the porch during the summer and trading gossip about everyone they knew . . . and everyone they didn't. In the winter, they took turns sitting in each other's kitchens drinking coffee instead of iced tea, not letting the cold stop them.

"What could Billie Jean have told her?"

Chip's eyebrows scooted up to his hairline. "You were with a woman last night. How long did you think you could keep *that* from your mother?"

"Shit. I suppose she's got me married."

"She wants you happy. Come on. She's been glaring at us for the past five minutes." Chip jerked his thumb to the front window where Ruby and Luna stood watching them.

Preparing to be interrogated, Mitch swiped the brush at the graffiti one more time, dumped it and the paint can in the garage, and followed his dad inside the house.

"Morning, Ma," he said, knocking his boots on the stairs

and letting himself in the mudroom. The house sat in the middle of a block in an older residential area. Autumn Bennett, Callie's new best friend, didn't live far away. He'd watched her come and go a time or two.

"Morning, Mitch. Coffee?"

"Sure. How're you doing?"

"The dryer started making noises."

"I'll check the lint traps and vent. Don't need a . . . fire." He couldn't remember a time since the accident he'd been able to say the word without it getting stuck in his throat.

"I'd appreciate it," she said, even though she knew he knew her husband could easily do the same job.

He settled in a kitchen chair and breathed in the scent of apple pie and cinnamon rolls.

Ruby plated him one without him having to ask, and despite the breakfast he's already eaten at the resort, dug in.

Chip sat in front of the TV, Luna laying on the floor next to him, and turned a local morning news program down low. He wanted to hear without appearing to listen, and Mitch bit back a smile.

Everyone was interested in his love life. His mother twitched with impatience, keeping her questions at bay while he ate, and he made her suffer, enjoying the fresh-baked cinnamon roll in silence.

The clock on the wall ticked away the minutes as Ruby anxiously sipped her coffee.

He scraped his fork against the plate to clean it of the last of the icing, and his mother couldn't help herself.

"Billie Jean told me you went to the hockey game last night," she said, trembling with excitement.

"I did," he said, rising from the table. He rinsed his plate under the faucet and slotted it into the empty dishwasher.

"With a woman."

A woman who'd be ice fishing right about now, if she followed through with her morning plans. "Yeah. She's staying at the resort. She's a bridesmaid in Marnie's wedding."

"I've been reading Autumn Bennett's blog. The wedding's causing quite a hullabaloo. Is it making your life tougher, honey?"

He had to give his mother points for tact, and she knew him well enough to know that if she pushed too hard, he'd clam up. That was his modus operandi when it came to anything about the fire, his burns, or his future. It shamed him that ninety-nine point nine percent of his life made his mother walk on eggshells when they spoke, but he didn't think it was too much to ask that she give him a break now and then.

This morning would not be one of those times.

"The resort's always full, Ma. It's not causing any more work than I usually have. As always, I'm thankful Desiree took a chance and hired me."

"You're smart and a good worker. She knew what she was doing. Now tell me about this woman. You brought her to the game?"

"Ah, no—"

"Billie Jean is never wrong, Mitch."

"If you'd let me speak, I'd tell you."

"I'm sorry, I'm sorry, but I'm just so happy I could burst."

She looked it, a smile lighting up her face, making her sparkle better than any makeup she ever found, even when his dad took her to Mall of America and let her loose in Macy's.

"I didn't bring her as much as she brought me. Asked me a couple of times before I finally said I'd go."

"I need to meet this woman," Ruby said, pouring him more coffee. "And she . . . and she . . ." She dropped into a kitchen chair and worried a paper towel between her fingers.

"She doesn't care how I look."

Chip looked into the kitchen, Luna perked her ears up, and tears filled his mother's eyes.

Good God. Had he been that pathetic these past seven years?

No, not pathetic.

Hurting so badly he dragged his entire family down with him.

"Mitch," Ruby breathed, dismayed.

"That's not what I meant. Of course she cares. She doesn't mind. She read about the accident, and she doesn't . . . blame me."

"Will you invite her over?"

"It's a little soon for that, isn't it? Besides, things are hard right now." No use trying to protect her. She already gone through it once, and she'd face this new wave of hostility as well. His dad wouldn't keep his mother from knowing about the things going on. Ignorance wasn't bliss in situations like this. It was dangerous.

"Why? What's hard? What do you mean?"

"Someone spray-painted my truck. Nasty things I'll need to have the body shop paint over. And Dad was cleaning up the side of the house when I got here."

Ruby shot Chip a dirty look. "We agreed not to keep secrets about things like that."

"I was going to tell you, but I didn't want you to see it. There's a big difference."

The frown on his mother's face said otherwise, and he held her hand. "You need to take care of yourself. We don't want a repeat of what happened before. You scared the hell out of me. I don't want you to have another heart attack because someone with his head up his ass couldn't let me have an evening at a high school hockey game. It isn't worth it."

"Then you didn't have a good time?"

He sipped his coffee to wet his mouth. "No." He'd lay it straight. "I went because she asked, and I wanted to make her happy. But if looks could kill, we would've been dead a hundred times over. Ed Dunlop asked us to leave after the first period." The old geezer's name had come to him last night while he tried to fall asleep.

Ruby covered her mouth with a trembling hand, and her eyes filled with more tears.

"He wasn't nasty, but he made it clear I wasn't welcome."

"Oh, Mitch."

"It's okay. Callie was enraged enough for both of us."

"Callie? That's her name?"

"Short for Callista." He still liked saying it. Her name made him think of water sprites and faeries.

"That's beautiful," Ruby said. "Are you going to see her again?"

"She asked me to go ice fishing this morning, but I turned her down. Dad, will you explain to Ma? Callie's going to realize that I don't mix with people and she'll back off."

"Well, son, I don't know—"

Impatiently, he shook his head and pushed away from the table.

Luna felt the tension and whimpered.

He stepped across the kitchen and brushed his fingers through the German shepherd's soft fur. After the accident, his parents adopted her to keep people out of their yard. Mitch would bet his paycheck that her ferocious barking had interrupted whoever spray-painted the side of the house.

"I do know. Women like fancy dinners and going to the movies. Callie proved it by just how many times she asked me to go to the game. She likes to be around people, and I don't. I tried, and the house and my truck were vandalized. I won't put you in danger trying to have a life when I don't deserve one. I'll take a look at the dryer, Ma."

He did the few chores around the house he grew up in and carried the paint and brush into the crisp air to add another layer to the words his father already covered up.

"I hope you reported this," he said, swiping viciously at the siding.

"Didn't think it was worth it," Chip said, zipping up his work jacket and keeping an eye on Luna as she sniffed around the yard, looking for the perfect place to pee.

He hunched his shoulders. With the way his family had been treated before, he agreed. "Probably not, but God help us if this gets worse. You need to create a paper trail, okay?"

"Yeah," Chip said, but he knew his dad would leave it alone, at least for now. The evidence on the side of the house was already covered up.

"I'll report the truck. Take some pictures and give them to the police."

Chip pushed his hands into the pockets of his jeans. "What you told your mom . . . you and this Callie . . . there's no chance?"

He thought of the way the blood drained out of Callie's face when Ed asked them to leave. She'd reacted in anger, not fear, but still, she wouldn't put up with that for long. He hadn't found anyone who would.

"Nah. She'll go home after the wedding. She lives in Decatur. It's fine, and I'm looking forward to it being done. The wedding isn't causing me more work, but I can't lie, it's hard to have so many high school classmates back in town. I want things to go back to normal."

Before the delusion he'd be welcome out in public. Before the spray paint.

Before the kisses.

"You can't keep on like this," Chip said, blinking against the sun. "You're too young to live your life like a hermit."

"Nothing's changed, Dad. All that's happened is that I've been reminded of my place. Say goodbye to Ma for me, will you? I don't feel like answering any more questions. I'll put this stuff away, then I need to get my truck to the shop. I don't want to look at it anymore."

"Keep in touch, son."

He nodded at the code. Keep his dad informed if anything else bad happened.

"Keep Ma safe, and you do the same."

CHAPTER FIVE

Undecided, Callie stood on the frozen water. She'd overslept and missed joining everyone for breakfast, and they'd left to go fishing without her. Marnie hadn't mentioned where on the lake they would be, and she could only hope they were off the resort's shore along with everyone else.

She didn't want to sit alone in her room, and Mitch said he had things to do that morning. She'd stopped at the dining room, wolfed down a bowl of oatmeal, two slices of toast, and a couple mugs of coffee, and trudged across the lake, the cold air blowing in her face, the sun glinting off the blinding white snow.

People sat all over the place, staring into little holes drilled into the ice in front of tiny houses that hopefully had somewhere to pee.

All that coffee hadn't been a good idea.

She shuffled over the frozen water in her boots, snow pants, and jacket, squinting against the sun because she forgot her sunglasses in her room. She'd brought her driver's license and debit card—she wasn't used to being without them—but that seemed stupid now. Where was she going to shop?

She searched the groups of fishermen for Marnie and the rest of her friends.

She hadn't seen anyone last night, but the arena had been crowded and she wasn't surprised she lost them in the sea of people attending the biggest hockey game of the school year. Maybe things would have turned out differently if Mitch had sat with a group of friends instead of her, an outsider.

Safety in numbers and all that.

Next time she asked Mitch to do something, it would be in a group.

And there *would* be a next time. She didn't give up that easily, but she had her way last night and now it was his turn. She looked forward to the walk through the woods he promised her.

"Can you believe the guts that took?"

"Don't you mean stupidity?"

She heard the grumble, an old man muttering to his fishing partner, and the disgusted reply, as she walked by a cheap fish house made of particleboard.

"He didn't belong there, that's for sure."

She moved on, blocking the sun with a mittened hand in front of her face. Too many people. She hadn't thought it would be this hard to find her friends, but on a sunny Saturday morning, everyone was enjoying the mild temperatures on the lake.

"Thank God Ed kicked him out," a woman said, sitting in a lawn chair near an ice hole that had a red and white bobber floating in the center. "He had no right trying to go to that game. What if those girls' parents would've been there? Why did he think that was okay? God Almighty."

She slanted a glance at the woman and her group.

"Mitch Sinclair needs to stay in the cave he crawled out of," another woman agreed.

Across the ice, Callie met her eyes, and the woman blushed and looked away.

She kept walking.

"Son of a bitch. Thinking he had a right to be there."

"Freak needs to keep to himself."

"Monster."

"Murderer."

She swallowed her tears and turned toward the resort. She wouldn't fish with these people. Not when they could be that cruel.

Ivy found her plodding across the ice. "Are you looking for a place to fish?" she asked, grabbing her arm. "What's wrong?"

She sniffled. "Everyone's talking about Mitch."

"I've heard. Come on. The resort sponsors a couple of ice houses, and they have some fishing holes ready to go. Sit with me. I don't want to be by myself."

She followed, grateful for a familiar, and kind, face. "Are you working out here?"

Ivy laughed. "Could you imagine a bar on the ice? There's plenty of drinking when it's five o'clock somewhere, but the resort doesn't supply it. I came out to get some air. I work from noon 'til close."

"You don't have much time."

"It's enough. I have my uniform on under my snow stuff. Want some coffee?" Ivy asked, leading her to a fish house that had several empty chairs, waiting for someone to plop into one and pretend to fish.

"Actually, I really have to pee," she said, embarrassed.

"There's a place inside. Have some coffee when you're done."

"Thanks."

After a short and desperate struggle with her snow pants, Callie gratefully sat on a toilet seat attached to a bucket. She felt better after relieving herself and filled a disposal cup with the resort's complimentary coffee. She stepped out of the dim shelter and into the bright sun where she sat next to Ivy who was watching people fish in the distance.

"It didn't go well last night," Ivy said, barely giving Callie a chance to settle into a creaky canvas chair.

"No." The way that old security guard kicked them out of the arena shamed her. Not for herself, but for Mitch. "But you already know that because everyone's been talking about it all morning. Did you invite me over to fish or to bitch me out for being stupid?" She deserved it. Mitch warned her, and she hadn't listened. She thought there would be *some* nice people at the game, but not one person defended them or even offered a friendly smile.

"Not to bitch you out, but to ask what happened. What I've heard ranges from Mitch having a good time to him getting his ass beat in the parking lot. I'm worried about him and I wasn't able to ask him. He spends Saturday mornings at his parents' house. I'll see him later, but you looked lost and I wanted to talk."

She sipped her coffee and tried not to feel used. Ivy saved her from roaming around like an idiot, and even if Ivy was using her for information, it was better than sitting in her room waiting for Mitch to pick her up to go on their walk. Which was exactly what she would have done.

"Are you and Mitch a couple?" She asked, squinting at Ivy.

"No. We're only friends."

"Do you want more?"

"No." Ivy paused. "Maybe I used to, a little bit, but not anymore. Besides, he doesn't see me that way."

"I guess it's none of my business."

"It is if you like him."

"I don't know how I feel. I've only been in town for a couple of days, and it's not like our first date went that well. He's probably mad at me for making him go. He warned me it would happen."

"What *did* happen?"

"Oh, Ivy, people were horrid." She squeezed her disposable cup. "I tried to pretend I didn't notice, but God. The glares, the swearing, and people didn't do it under their breaths, either. After the first period, arena security asked us to leave. I was humiliated on his behalf. Livid."

"He went with you to show you that. I saw him while he was getting ready to go. I was on break, and sometimes I nap in his room."

She raised her eyebrows.

"Doubles are hard and I work them a lot. I need the money."

"I get it. I'm sorry."

Ivy shrugged and stared into the icy horizon. "It is what it is."

"He wanted me to see how people would treat him?" she asked, picking up the thread.

"Yeah. You needed to what would happen so you'd leave him alone."

"He said that? That he wants me to leave him alone?" Hurt and humiliation burned her throat.

Ivy's cheeks pinked. "It's what he said before the game, but I don't know how he feels now."

She nodded. Mitch's kisses had to mean something, and if this was Ivy warning her off him, then the bartender didn't know whom she was dealing with.

Callie walked into fire.

She was tougher than she looked.

"I can't speak for Mitch, but he invited me out on a walk later this afternoon. I guess he'll tell me then," she said, feeling childish enough to needle a woman who only wanted to protect a friend. "I'm sorry. I didn't mean anything by that."

Ivy surprised her by taking off her mitten and placing her hand on Callie's arm. "He's tried to date, and no one has been strong enough. No one can hack it. Can you?"

"I don't know," she said honestly. "I really don't know."

"I guess you'll find out."

A man dressed in jeans, a black leather jacket, and sunglasses that hid his eyes crunched over the ice flanked by two men dressed similarly. They were grinning, arrogant and confident, cruel in their superiority.

Callie knew the type, and she grimaced in disgust and a small hint of fear.

"You're the girl who was with that fire freak last night."

"Who are you calling a freak?" she asked, standing from the chair, her palms damp inside her mittens, already plan-ning Mitch's defense. She couldn't fight all three of them at once, but she could handle the one mouthing off.

"I'm calling that murderer a freak," he said, stepping forward. "He's got no business going to a hockey game. He needs to remember what he did."

"I'm sure he does," she bit out, "every time he looks in a mirror."

"Nothing less than what he deserves. Keep your freaky-assed boyfriend at home and no one will get hurt."

She didn't like the sound of that, and she narrowed her eyes. "Are you threatening me?"

Ivy sprang off her chair and stood next to her, her breath coming out in angry puffs.

He tilted his chin in defiance. "Little burn boy hiding behind his women. Yeah, that's a threat. He'll get what's coming to him if he doesn't listen."

Callie barreled toward him before she could stop herself, and the jerk scrambled back but not fast enough to stay clear. She hooked her foot around his leg and yanked as she shoved on his chest, pushing the bastard flat on his ass onto the snow and ice.

His two buddies gaped at her.

"Listen here," she snapped, hands on her hips, "I don't like threats, especially by cowards like you."

"I'm calling the cops," Ivy said, pulling her cell phone out of a pocket in her snow pants.

"That's not necessary, is it?" she asked pointedly. She kicked the man's boot. "Get out of here."

"You're next," he said, standing. He brushed snow off his jeans. "You think I'm going to let this go? Think again, bitch."

She'd been called worse, and she only pursed her lips as the three assholes walked away, swaggering, pushing each other while they guffawed.

The one she tripped looked over his shoulder, pointed at her, and glared.

"Idiots," she hissed.

"Where'd you learn that?" Ivy asked, awed.

"My dad made me take self-defense classes. Plus, I grew up with two brothers. That guy's bark is worse than his bite. At least, for now." She sat and chugged the rest of her coffee. "God, Ivy. That's what Mitch means, isn't it?"

"Yeah."

She stared at the fishermen who cast them furtive glances. No one but Ivy stepped in to help her.

Autumn slid over the snow, clutching a notebook in one hand and a pen in the other. "I saw what happened but I was too far away to do anything. Are you okay?"

"Yeah, we're fine. Where were you guys last night?" she asked, annoyed she and Mitch had to sit alone.

Autumn blinked. "I was with Leah for most of the game. I looked, but I didn't see you. Marnie and James were there, somewhere. I'm sorry we didn't sit together."

"I was just thinking about Mitch, that's all," she said. "I'm sorry. I didn't mean to take it out on you."

"It's okay. Everyone's used to how he's treated by now."

"That doesn't make it right."

"No, it doesn't."

"I thought the town was divided. It doesn't feel like it."

"Didn't Mitch tell you anything?"

"He doesn't talk about it."

Autumn move a chair closer, sat, and rested her notebook on her lap. "Let me tell you a few things that you weren't able to read in the paper. Maybe it will make things a bit clearer."

She leaned in to listen.

Mitch knocked on Callie's door, his heart in his throat. He wanted to see her, spend time with her, but afraid she changed her mind, he almost bailed on their afternoon walk. Only the idea of not talking to her anymore propelled him down the hallway, and he was rapping on her door before he could talk himself out of it.

She answered dressed in jeans and a sweater, lighter strands streaking her brunette hair, brightening her face. Her guarded look made him wish he'd given her an excuse after all, check on that hot tub alone, but he asked, "Are you okay?"

She paused, biting her lip. "Listen, I don't want to make things harder for you."

"You heard about my truck then." He let out a sigh.

She frowned. "What about your truck? No, I didn't hear anything. Are *you* okay?"

Dammit. He wouldn't have mentioned it if he hadn't thought that's what she was referring to. He could've picked his truck up without telling anyone and no one but his parents would have been the wiser.

"Let's talk while we walk, okay? That is, if you still want to go."

"Yeah, I still want to go. Come in. I have to put my stuff on."

He hesitated.

She growled low in the back of her throat, and he smiled. "If I invite you in, it's okay."

"I'm sorry. It's just, you get into the habit of being cautious, and it's hard to stop. I *can't* stop. I'll always have other guests to deal with after you leave. Guests who won't want me in their room, even to fix something."

"Did it ever occur to you that you make things harder on

yourself?" she asked, grabbing her jacket. "That you ask to be treated that way?"

"I don't understand what you mean," he said, stiffening. He didn't ask to be Rocky Point's outcast. He didn't ask to be treated like the town's pariah.

"I mean, I talked to Autumn this morning. And Ivy, too."

He turned and walked out of her room. He didn't need to hear this.

She followed him, slamming the door shut. She stopped to lock it, and that gave him time to stride half a hallway ahead of her.

But he wanted to be with her, even if she spent the whole afternoon ragging on him, and he slowed and waited for her to catch up so they could walk down the stairs together.

"I suppose you're going to tell me what they said," he muttered, yanking on his gloves.

"Well, it wasn't Ivy. Don't be mad at her. She was only looking out for you, and she gave me a big bowl of 'I told you so' served with a side dish of 'maybe you'll leave him alone now.'"

"She's been hurt."

"Haven't we all?"

He scoffed. "Have you?"

"Mostly by men who can't handle what I do."

That stopped him, and he leaned against the glass doors that would let them out the back of the resort and to the trail that led to the cabins about a quarter of a mile away. Callie could make it. He'd watched her run six miles in under an hour.

"And what's that?"

"Why? So you can dump me? Tell me it's you not me? It's what I get from everybody else."

"We aren't doing anything. I don't think it would be considered dumping if we stopped talking."

"Then what was last night? What were those kisses? That I liked very much, by the way."

He laughed. God, he'd missed arguing with a woman. He felt like they were fighting about ten different things and he was loving every minute of it.

Hooking an arm around her neck and pulling her close, he said, "Come on."

"Kiss me first, and then tell me it's nothing."

He could kiss her and pretend it didn't matter. He could kiss her and admit she stirred up a bunch of feelings he hadn't felt in years, feelings he thought he'd never feel again. And maybe, feelings he didn't want to feel, because falling in love with Callie Carter would end in nothing but trouble. He could avoid kissing her and try to distract her with something else, but she was too smart for that.

Why deny himself something he wanted? This one small thing?

He tilted his head and rested his mouth on hers, and she moved her lips, inviting him to take more.

He hugged her closer, accepting what she offered, and she wrapped her arms around his neck.

Tasting her, wanting more, he slipped his tongue into her mouth and had the pleasure of hearing her moan.

She broke the kiss and said, "See? You can't tell me you don't feel something when we do that."

He felt something, and so did his cock. It throbbed against the zipper of his jeans. "Besides lust?"

She looked down at her boots, their legs tangled together. "It's more than that," she whispered.

With a finger under her chin, he asked her look at him. She wasn't crying, but the pull around her eyes told him he hurt her. "It's more than that."

She smiled, and suddenly, nothing else in the world mattered.

He was in deep shit.

"What did Autumn tell you?" Mitch asked, leading her down the trail. He'd never brought anyone with him, not even Ivy. He hadn't wanted to give up the solitude he could find for himself, and bringing Callie with him today was like shooting himself in the foot. He'd never be able to walk this trail and not think of her, or the kiss they shared before they came outside.

"That the town was divided after the accident. That you had people on your side."

"I wouldn't say it was fifty/fifty, but I had people who believed me," he said, unsure of where she was going with this direction of conversation.

"So where'd they go?"

His mind blanked. "What?"

"Where did they go? These past seven years since the accident?"

"What does that have to do with anything?"

"Well," she said, walking through the snow beside him, easily, steadily, as he knew she could, "they didn't just disappear. How did you know they were on your side?"

He thought back. "There were a couple of churches that set up their Sunday offerings to go to me and my mother to help pay our medical bills. People brought over food, sat with Ma, drove me to the clinic for my appointments after I came back from Decatur. You know about some of that?"

She nodded. "I read about it."

"They helped my dad split his time between us. It was hard for him to choose, and he had to be careful too, since the people who blamed me started shit he had to deal with."

"But you did have the support of some people in town."

"Yeah."

"Then where did they go?" she asked again.

"I don't know. Hell, Callie, they could have changed their minds. It's been seven years. Who knows what kind of gossip they heard."

"Or was it you?"

"It's always been me. I don't know what you're getting at."

"I'm getting to the fact that when people act guilty, people start to think they *are* guilty."

"What?" He stopped in the middle of the trail. They were almost to the salt lick he put out for the deer, and if they didn't quiet down, they'd scare them off. He wanted to watch the deer with Callie. Wanted to sit on a fallen tree in the quiet, maybe steal another kiss.

"Think about the past few years. How have you behaved? Did you stop going out in public? Did you stop going to the store? Stop going to the movies? To the bar? Did you stop dating?"

"You know the answer to all that," he said, fury bubbling under the calm. How did she tag him so well?

"Why? Because of how you look?"

"You really think I'm a bastard, don't you? No, it's not because of how I look, though that plays a big part of it. It's because of those girls."

"Exactly."

He scoffed. "There's a difference between guilt and remorse."

"And how will people know which one you're feeling if you hide?"

The denial was quick on his lips, but hell. He'd been hiding. He knew it, and she knew it. He didn't have any friends except Ivy, and he didn't have to step one foot out of his comfort zone to spend time with her. Did a couple of things for his dad in town, and if he thought about it, that was his dad's way of prying him out of the house.

When he dropped off his truck, the guy filled out the work order and told him when it would be ready. Mitch shook his hand and walked out of the office. There hadn't been any smirks, or leers, or swearing under his breath. Not even a comment, rude or otherwise, about what was sprayed on his truck. A simple business transaction that others took for granted but had left him reeling.

"You teach people how to treat you, Mitch."

"And how have I taught you to treat me?"

She stepped next to him, pulled her mitten off, and brushed her fingers along the scarring on his cheek, across his jaw, and down his neck. He still couldn't get over the fact she could touch him without flinching. "With compassion and kindness. I'm starting to . . . care about you."

He cuddled her to him. "I'm starting to care about you too, and that scares the hell out of me."

They straddled the log, her ass wedged firmly between his legs, his arms wrapped around her, and watched as deer poked around the clearing. A huge buck, it had to be at least ten points, majestically held court, and the three does with him blinked at Mitch and Callie with curious eyes but made no move to leave.

Content, she could've sat there all day, but he released her, and she bit back a sigh and stood as well. He had a job to do, and even though it was technically his day off, the resort needed the cabin in working order for a check-in that night.

She followed him down the trail, the deer ignoring them in favor of the salt lick. She held his hand and kept a smile to herself when his lips twitched.

He hadn't had much to say about her comment, but she wasn't finished talking to him about it, either. Let him chew on it because everything Autumn said to her that morning made sense. "Let me interview him for the blog," Autumn said. "Just something light, something fun. Nothing too heavy or it will feel like he's defending himself, and he doesn't need to do that. No one will forget those girls, but life goes on and he has a right to his. Ask him if he'll talk to me."

Callie promised to ask, but if Mitch wasn't ready, she wouldn't push.

They broke through the woods and into a snowy cul-de-sac where five cabins sat in a half-circle, the woods hugging them from behind. "God, these are fabulous."

Mitch pointed. "Logan Draper's in that one," he said. "I've heard he's one of James's groomsmen. That one and that one are empty. That one has the hot tub I need to check on, and the other one has a couple staying in it."

"James's aunt needs a place to stay. She wants to go to the wedding but she can't because there aren't any rooms available. Why doesn't she stay in one of these?"

"She probably can't afford it. They run a few hundred a night, and at two weeks . . . Desiree tries her best to keep them full. They might be booked."

"Logan must be doing all right."

He shrugged. "You'll have to ask him. I lost track of him after graduation. He went to Decatur with James and never came back."

She followed him up the cleared path to the cabin, and he unclipped a keyring off the belt loop of his jeans and opened the door.

"Take off your boots, will you?" he asked. "Housekeeping has been in here already. Desiree wants me to make sure the hot tub's working, but I won't need long."

"Okay." Callie slid her boots off her feet and walked around the cabin, her socks padding against the hardwood floor. "This is really nice," she said, skimming her fingers over the counter in the small kitchenette.

The beams in the ceiling had been left exposed, giving the cabin an airy feel. A king-sized bed was centered in front of a large picture window that looked into the snowy woods, and a huge stone fireplace took up half the wall. Kindling and logs were bundled in an iron basket near the hearth.

"It would be amazing to stay here," she said, sitting gingerly on the edge of the mattress. She didn't want to mess up the bedding.

"You and whoever you're with better get along," Mitch said, kneeling by the hot tub.

"Why do you say that?"

"Because there isn't a TV in these cabins. There's Wi-Fi, but it can get spotty when it snows."

"That wouldn't be bad. You know, when there're other things to do."

The tops of his ears tinged pink and she laughed.

He cleared this throat. "You mean like fishing and cross-country skiing?"

"I mean, sitting in the hot tub, sipping on a glass of wine, then crawling into bed . . . and . . . reading a book all night."

He turned away from the hot tub and gave her a wry grin. "Is that what you'd do all night?"

"It's what I do now."

"You're too pretty to be by yourself." He cleared his throat again and fastened the back of the hot tub in place. "I think this looks okay. I'll fill her up to be sure, and then we can head out."

"No rush. What are you doing later?"

"I'm always on call and usually stay close to the resort. Stop in the lounge and see Ivy. How about you?"

"I'm not sure. Probably hanging out with Marnie. It's what I'm in town for."

He turned the water on and sat on the bed with her while they waited.

She wiggled out of her jacket.

He coughed. "What are you doing?"

"It's warm in here."

"Yeah, I guess it is." Mitch took his off and tossed it on top of hers.

Steam began to rise from the tub.

"It looks like the water's hot," he said.

"That's good, right?"

"Well, hot tubs should be hot," he agreed, his lips twitching.

"Why is it so hard to make you laugh?"

He squeezed her thigh. "Because I don't do very much of it."

"Mitch."

"It's okay. Let me turn the jets on to make sure they're working, and then we can get out of here."

"All right."

He turned the water off and turned the jets on. Bubbles exploded in the tub.

He looked competent, confident. When she looked at him, she didn't see his scars. She saw a kind, a generous man, and a lonely one, struggling to find his place in a world that didn't want him.

But she did.

They were alone, and neither of them had anything to do for the rest of the day.

She could seduce him.

He'd already brought up lust.

She would show him love.

Here on this bed. She would show him how much he'd come to mean to her because, God, she was falling in love with him.

Electricity zinged around the room, bouncing off the walls like a ball in a pinball machine, and Mitch's hand trembled when he turned the jets off.

Something changed, though Callie looked the same sitting on the bed, waiting for him to finish his job. He opened the drain and stood awkwardly by the wall, but when she held out her hand, he had no choice but to cross the room and take it.

She stood and placed his hand on her breast. Gently, she kissed him.

She tasted sweet and full of promise. Of a future that maybe he could have if he took it. If he was brave enough.

If it was his to take.

If it was hers to give.

"Make love to me, Mitch," she whispered against his lips. "Please."

His brain said yes, his cock said hell yes, but his heart writhed. "I can't."

"Why? Did the fire hurt you?"

"No. Because I'll never be able to forget you if I do."

"Who says you'll need to forget? Who says we have to stop seeing each other? I live two towns away. Not two states. Not two countries. We could make it work."

She wrapped her arms around his waist and rested her cheek against his chest.

He rubbed his hands up and down her back.

Eventually, enough evidence would stack against him and she'd finally understand why they couldn't see each other, why it was impossible for him to be in a normal relationship, but until then, why not take what she offered? Why not, because he wanted it, and God, she could touch him without flinching and he'd never find another woman who could.

"I don't have anything with me. I'm not in the habit of carrying birth control."

"I'm on the Pill."

He cradled her face in his hands. Her huge brown eyes peered at him with hope and desire, and desperately, he captured her mouth, sliding his tongue between her lips.

There was nothing stopping them now, stopping him, from taking her. She offered, and he accepted.

She kissed him back with just as much passion, and he

shoved his hands under her sweater, needing to feel her skin beneath his fingertips.

"Please, Mitch," she said, tipping her head back.

He didn't waste a second, nibbling at the delicate skin beneath her jaw. He leaned away to pull her sweater over her head and revealed a pink lace bra. "Pretty."

She laughed. "I have matching panties, too. Wanna see?"

"Yeah."

He was patient, holding her in his arms, cupping her ass and hugging her close.

She rubbed her lips over the scars on his neck, across his throat to the other side of his face.

He throbbed, but he wanted to go slow, make it last. Make it good for her.

Kissing down her collarbone to her breasts, he teased one of her nipples through the lace, and she forked her fingers through his hair.

Kneeling, he kissed her flat belly. He paused, his fingers on the button of her jeans.

He looked up at her.

"Don't ask me if I'm sure, because I am."

"Okay."

He pushed the button through the buttonhole, pulled down the zipper, and slowly drew the soft material over her toned legs. Legs that could kick the crap out of him on the treadmill. "You're so beautiful. Lift your feet up."

She raised her feet, one by one. He tugged her jeans off the rest of the way, and on his knees, worshipped her the way she deserved.

"You're right. They match."

"I told you. Can I undress you now?"

"Not yet. I want to . . . can I touch you?"

"This whole thing would be difficult if I said no."

The corner of his mouth lifted. "Right."

Gently, he moved her panties aside, and she widened her legs.

"Please, if I do something wrong, don't pretend you like it," he said.

"I won't. Will you touch me now? Stop talking."

"Not even to tell you how beautiful you are?"

"You already said it. Show me."

He explored her sweet spot, probing until he found her slit. She was already wet beyond his imagination, and she mewed when he slipped a finger inside her. He pulled the material aside even more and licked her. Her muscles contracted around his finger.

She whimpered.

Disappointed, he asked, "Do you want to come like this?" If she did, then she wouldn't want to continue. She could put her clothes and walk away.

"No. Stand up and let me undress you now."

"Are you sure, because—"

"I know what you're going to say, and you're beautiful, too. Come here."

Callie knew what the poor man was thinking. If he'd gotten her off right then, she could get dressed and that would be that.

Stupid. She told him she wanted him, and she meant it.

She wanted to feel him inside her. She wanted to meet his eyes as he left a part of himself behind.

And stole her heart.

She unbuttoned the flannel that had the Rocky Point Lodge embroidered over the pocket. He wore a white, ribbed tank top under it, and she heaved a huge, exaggerated sigh, hoping to dispel some tension. Because there was some. He wanted to go slow and enjoy her, but she bet if she volunteered to lean over the bed and all he'd have to do was pull his pants down to nail her, he would have taken it out of fear.

"So many layers, Mr. Sinclair," she teased, pushing off the flannel.

"It gets cold," he said, dropping his shirt onto the floor.

"Hmmm." Callie tugged the hem of his tank top up and feathered her fingers over his abs. He'd make a wonderful firefighter, as fit as he was. Six pack, pecs, shoulders, biceps. He'd have no problem carrying someone out of a burning building. Even with all the equipment weighing him down. "You have one fine body."

The scar on his right side shimmered in the light shining through the window. Pink, but duller now than if it was new, it still looked painful. She wanted to smooth her lips over the burn, down his neck, his shoulder, his ribs and lower.

"You're the only one who's seen it in a long time."

She unbuttoned his jeans. "You know, for some reason, I like that. Take the rest of your clothes off, okay?"

"What are you going to do?"

"Get into bed?"

Dammit. The bed was ready for check-in. She should've waited until they were in her room before she tried this, but the timing had been right and she didn't want to let the chance slip away. Before she lost her nerve, she turned down the bedspread and sheets and slid into the cool softness.

Yes, it was right they do it here, alone, with the trees of Rocky Point their only company.

He took his jeans off and threw his tank top on the floor near his flannel shirt. Uncertainly, he stood at the foot of the bed wearing only black boxer briefs, letting her look, until she crooked her finger. "It's okay, Mitch. If I wanted to change my mind, I would have five minutes ago. Your scarring doesn't bother me, I promise."

No, visiting her mother in the burn unit of Decatur's primary hospital, she'd seen much worse. For a second, she wondered if her mother had been Mitch's nurse, but he slid into bed and her mind moved on to other things.

She licked one of his nipples and brushed her fingers lightly over his hard cock.

Suddenly, he reversed their positions, pushing her down into the pillows and kissing her, rubbing his cock against her leg.

"Don't you want to go slow?" she asked, laughing.

"I'm trying, but you're breaking a pretty long streak for me," Mitch murmured into her neck.

"Oh, well then." She sat up and unfastened her bra's hooks. "I wouldn't want to hold us up with silly kissing."

"Maybe a little bit more," he said staring at her breasts. "Callie, you're gorgeous. How are you single? You should be . . ."

"Barefoot and pregnant?" she asked, wiggling under the heavy bedspread.

The smolder in his eyes told her yes, that's exactly how he wanted her. He sucked her nipple into his mouth and nibbled at the sensitive skin.

Her breasts grew heavy at the thought of carrying his child, as if her body wanted that more than anything.

Awkwardly under the sheet, he pulled his briefs off, and

she wiggled out of her panties. She laid back against the mound of pillows and spread her legs, letting him settle there like he'd always belonged.

He nudged her clit, pre-cum wetting the tip.

"Please, Mitch, now. Don't play."

"Tell me if it hurts."

It would maybe hurt a little, if only because it'd been a while for her, too.

He went slowly, gently sliding inside her, withdrawing, pushing, withdrawing, until he was as far as he could go. Or so she thought.

Lifting her hips with a hand under her ass, he thrust, his tip hitting her center, and she cried out.

She wrapped her arms around his neck as he rammed into her, lost in the need, lost in the resentment he didn't have a healthy sex life because of the accident.

Let her pay for that.

It would be her gift to him.

Groaning, he came, propping himself over her with one hand, holding her to him with the other, his cock twitching as he emptied.

He caught his breath. "You didn't come."

She smacked a kiss to his cheek. "You were in it to win it."

Swearing, he pressed his forehead to hers. "I wanted you to tell me."

"I didn't tell you because I wanted it to be good for you. It can still be good for me. Was I enough?"

"You're everything I want."

"Good."

He slid out of her and she tensed. "Ah."

"Dammit, I knew I was too hard on you."

"You were rough, but I liked it. Really."

He looked away.

"Mitch. Don't do this, please." With a hand to his cheek, she forced him to meet her eyes.

"I don't want to hurt you."

"I know. But we will. Hurt each other, somehow, some-day, won't we?"

He tucked her into his side and she licked the sweat that misted his skin. He didn't say anything, and she assumed he was done talking about it. That was okay. She was done talking about it too, for now. Her insides were vibrating like a rubber band stretched too tightly, and she needed the release.

She spread her legs. "Help me out, please?"

Propping his head on his hand, he said, "Of course I will. Like this?"

His thumb rubbed her clit, and he pushed two fingers inside her. She was soaking wet, full of his cum. "That doesn't hurt does it?"

She lifted her hips in response. "No, yes, but I like it."

"Do you want three? Can you handle it?"

"Yes, please." She sucked in a breath, preparing herself. She liked three, but it hurt.

Slowly, with his thumb massaging her clit, he eased three fingers inside her. It pinched and she reveled in the pain. She kissed him. "Like that, yeah," she whispered against his lips.

He found a rhythm, and her hips matched his short, forceful thrusts.

He sucked her nipple into his mouth and bit.

She arched her back, encouraging him to bite her harder. "I'm coming," she panted, and he rubbed furiously at her clit.

She convulsed around his fingers, but she didn't let his

head come up from her breast. In response, he bit harder, and she rode the crest of her orgasm with the added pain.

Slowly, she came down, and sank into the mattress, spent.

He pulled his fingers from her, tenderly, so, so gently, but before he could dry them on the sheet, she snatched his hand out of the air. She licked their cum off his skin, and he stared at her, his cock hardened against her leg.

"You like that? Watching me do that?" she asked.

"Do you like how it tastes?"

"It's a part of us. What's not to like?" She sucked his finger into her mouth, swirling her tongue around the tip. "You were lucky you didn't lose any of your fingers."

Sated, he settled onto a pillow. Her teeth grazed his fingertip and he shivered. "Yeah, I was. I was fortunate the doctors were of the 'wait and see' variety. It took a lot of physical therapy, and occupational therapy, for my range of motion to come back. Especially since I'm right-handed. As the years have gone by, I've learned to do things with both hands."

She didn't want their lovemaking to turn heavy, and she said, "Will you show me?"

He nuzzled her temple. "Definitely. I'm sorry if I bit you too hard."

Her nipple throbbed, but in the best way. "I liked it. I liked it all."

"Good. But we should go now. I have to figure out how to change the sheets without getting anyone in trouble. Maybe if I can convince Carmen to give me clean bedding, I can do it myself."

"I'll help you, since this was my idea. We both have perfectly good beds barely half a mile away."

He laughed, and with the sun floating through the

window, his whole face lit up. She tumbled the rest of the way. She'd put that smile on his face, and in turn, he brought joy and hope to her empty heart.

"I'm so glad I didn't turn this down."

She brushed her lips against his. "Then never think you can't ask. I'll never say no," she said, meaning it in more ways than one.

Even if her father's voice was in the back of her head asking her what in the hell she thought she was doing.

She'd make it work. Somehow, she'd convince him they belonged together. She still had the better part of two weeks.

Maybe, she thought, as he kissed her outside the cabin, it would be easier than it seemed.

CHAPTER SIX

They managed to change the sheets without Desiree knowing, and Mitch owed Carmen a few favors for keeping the request to herself. He shouldn't have taken the chance. He'd lose a lot more than Callie when she went back to Decatur if he didn't have a job after the wedding.

Marnie cornered her in the hallway as they were making plans to spend the rest of the evening in her room eating pizza and watching TV, something so normal the thought of it dried his mouth, and asked her to join them for dinner. He'd been invited too, in the casual, off-handed way that said Marnie didn't give a shit if he joined them or not, and torn between his own wants and what Callie needed to do, he shooed her off.

Marnie had taken her hand and dragged her down the hallway. She looked over her shoulder at him the whole time.

He'd find something else to do. Being alone on a Saturday night wasn't a new experience. His room was hooked up to cable and internet like all the others, and he could eat pizza and watch TV by himself. Before that, he'd have a drink and talk to Ivy, if the lounge wasn't busy and she had a few minutes.

Same shit, different day.

Meeting Callie hadn't changed anything.

Except for how he felt inside. Thinking about her licking their cum off his fingers made him hard all over again, and when she offered herself, even after he hurt her, it had humbled him in a way he couldn't explain.

The front desk texted him to take a look at a tub drain in a room on the first floor, and that's where he bumped into Jared Hollister.

Mitch ducked his head, hoping the man would pass him by. As the manager of the arena, he'd know what happened, and Mitch didn't need a second round of, "Stay home, murderer." Ed had driven that point home loud and clear, and hell would freeze over before he attempted to go to another game. Even with Callie.

"Hey, Mitch," Jared said as he tried to slink by.

He stiffened. Dammit. Jared wasn't going to let this go.

"Yeah? Is there something I can do for you?" At least he could approach this as a resort employee.

Jared shifted his weight from one foot to the other. "Ah, I heard Ed Dunlop kicked you out of the arena last night."

"Yeah, sorry about that." Get it over with, take the blame, move him along. "It won't happen again."

Frowning, Jared pinned him with a heavy stare. "What are you talking about? I'm sorry Ed thought he had the right to do that. I told him to leave you alone, but he didn't listen. Ed wasn't happy I took your side, and that's putting it mildly."

"It wasn't my side."

"No, you're right, it was the side of doing the right thing, and he didn't agree. I had to cut him loose. He doesn't work at the arena anymore. I don't know if that was smart because I sure as hell don't want this to turn into a fiasco." Jared adjusted the ball cap on his head. "If he comes at you, tell me. It'll be my fault."

He wouldn't breathe a word of anything to anyone, but he nodded. "I appreciate it."

Jared jerked a thumb behind him. "I've been ah, kind of hanging out with Leah. She took a spill in the water when everyone was fishing this morning. Were you out there?"

"No. Is she going to be okay? That water's damn cold this time of year."

"Yeah, I think so. She's sleeping right now. The swim didn't do her any good, but I didn't mind warming her up." He jiggled his keys. "Anyway, maybe the four of us, or six of us, whatever, we'll meet up sometime. This wedding stuff is going to make a long two weeks."

Mitch blinked in surprise. Jared was inviting him out on a double date? Triple, with Marnie and James. God. He'd have to blow the dust off his social skills. "Thanks. Yeah. I'm sure Callie will be all over it."

"You like her?"

Now he was gossiping? Jesus Christ, what was the world coming to?

"It's only been a couple of days."

Jared looked up at the ceiling. Must be where Leah's room was located.

"It doesn't take much though, does it?"

"No." No, it didn't.

"She's a firecracker, too. Callie, I mean. I heard she kicked some ass on the lake today."

"What? She didn't say anything."

Jared raised his eyebrows. "Yeah, a couple of pricks came after her and Ivy, gave her a hard time for being out with you last night. Callie took one of 'em down. She didn't tell you?"

"No. Not a word."

"Be careful. I'm ashamed to admit Ed probably started the whole thing kicking you out of the game. I had my own hassles and didn't know until it was done. I'm sorry about that. Keep an eye out, yeah?"

"Yeah. Thanks for the heads up."

"Yeah. Catch you later." Jared continued down the hallway, jiggling his keys.

Anger burned his throat. There was no chance he'd let Callie take his punches for him. Absolutely none. He never would have made love to her if he'd known.

Why? a little voice asked. *Isn't it nice someone sees who you are despite the accident?*

Yeah, sure it was, but he had enough to worry about. His parents were already innocent bystanders, and he didn't need to add Callie to the list. He'd talk to her as soon as he could.

But he couldn't tamp down the smile. She'd kicked ass. Well, he never did.

Good for her.

"I've arranged for you to visit the fire department there."

"You what?" Callie asked, stopping in the middle of the hallway after dinner. Marnie had been full of all sorts of news, and she had a lot to tell Mitch if he wanted to meet for dessert, coffee, and maybe some more hot sex.

"Fire Chief Mike Bakersfield will be waiting for you to stop by," Ace Carter snapped.

"Why? This is my vacation. I don't want to think about work."

"Be cordial. You're representing Decatur."

"I'm sure he knows everyone in Decatur," she said sarcastically.

"He doesn't know you, and he said he'd love to have you visit the station. Don't disappoint me." Ace paused, and a female voice drifted to her through the phone. "Your mother wants to know if you've talked to Brandon. He, ah, won't take our calls."

Probably because his therapist told him not to. Which made her feel pretty damned special he'd spoken to her for a few minutes the other day. "He's . . . busy when I call. They encourage you to write letters," she said, hating herself for lying. But as much as she loved her mother and knew she worried about her son, Callie would protect Brandon from their father.

"He needs to toughen up, like Zach. Like you."

She wasn't tough. Thirty years old and doing whatever her father told her to do made her a coward. "Brandon thought he was going to die. There's no coming back from that, Dad."

"It's in our blood. It's what we do. You can't hide from it. You think I haven't put myself in dangerous situations since I was a rookie? It's what my father did, and it's what his father did. Fire runs through our veins, Callie. Don't you ever forget that."

Like he'd let her.

"I know."

"Are you keeping up with your workouts?"

She hadn't today, unless she called scorching hot sex with a maintenance man working out. "Yes."

"Good. No slacking."

"Yes, sir."

"Goodnight, Callie. Your mother says hello."

"Tell her hi. Goodnight."

She disconnected the call. Shit. Visiting Rocky Point's fire department was the last thing she wanted to do, but now she was stuck. Her father would check up on her to make sure she did it.

She backtracked to the reservation desk. She wouldn't wait for Mitch to find her. After the conversation with her dad, she'd find him and let him kiss the crappy taste out of her mouth.

The woman at the reservations counter lifted an eyebrow at her request. "Do you have a concern, ma'am?"

"Oh, no. I was looking for him to . . . tell him what a great job he did with my . . . outlet." She stifled a laugh. Marnie would get a kick out of that.

"His room is located in the service hallway near the pool. That information is usually kept private, however. Are you sure there's nothing I can help you with?"

"No, that's fine. I'll only need a second of his time."

"Do you need directions?"

"Yes, please."

It took her longer than she thought to find his room, but when she finally faced his plain brown door that had a gold nameplate fastened to the wood that said MAINTE-NANCE in elegant script, she paused before knocking.

Before she could summon the courage, the door swung open.

"Callie."

"Hi." Shit. He didn't look happy to see her. "I wanted to say . . . goodnight." It wasn't what she wanted to say, but the scowl on his face didn't leave room for anything else.

"I was going to find you."

"You were?"

"Yeah. Can we talk in your room?"

"Sure," she said, relieved. Mitch didn't seem like the kind of man who would blow her off after an afternoon of making love, but she'd been wrong about men before.

She didn't want to believe that about him, and the easy way he held her hand as they walked down the empty hallway made her heart beat at a steadier pace.

"Did you want to order some coffee? Dessert?" she asked.

He paused.

"Or maybe you're wanting a little of this?" she asked, pushing him down on the bed and straddling his lap.

"I wouldn't mind, if you're offering," he said, tangling his fingers in her hair and taking her mouth with his.

He had him out of his clothes in five seconds, and ten seconds later they were under the sheets and bedspread, his hands roaming her body like they hadn't had sex six hours ago.

She came the moment he slid into her, and he followed soon after.

"That was nice," she said, cuddling into his side, catching her breath.

He brushed his fingers down her back, tickling her. "I've had more sex today than I have in four years."

She rested her chin on his chest. "You were able to find someone? After?"

"A couple of women slept with me to see the scars. They didn't admit it, but after the one time, I never heard from them again."

"That's terrible," she whispered, forcing back tears of humiliation for him.

"I was lonely enough to think that what I looked like

didn't matter. A couple of years later, I met a woman and we spent some time together. When things became . . . intimate, she realized she couldn't and was kind enough to tell me."

"How nice of her," she said in disgust.

"When you're faced with rejection on a daily basis, a little honesty can go a long way. Like today."

"What about today? Do you regret what we did this afternoon?" She thought they connected. He hadn't told her anything like "I love you" and neither had she, but that hadn't stifled the emotions she'd experienced when he sucked on her nipple while she came, his fingers deep inside her.

He brushed the hair away from her face. "Jared Hollister came to see me this afternoon."

"For what?"

"He wanted to apologize for Ed Dunlop kicking us out of the game last night."

She scoffed. "Good. Someone should have."

"No, it wasn't right, but he also said something else that I found rather interesting. Something I would've preferred to hear from you."

"I have no idea what that could be."

"Jared said Autumn told him—"

"I wasn't keeping it from you. I still think it's a good idea."

"Wait. What's a good idea?"

"That you talk to Autumn. She's interviewing people for her blog. She wants to ask you some questions about working at the resort during the wedding." At least, that's what she thought it would be about. Autumn said she'd keep it light, and Callie believed her. "Besides, what's this 'he told me' and 'she told him,' stuff? You can ask me a question, Mitch." It irked her that Jared said something that would make him annoyed with her.

"Autumn wants to interview me? I'm the least interesting guy in Rocky Point."

She covered her breasts with the sheet. She didn't want to talk about this naked. "She's the journalist. I would assume she knows how to do her job."

"Do you want me to?"

"Don't do it because I want you to. If you feel good about it, then yes, I think it would be good for you. But if the thought of being in the public eye makes you uncomfortable, don't. She's only trying to help. She said people have forgotten you're a person, and I agree." She turned her back, fighting tears. She'd given him the power to hurt her, and in such a short amount of time, too.

"Hey. Come here."

She let him cuddle her against his chest, wrapping his arms around her. "I'm sorry. I didn't mean to snap, but that wasn't what I was talking about."

"There's nothing else."

"Autumn said you got into a fight on the ice."

She sat up again. "*That's* what you're upset about? I wasn't going to let him call you a murderer to my face. My father may be a tyrant, but there's one thing he taught me, and he taught me well. Stick up for yourself. Don't let anyone bully you or treat you like crap. It doesn't matter who they are. It could be anybody, and *nobody* deserves that."

"I don't need—"

"Everybody *needs*, Mitch. Even you. Especially you. And if you don't like that a woman gave it to you, too bad." She placed a hand on his cheek. "That was before we made love today. Before I knew how you felt about me. I was already feeling something. Are you going to punish me for that?"

Mitch grabbed her wrist and pressed a kiss to her palm. It hadn't escaped his attention she'd defended him before they slept together. That she would do that for someone she considered only a friend made him respect her more. "I can't say anything when you put it that way, but I can't watch you get hurt, Callista. I can't watch you get hurt because of ignorance and hate. I already look out for my parents. This morning—" He pursed his lips. He hadn't wanted to tell her, but he'd accused her of keeping secrets, so what did that make him?

"What? Are your mom and dad okay?"

"For now. Someone spray-painted the side of their house. My dad was covering it up when I got there this morning."

"Do you think it was the same person who threatened me on the lake?"

"No way to know, I guess. Especially since you probably don't know who it was."

"No. Ivy didn't either. At least, she didn't tell me."

"I'll talk to her later."

Her eyes flickered.

"What?" he asked.

"Nothing. Should I order dessert? Do you like cheesecake?" She slid out of bed and put on the robe she wore the, day he fixed her outlet. Her skin glowed in the dim light shining from the small lamp on the desk.

"All the flavors are good here."

She stopped her reach for the phone. "Of course. You probably eat resort food all the time. Do you want something else? Coffee? Or nothing?"

"I want to know why you got out of bed when I said Ivy's name."

She shrugged. "No reason, except she said she used to like you that way and she warned me off if I wasn't going to . . . take this seriously, I guess."

"It's none her business what we do," he said, digging through the clothes on the floor to find his briefs. "She's been hurt pretty badly and doesn't want the same thing to happen to me. We're friends, that's all."

"With benefits? She said she uses your room to nap."

"We went through my sexual history since the accident. I didn't mention her because there wasn't any reason to. Why are you giving me a hard time? Do you want me to go?"

"No. I . . . No. It's fine. I'm sorry."

He realized what was bothering her, and he felt like a moron for not figuring it out sooner. He stepped next to her and made her look at him. "There's nobody else. There's only been you since the moment you opened your door so I could unclog your drain."

That brought a smile to her lips, and he sagged in relief. He hated fighting. With anyone. Hated more that if she left Rocky Point angry, he might not ever see her again.

And that brought the same amount of fear into his heart as thinking of his parents being targeted because of him.

"It's stupid I'm jealous," she said, resting her cheek against his chest.

"No, it's not. It's sweet. But the past few years have been tough and I need things slow. I want to enjoy you."

"I want that, too."

He kissed the top of her head. "Good. The turtle

cheesecake is the best, and I wouldn't mind a cup of coffee. If you tell the kitchen I'm with you, they'll send it up no charge."

"You don't mind?"

"That the staff knows I'm seeing you? No, but Desiree will tease me about it. I'd like to keep us discreet, for now, if that's okay."

"Who's Desiree?"

"The manager here. She told me I could date you as long as it didn't cause problems. She keeps things professional."

"Don't worry, I won't tell. We don't need to let the kitchen know, either. I can afford dessert."

"How about we take turns?" He planned to spend as much time with her as possible.

Picking up the phone, she grinned. "Deal."

He stayed with her that night, spooning her, and he had dreams, the bad ones, though they were never worse than what had happened in real life. The screams echoed in his head as he opened his eyes to the sunny Sunday skies.

Callie slept sprawled across the mattress, her lips parted.

He resisted the urge to kiss her awake.

They'd made love near morning, but it hadn't been enough to erase the dregs of the nightmare and misery scratched his throat raw. He hadn't woken her, and he was grateful.

He didn't want to explain that after seven years he still hadn't been able to move on. That the girls' bright blue eyes still peered at him, helpless, though by the time he'd realized they weren't with them on the shoulder of the road, it had been too late for them to look at him, or anything.

He hadn't tried to move on, preferred to suffer as penance.

Callie didn't blame their deaths on him, but he blamed himself.

Was she wrong? Or was he?

She blinked her eyes open, hazy with sleep. A smile curved her mouth. "Good morning."

"Hey. I was going to get out of your way and let you sleep."

"You don't want to take a shower? Stay and order breakfast?"

Showering with a woman was a luxury he didn't think he'd ever be allowed to experience again, and he almost said yes. But he'd met Callie only a few days ago, and last night he said he wanted to go slow. Slow didn't mean breakfast in bed or taking long, leisurely showers. Or making love to her, her back pressed against the tile as he devoured her neck, her legs wrapped around his waist while he emptied himself inside her.

Slow meant distance, and he needed it.

To breathe.

To get a fucking grip.

His phone chimed, and he searched the pile on the floor for his pants.

His mother, up bright and early to badger her only son. *When can we meet Callie?* her text asked.

The woman in question hadn't moved, didn't look like she even woke up. Her eyelids were closed, her lips parted, her breathing shallow. If he left now, she'd fall back asleep before he shut the door.

"Who's that?" she whispered.

"My mother. She wants to meet you."

She swallowed, and the sticky sound echoed in the quiet room. "Today?"

Hell no, not today. Not tomorrow or the next day or the next.

That wasn't what slow meant.

"I'm free all day. Marnie doesn't have anything planned."

He stared at his phone.

"Mitch."

"What?"

"Tell her we'll be there for lunch, and then come back to bed."

"Callie."

She held out a hand, but it didn't reach him. He met her the rest of the way and laced their fingers.

"Please?" she asked, tightening her grip.

"Do you always get what you want?"

"Not always."

He answered his mother. *We'll be there for lunch at noon.*

He could picture her doing a happy dance around the kitchen, spilling her coffee in her glee.

"Thank you."

"You're welcome." He brushed his fingers over her cheek.

She turned her head, and his fingertips skimmed over her lips. "Make love to me, Mitch."

He slid into bed and fell into her soft heat.

This wasn't terrible, he told himself as he nestled between her legs. He didn't mind this wasn't as slow he thought they should go.

Maybe he should take what he could get, while Callie still wanted to give it to him.

Mitch showered in his own room. He needed a change of clothes and a few minutes to himself.

Things were going too fast, and he was enjoying it way too much. They hadn't talked about what they would do after Marnie's wedding, and he couldn't demand answers because she probably didn't have any.

His quiet world was being tipped upside down.

"We're going to have to take your car," he said when he met her in the lobby. He asked she meet him there to keep them from ending up in bed again. He could easily spend all his time with her making love, making up for the years of loneliness. But they couldn't build a relationship on sex, and he needed more than the physical to fill the holes in his soul.

They barely knew each other, and he needed more.

He didn't know her favorite food or her favorite color. Her body was becoming familiar though, and he'd quickly learned the fastest way to make her come. How long she'd let him tease her before she reached her breaking point.

"Why?" she asked, her voice jerking him back to the resort's lobby.

"What?"

"Why do we need to take my car?"

"I didn't tell you . . . my truck was vandalized the same night someone spray-painted my parents' house. It's in the shop being painted."

"Did you report it? Do you know who did it?"

"The cops said they'd look into it. I showed them a few

pictures I took before I dropped it off. The resort's parking lot is equipped with security cameras. Maybe they picked up something."

He followed her into the chilly morning, a puffy white cloud hiding the sun.

"This is because we went to the game," she said, unlocking a mid-sized black car parked near the front door.

"Probably."

"I'm sorry. That was my idea, and I forced you to go." She settled in the seat and rested her head against the steering wheel.

He climbed into the passenger's side and smoothed his hand over her hair, tangling his fingers in the silky strands. People took for granted how something so simple could bring so much peace. To have the chance, that someone would to allow it. She didn't shrink away, she didn't glare. She simply let him touch, and his heart heaved. "Callie, I've been the target of stuff like that for a long time. It's nothing you did or didn't do. It's okay. I haven't told you how pretty you look this morning."

"I didn't know what to wear. It's been a long time since I met someone's parents."

"Why aren't you dating anyone?" He stilled. Dammit. This wasn't the time to ask something like that. After his heart had already started scrabbling down this slippery slope.

She started the car. "My father is a very hard man, and I have two older brothers. It takes some hearty stock to get past them to date me. Most don't make it."

"That doesn't sound encouraging," he said, relieved they weren't talking about his truck anymore.

She laughed, maneuvering the car out of the parking lot. "Brandon's the middle child and more like Mom. You'd like her. Very mellow, quiet. My dad's the complete opposite. He's always on the verge of exploding over something. I think she saves him from having perpetual high blood pressure. Zach, the oldest, is the spitting image of our dad, in all ways. He's married, and my sister-in-law is pregnant with their second child." A shadow flitted across her face, and she tried to hide it, looking out the window. "You'll have to give me directions."

He rested his hand on her thigh. "Do you want kids?"

"Yeah." She drove through the streets, quiet this time of day. "I can feel it, when we make love, the pull of it. Can you?"

"You said you were on something." He teetered between wanting a family and keeping as far away from anyone who could hurt him as possible.

"I am. I'm never going to lie to you, Mitch. If I say it, I mean it. I'm on birth control. But that doesn't mean I don't think about a family . . . anyway. This is it, huh?" she asked as she parked. "It's pretty. You grew up here?"

He stared at the house as if he were a stranger. On the small side, though the basement gave it more space than it looked like it had. Even from the distance, the fresh paint covering the nasty words stood out against the old, dull color. This summer he'd give the entire house a fresh coat of paint. The winter's temperature made it impossible now.

"Yeah. My dad started at the paper mill the day after he graduated high school. He retired with a good pension right before they shut down two years ago. It makes the resort's business more important than ever."

"What does your mom do?" She turned the car off and pulled the key out of the ignition.

"She's been a homemaker since she married my dad. She sold cosmetics for a while, she liked inviting people to the house and throwing parties, but after the accident, she had to stop. No one would buy from her."

"I'm sorry."

"It's okay. Come on, she's trying not to let us see she's been staring at us since we parked."

She leaned over the middle storage compartment and cupped his scarred cheek in her hand. "Let's give her something to watch, then."

He met her lips, soft, her breath hinting of coffee. He could fall in, kiss her forever.

She slipped her tongue into his mouth, and he moaned. "Callie," he said, leaning away. "I can't go in there hard."

"Well, you made me wet. Think about that while your parents are sitting across the table from us."

She scrambled out of the car, giggling, and he followed, slower, using the protection of the vehicle to adjust his cock.

Ruby greeted Callie at the door, and he prayed for all their sakes his mother didn't fall in love with her, too.

He couldn't deny he was falling in love, didn't want to deny it, wouldn't deny it, either, but he didn't know where it would lead.

His future seemed bleak and murky, a pinprick of light far in the distance resembling Callie, but when he reached out, the picture wavered then disappeared, stealing all his hope with it.

"You shouldn't have gone through all this trouble," Callie said, standing in the middle of the cramped kitchen. She'd already had a tour of their house and had been introduced to Luna, a huge German shepherd that slowly crawled into her lap when she sat on the couch in the living room, and had peeked at the snow-filled backyard.

Mitch's dad, "Call me Chip," had leaned back and watched her, not having much to say, and she wondered if he would have acted differently toward her if Mitch hadn't been hurt in the accident.

"It wasn't any trouble at all," Ruby said, gesturing eagerly at a chair and inviting Callie to sit.

She sat at the table laden with cold cuts and vegetable fixings to make homemade submarine sandwiches. Three different kinds of chip bags were open and waiting. Chicken noodle soup simmered on the stove ready to be ladled into bowls.

A simple Midwestern lunch, and she dug in.

Ruby beamed, and Mitch settled into a seat next to her, his hand brushing her arm. Close.

His mother didn't miss it.

"You're from Decatur?" Ruby asked, putting together her sub.

She held up a hand, chewed, and swallowed the chip she popped into her mouth just as Ruby asked the question. "Yes. I'm Marnie's neighbor. Our townhouses are connected."

"Oh, you own your own home. You must do well for yourself."

She shrugged. Firefighting didn't pay terribly, but being a rookie wasn't lucrative. Her father always said the want to help had to be in the blood, that the satisfaction of the job paid as much as the paycheck. Over the years she'd managed to move up the pay scale, but she was unwilling to take on more responsibilities to earn another bump. "I do okay. I have a couple of years of college behind me, and that helps. Mitch, you never said why you wanted to be a bus driver."

Ruby stilled, though her fingers dug into the bread of her sandwich.

She looked around the table, hoping the subject wasn't taboo. They'd had several years to deal with it.

Mitch set his soda can on the table and the clink echoed through the silent kitchen.

Even Luna, who sat near the table hoping for scraps, seemed to be holding her breath.

"I did two years at the community college after high school. Most kids do, since it's cheaper to get the general classes out of the way, then they transfer somewhere else." Mitch picked a chip up off his plate and scraped his thumbnail over the orange cheese. "I didn't know what I wanted to do, and my name was on the waitlist at the mill. Dad couldn't get me in. There aren't a lot of employment opportunities around here, you know?"

She nodded. Rocky Point wasn't like Decatur. In Rocky Point, minimum wage jobs could be found easily: fast food, a clerk at the drug store. Stocking shelves at the hardware or grocery store. Ticket collector at the small movie theater. But to make a living wage, those positions were already full, and an opening didn't come along very often.

"I did odd jobs, but nothing that would let me move out of the house."

"All he could talk about was moving out." Ruby sighed and fed Luna a small piece of bread.

"I was twenty, it's what men do at that age," Mitch said. "It's what we're supposed to do at that age."

"At least he didn't go into the military," Ruby said to her, and Chip patted her hand. Judging by the lines that suddenly crowded Ruby's face, she guessed that had been a real worry. And a realistic one. Several of her classmates had gone into the military, thrilled at the prospect of being sent overseas. She hadn't wanted to, but her father said serving their country was another acceptable choice. The military hadn't appealed to her, and she'd taken the easiest path presented to her.

"Lots of young people enlist. No shame in it. Things might have turned out better," Mitch said.

Callie took another bite of her sandwich and waited.

"I was working part-time for the city road crew when the positioned opened, though it really wasn't what I wanted to do. I was twenty-five and I considered dealing with kids at seven-thirty in the morning a form of torture, but it was full-time and that year they added a sign-on bonus that would payout over five years. Needless to say, I didn't earn the full amount."

She chewed and swallowed. She wouldn't let the topic bring them down, and she asked a lighter question. "Did you like it?"

"Bus drivers should be paid more. They put up with a lot of shit." He glanced at Ruby. "Sorry, Ma. But yeah, after I got to know the kids, and they got to know me, it was almost fun."

"What did you do between runs?"

"There wasn't much time between. I drove bus for the elementary, middle, and high school. They had staggered start times, and I only had a couple hours to eat lunch."

"Would you want to do that again? Drive a school bus, I mean?"

Ruby sucked in a breath.

Chip leaned back in his chair.

"I can't be around kids, Callie."

"Oh." Was he telling her he didn't want to have a

family, or was he saying he could never have a job where he worked around children?

She met Ruby's pinched eyes across the table, and she didn't think now was the time to ask. Besides, she'd pushed enough, and she didn't want to ruin lunch.

"What do you do now that Mr. Sinclair has retired?" she asked them, and the question dispelled the tension.

"Nothing much," Chip said, joining the conversation for the first time. "We fish. Take walks through the park down by the lake. Ruby and I, we like to read a lot and we're part of a book club the library hosts every month. We live quiet lives."

"Because of what happened?"

"Some," was all he said and scooped more sour cream and onion chips out of the bag.

"Autumn Bennett wants to interview Mitch for the newspaper's blog," she said, nibbling at the last of her sandwich.

"Callie," Mitch said, warning in his voice. "This isn't the time."

"Well, she does."

"Mitch, why don't you help me in the garage for a minute? The truck's been acting up again," Chip said, pushing away from the table. Luna drooped in disappointment.

"Will you be okay?" Mitch asked, squeezing her leg underneath the table.

"Yeah, sure."

Ruby remained silent until Mitch and Chip closed the door that connected the house to the garage.

"He really likes you," she said, balling a paper towel in her hands. "He'll do it, too, if you beg him enough."

"Do what?"

"The interview."

"Oh. I don't understand why he wouldn't. Autumn said the town was divided, that it was Mitch's behavior that turned the others against him."

"It wasn't his behavior, Callie, and I'm surprised Autumn Bennett would stick her nose into something like this." Ruby lifted a bag of chips off the table, the plastic crinkling, and rose from her seat. "I know she's a reporter, but this was a long time ago and she wasn't even in town when it happened. She was living in Decatur. She doesn't know a thing about what happened here."

"I don't either. What *did* happen, Mrs. Sinclair?"

"Town was *not* divided. That's bullshit talk from someone who doesn't want to admit that the whole of eight thousand people ganged up on us, excuse my language. The girls' mother and father, and their families, they did everything they could to blame Mitch. Every kind of investigator they could dredge up talked to Mitch, looked at that bus, talked to the semi-truck driver until he started saying he was gonna sue for harassment. They checked into Mitch's background, and it's a good thing my boy was clean. If anything, *anything*, would have even hinted that Mitch left those girls to burn on purpose, he'd be in prison right now." Ruby crushed the bag of chips, the crunch mixing with the grief in her voice.

"Then why didn't you leave?"

"Because that would have been as good as admitting Mitch was guilty. We had to stand our ground. The girls' funeral was the hardest part. Hate mail, people doing things to our house, breaking our trucks' windows, slashing our tires. We adopted Luna from the shelter, and two weeks later we found her barely breathing, laying in our backyard, poisoned. Chip had to take her to obedience school in

Marengo to teach her not to accept food from anyone but us. Yes, things have quieted since the accident, but you bringing him to that hockey game has brought up a lot of the hurt all over again."

"I didn't know," she murmured.

"He didn't tell you, or you didn't listen?" Ruby sank onto her chair, her shoulders shaking. "He loves you. I can see it on his face. It's been heartbreaking watching him try to find someone since the fire. My boy doesn't deserve what he's been through." Her voice cracked. "He's thirty-six years old. He should have a wife waiting for him at home, children to play with, family vacations, and presents under a Christmas tree. In this little town, staying here, he'll never have that. Then he meets you, and you can see. You can look at his face, look into his eyes, and see the man he used to be. Why? Why can you do that? Why you?"

She pushed the sleeve of her sweater up her arm. The scar that marked her skin from Marnie's grease fire sparkled in the light shining through the window behind her. Scar tissue was almost . . . pretty, in a way. A badge of honor, perhaps, or stupidity, in her case. Glossy pink in some areas, dull in others, blending into the color of her skin around the edges. A doctor may have done better, but she'd treated the burn herself, could still feel the sizzle and the pain. She'd called nine-one-one and told dispatch she already put the fire out, but they sent a truck anyway. Ace had torn her to shreds for her carelessness and disrespect.

Fire deserved respect.

No one knew that better than she did.

She traced the scar, the wormy feeling Mitch described under the surface, though what he felt must be a million times worse than what she did whenever she touched her injury.

"Because I know what fire can do to people. Because I know that under the scarring there's a person, a person who has feelings, who can be hurt. Someone who has lived through that kind of trauma . . . their compassion, their sympathy and empathy toward other people is doubled, tripled . . . but it makes them vulnerable, too. I get it. But Mrs. Sinclair, he did nothing wrong."

"Tell that to the mother of those girls, Callie. You don't have children, not yet, but the time will come and you'll love that baby with everything you have. You'd walk through fire for that child, you'd take a bullet, because that's what mothers do. And if anyone hurts her, I don't care who it is. The school bully who hits her, a teacher who doesn't like her, a pediatrician who's too rough, anybody who even looks at your child the wrong way, there'll be hell to pay, won't there?"

She gritted her teeth. She didn't have children, but she knew without a doubt what Ruby said was true.

"You think your child will be safe on a school bus, you think nothing will happen. But one day it does, and it comes out that the only adult who could have prevented such tragedy did nothing."

She opened her mouth to defend Mitch, but Ruby cut her off.

"What it looks like, and what it *is*, are two different things. You're young, but you're old only enough to know that."

"Yeah, I do."

"Then you think like a mama and what you'd do if you lost your only children in an accident you believed with all your heart could've been prevented." Ruby grasped her hand. "You've been here for only a few days. Mitch has lived with this for seven years. You think you'll swoop in here, wave your magic wand, sprinkle Rocky Point with fairy dust and everything will be okay? And God knows, with the way Mitch looks at you, he'll let you try, consequences be damned."

"That's not—" She stopped. That's exactly what she thought. The fact that she'd be taking on the entire town, instead of only half like Autumn led her to believe, meant nothing. She thought was helping, when in reality, she was doing the complete opposite.

Ruby wiped a tear off her cheek and stood to her feet. "Don't hurt my boy. He's been through enough already. Now, help me put the leftovers away, will you?" She paused, sniffling. "I didn't think he'd bring you."

She tried to smile. "I asked him to."

"See? He'll do whatever you want. That's power, and you need to use it wisely."

Or you'll break his heart. She heard it, even if Ruby hadn't said it out loud. She didn't need to. Ruby accused her of not listening to Mitch, and she hadn't. She hadn't listened to Mitch, and she hadn't listened to Ivy, either. She'd listened to Autumn, who hadn't even lived here at the time. Because she wanted to believe things couldn't be that bad. But they were.

She understood now, and things needed to change. Mitch deserved a life.

She didn't plan to swoop in, make things perfect, and then leave again.

She wasn't going anywhere.

"What do you think Ma's saying to her?"

"Nothing she doesn't need to hear."

"You don't like her."

"I didn't say that."

"You didn't need to."

Chip opened the garage door, letting in the frosty December air. They didn't need the light, but it was a habit now, to keep watch over the house.

The block was quiet though, empty except for Callie's car parked across the street.

No, his dad didn't need to say he disliked her, and right from the minute she stepped into the kitchen, too, if Mitch had read his father's cues correctly.

"It's not her." Chip popped the truck's hood and checked the oil, wiping the dipstick on a rag, not meeting his eyes.

"Then what?"

"She's naïve."

"Yeah." He couldn't argue with that. Callie came from a large city where nasty things happened and people went about their business. The same couldn't be said about this town. Even though the Decatur and Rocky Point were separated by only three hours of drive time, people lived, and suffered, in drastically different ways.

"Do you like her?" Chip asked.

He liked when she wrapped her legs around his waist, pulling him closer. He liked when she whispered in his ear, his bad one, and could lick his earlobe without cringing. He liked she would give him a blowjob, that the scars that marred the right side of his body didn't turn her off. He liked that when he touched her with his right hand she didn't freak out, as if she were going to catch a disease.

He took too long to answer.

"Besides the sex, son."

He scowled. "How did you know?"

"I might be your father, but I'm a man first. I know you've been intimate. She was nice about it?"

Blushing furiously, he said, "She never said anything."

"That's good." Chip shoved his hands into the pockets of his jeans. "I don't have to tell you to be careful."

"She's on the Pill."

His father looked at him out of the corners of his eyes. "That's good to know, but that's not what I'm talking about. People don't want to let this go. It might've felt like it faded away, but it's there, simmering."

"I know. I won't let you and Ma get hurt again."

"It's gonna happen, Mitch. The cops don't have our backs. They do the bare minimum they can get away with, nothing's changed there. You'll do what Callie wants. And maybe she has a point, maybe it's time to start defending yourself. It was a long time ago and you did everything you could, but if this is something you're going to choose to do, do it right, and do it all the way. Me and your mom, we'll stand with you."

"Thanks. We're only talking about an interview with Autumn, and Callie says it won't be about the accident."

"When you were in the hospital in Decatur and your mom was in the hospital here, those were pretty dark times for me."

Mitch blinked. His dad had never talked about this before.

"You two are my whole family. Besides my Luna girl. Sinclairs don't give up and we don't back down from a fight, but your grandpa, he always said we were smart enough to know when enough was enough. Knowing you can't win isn't the same as giving up, Mitch. Remember that."

"Yeah, I got it."

"Let's go inside, then. Your mom's got pie."

"I better see if Callie needs rescuing. Ma can get a little intense."

"Your mom, and me, too, we have a right to be concerned. We're afraid that down the line, Callie isn't going to be the one who needs the rescuing."

CHAPTER SEVEN

Callie drove them through town to the resort.

Christmas decorations on Main Street struggled to exude holiday cheer, red and silver candy canes and green Christmas trees made of tinsel attached to the street-lights barely sparkled in the sparse sun and freezing wind. Some braved the weather to hurry down the sidewalk, poking into the stores that were open to Christmas shop or beat off the doldrums of staying at home. The Rocky Point Supply Company had its share of visitors, people looking to gossip and see what Leah was doing to the store, and despite the lunch hour having come and gone, the diner looked crowded.

The talk with Mitch's mother drained her. She could use a nap, or a soak in the hot tub in the pool area, or, if she was being responsible, a two-hour workout.

Silently, Mitch stared out the window. She would've thought he was mad at her except he twisted their fingers together on his thigh, and she drove with one hand on the wheel.

They were moving too fast, and it made him uncomfortable. She couldn't blame him, not after the stories he told her about the other women. To find someone who accepted all of him, and she did, more than anything in the world, well, she'd give him time to sort it out.

His mother knew him better than anyone, and if she thought he was in love with her, she could afford to wait.

"I think I'll take a nap when we get back. I know we've been spending a lot of time together and it must have messed up your schedule. Don't feel like you have to entertain me, especially if you have other things to do. Marnie said I didn't have to be here for the full two weeks, but I took the time because I needed the break. That's all."

"The future makes me nervous."

She squeezed his hand. "I know. Me, too."

"I'd like to talk to Autumn, if she still wants me to."

She turned her car onto the resort road and began the slow climb up the hill, her wheels skidding. "Your parents don't think that's a good idea, and after what your mom told me, I don't know. I want it to be good for you, but it's only a little blog post and I'm torn. Will it be okay because it's only a little blog post? Or will it cause so much trouble the little blog post will end up turning into a massive mistake? Autumn says it will help. I agreed with her, but now I'm beginning to think she's the only one who thinks so."

"I don't want to be the only resort employee she interviews. If she'll interview Ivy, and Desiree, and a few others who work at the resort, then it won't seem like she singled me out."

"That's a good idea. But I think she did, you know. Single you out. Because I started asking questions. Because she thinks we're together." She liked the sound of it, the together part.

He didn't say anything, and she didn't push.

She parked her car, farther away from the lobby doors than before, and turned the engine off. She looked over the wooded area. So many trees, so much snow.

She unlatched her seatbelt and reached for the door handle to get out, but he stopped her.

"Is that what we are? Together?"

What was she supposed to say to that? If she said no, she'd sound like she didn't want him. If she said yes, she'd sound like a presumptuous bitch. There was no good answer, and she laughed, a bit rueful. "You said you wanted to take it slow."

He cupped the side of her face with his warm palm, and she leaned in, closing her eyes. "I did, but that doesn't mean we're over, or that I won't want more . . . later. I'm afraid if —" He stopped and looked out the window, his lips pressed into a thin line.

"You're afraid if we go too slow, I'll disappear."

"Yeah."

"I like you, Mitch, and if I've acted like a desperate whore, that's my fault. I know you didn't want me to meet your parents today, but I think it worked out. Your mom told me a few things I didn't know, a few things I should have known. About the accident, about the way you were treated. I grew up in a houseful of men, besides my mom, of course, and I was taught to fight. It's not a reflex to back down, even when I should. You'll have to rein that part of me in. I don't want to hurt you because I was blind or stupid."

He traced her eyebrow down her temple, to her cheek. "Thank you for that."

"You're welcome. Thank you for letting me meet your parents. I know they didn't like me, but maybe they would have, if things were different."

"They're worried."

"I know."

"You'll tell Autumn I'll do it?"

"Yeah. I'll ask her where she wants to meet you."

"You won't be there?"

She climbed out of her car and slammed the door. "Do you want me to be?"

"If you wouldn't mind." He leaned against her car's back fender and squinted against the sun into the woods.

Maybe he'll take a walk out there later and invite her along. She liked the deer. Almost as much as she liked being with him.

"Okay."

"Are you coming inside?"

"I'm going to sit out here for a minute. I'll let you know as soon as I hear from Autumn."

He brushed his lips over hers. "Sounds good. Don't stay out here too long. It's too cold."

"I won't. I'll see you later"

She perched on the trunk of her car and breathed in the frozen air long after Mitch went inside the resort.

Her heart twisted.

Don't hurt my boy.

Nothing about this was going to turn out right. She started an avalanche throwing a tiny snowball, and she wished now, with all her might, she could take it back.

Stupid hockey game.

She texted Autumn and told her Mitch agreed to the blog interview. After looking longingly at her bed, she pulled up her big-girl panties and changed into her workout clothes. What did Mitch normally do on Sunday afternoons? Spent time in the woods more than likely. He'd seemed at peace watching the deer. She was glad he could find a sense of wellbeing somewhere, but it saddened her it had to be in the middle of the woods alone.

She sat in the hot tub after her workout and chatted with a few other guests who were also in town for Marnie's wedding.

Mitch never did surface, and when Autumn texted her a time, she leapt at the chance to touch base with him. Only a few hours had gone by, but he wasn't the only one thinking this relationship was too good to be true. It wouldn't surprise her if he broke things off because it would be too complicated to continue, but it would hurt her, too.

The pull to wrap her arms around him, to twist and writhe until they were two halves of a whole, scared her.

Her fingers trembled when she texted him. *Autumn said she can come by the resort tomorrow morning before you start your shift. She'll meet us in the dining room at 7:30 and offered to buy us breakfast for our trouble.*

She hoped he'd call her to talk about the interview, but when her phone chimed, the number of Brandon's rehab center glowed white on the screen instead of Mitch's name.

"Hi! How are you?" she answered, happy he was taking the initiative to reach out. The first couple of weeks after he checked himself in he hadn't spoken to anyone.

"Hey, Callie. How's the middle of nowhere?"

"Good. Relaxing. I just got done working out. Thinking about a nap, but it's probably too late now."

"You're still working out? That's one thing I don't miss. I still run, but damn, all that weightlifting was a pain in the ass, sometimes literally."

"I have to. You know how important it is."

"I know."

"How's therapy going?" she asked to steer them away from their father and their jobs.

"Making progress. My main therapist is pressuring me to ask Mom and Dad if they'll attend sessions with me. I know Mom would, in a heartbeat, but Dad . . ."

"Dad understands therapy has a place, but he thinks it should be to get you back on the truck, not further away from it."

Brandon sighed in frustration. "Yeah. I don't want to be a firefighter anymore. What will he say when I finally tell him that?"

"That you're a coward." It wasn't time to mince words, and why bother? Brandon's question wasn't rhetorical. "What would you do if you weren't a firefighter anymore?"

"I still want to help people. There are other ways of helping people than hauling them out of burning buildings."

"You mean like emergency services, or becoming a therapist?"

"Something like that. I need to help, that's in our blood and I'm not fighting it, but I can't be around fire anymore. I can't." His voice broke on a slight sob of misery.

"I understand, and it's something I've been struggling with too. The weight of it."

"Maybe it wouldn't be so hard if Dad wasn't such a prick."

"Yeah, that too."

"How's your guy? Still seeing him?"

"Yeah, I am. Do you remember a bus fire a few years ago, here, in Rocky Point? The Decatur paper ran it for a day, maybe two, but they dropped it because of that bridge collapsing the same week. Anyway, the bus driver wasn't able to save all the kids. Do you remember that?"

Brandon paused, his breath coming over the phone in a quiet stream. "Kind of. That was . . . shit, six, seven years ago? You were just starting out in the department, right? Why? Is that who you're seeing? Sweet Jesus Christ. Out of anyone in the whole town, you pick a guy who has a history with fire worse than us. Does he know you're a firefighter?"

She opened her mouth to say, "Of course," but did he? "I don't think it's come up. Why? Is it bad?"

"It won't be good. Let's just say since I was trapped in that building, dating someone who has a relationship with fire isn't going to be first on my list of things to do. If you like him, tell him. *Soon*. Or he'll break your heart when he dumps you."

"He wouldn't dump me over that."

"Is he still struggling with it?"

"Yeah. The people in town still treat him like shit, too."

"Then he'll dump you over it. No one wants to see their nightmares every time they look at someone, especially someone they love. You know what kind of hell that would be for him. Get your head on straight, little sister. Your vacation's turning your brain to mush. I'll talk to you later. Jeopardy's on in the common room, and I have a friendly little wager with the nurse who dispenses my meds I can knock her socks off."

"That doesn't sound like a game of Jeopardy. That sounds like something else." She tried to joke, but her brother's advice squeezed her lungs until she couldn't breathe.

"I didn't say she wasn't pretty, and we talk a lot about the medical profession. It's something I'm looking into."

"Good for you. I'm glad you called, Brandon. I love you."

"Love you too, Callie. Take care of yourself."

The call disconnected and her cell phone beeped. She dropped on the bed, her heart racing.

Brandon had to be wrong. Mitch wouldn't dump her over her job. That was stupid.

Marnie texted her, inviting her to go swimming at the pool the next night. Beyond that, she didn't hear from anyone, and the silence put her on edge.

She'd have to trust Mitch to show up at the interview. She wouldn't badger him about it. If he changed his mind, maybe Autumn would interview her again, or she'd treat Autumn to breakfast to pay her back for the wasted hour.

Not hungry, and not wanting to sit around in her room, Callie dressed in her winter clothes and headed out to the lake. The snow crunched under her boots, and the stars twinkled. The Auroras slithered across the sky in bright greens, and she kept going until the resort was but a speck of bright light against the dark.

She walked, her heart growing heavier with each step. If she never turned around, how many people would miss her if she faded away? She tried to ignore her heart when it whispered no one would care at all.

Sluggish, Mitch met Callie and Autumn for breakfast the next morning. An emergency had come up in the laundry room last night, and Carmen called his cell, panicking. There wasn't any reason for her to be scared of Desiree, but ever since she'd been promoted to head laundress of the resort, she took her position seriously. Never one to pry, he never asked why she freaked out over circumstances that were out of her control, only fixed things the minute they broke to give the older woman peace of mind. Last night was no different, and he'd spent hours past his bedtime repairing a washer that had a busted hose.

He hadn't seen Callie's text until he'd fallen into bed almost asleep, and she probably thought he changed his mind and would blow off the interview.

Being five minutes late didn't help, and she sat with Autumn, her shoulders hunched, shadows under her eyes. Maybe something else was wrong. Her pallor seemed much too serious over what she called a little blog post.

"Good morning," he said, sliding into the chair next to her.

"You came," she said, smiling in relief.

Mitch brushed some of her hair away from her face, his fingers lingering near the corner of one of her anxious brown eyes. Autumn studied him as he held his hand to Callie's temple, but he didn't care. "Did you think I wouldn't?"

"A little."

"I was in the laundry room late, fixing a washer for Carmen. She's in charge of washing the linens for the resort. You know, towels, sheets, pool towels, napkins, that kind of thing," he explained when Callie frowned.

"That must be quite a job," she said.

"She's in charge of a small staff, and it makes her feel better when her machines are working."

"I can't blame her," Autumn said, holding a carafe of coffee over his mug. "It's really busy around here. Do you want some?"

"Yeas, please."

He didn't know Autumn well. They'd gone to high school together and she'd had a crush on Cole McClure, the photographer who followed her all over the place like a puppy now. Mitch expected him to be lurking around, ready to take his picture, something he wasn't looking forward to at all, but it came with the territory, and like the game, he'd do it because Callie asked.

"How are you?" Autumn asked as she poured coffee.

Did she mean on a superficial level, like most people meant it? How are you? *Oh, I'm fine, how are you?* Or did she mean something more? How are you? *I'm okay, except, I'm afraid someone will hurt my parents because I wanted to watch a hockey game with the woman I'm falling in love with. And, you know, finding nasty words spray-painted on my truck wasn't that great, but, hey. I have a job and a roof over my head. Things could be worse.*

Autumn tilted her head. "Mitch? I was wondering how you're doing. I'm a reporter, not a shrink."

Embarrassment heated his face. "Sorry. Overthinking."

Callie rested her hand on his thigh.

"It's okay." Autumn laughed. "I'm kind of surprised how put out this can make people. It's a blog post and I'm asking a few questions. Not a big deal. I'm lucky Marnie's having her wedding here so I have something to put on the website. It's difficult to think up topics that would be worth someone's time."

"And you think an interview with me is?" he asked, raising his eyebrows.

"She interviewed me, and I'm pretty boring," Callie said.

"I doubt that." He sipped his coffee and hoped Autumn didn't ask if he was reading the blog series. It's not that he didn't care about Marnie's wedding, it's that he didn't care about almost everything, and that included wedding ceremonies he wasn't invited to.

That brought on a whole other set of issues. He wanted to be Callie's date if she asked him, but deep down inside, he hoped she didn't ask to take the decision out of his hands.

"I haven't posted yours yet, either, if you've been waiting for it," Autumn said to Callie. "I lost it somewhere, and I need to find where I saved it on my iPad, otherwise I'm going to have to ask you the questions all over again."

"That's okay. I have plenty of time."

"When did she interview you?" he asked.

"The day I got here. At Marnie's get-to-know-you thing."

He smiled, remembering her clogged drain. "We'd already met."

Callie beamed. "Yeah."

"You guys are cute together," Autumn said, appraising them with a faint smile.

"I don't think I've ever heard anyone use the word cute to describe me . . . at least, not since the accident," he said. No point in avoiding the obvious.

"It's not about that. It's about . . . all of it." Autumn waved her spoon around in a circle. "You guys click."

Maybe that was as simple as it needed to be. He sat back in his chair, his mind working furiously through Autumn's words. They clicked. God knows he'd felt it the minute he saw her, and she'd felt the same.

He kissed Callie's cheek. "Yeah. We do."

"Anyway, let's get this going. I know you need to get to work. I appreciate you taking a minute to talk to me."

"It's no problem, but I don't know if I have anything to offer."

"Callie told me one of the conditions, well, the only condition, I guess, is that I interview other people who work here, and that's fine. In fact, it's a great idea. I have to admit,

I hadn't planned on it, but what the hell. It will give me even more to add to the blog."

"I'm glad I could help," he said, trying to keep the sarcasm to himself, but failing by the wry look Autumn shot his way.

"Don't be like that. I know we haven't talked much, not since high school, and even then, the best I can say is that we were civil to each other in the hallways. But I didn't think, I mean, I didn't think you would—"

"You don't have to apologize for not talking to me after you came back to town. Everyone knows Cole and your sister give you a hard time, and I know how much you work, even if you say blogging isn't difficult or worth anything. We have jobs. It is what it is."

"Thanks. We should go out. All of us," Autumn said, circling her spoon again. "Marnie would love having us together. She's throwing a pool party tonight, if you want to come."

"I appreciate the invitation, but I'm not ready for something like that. If you plan to do something with your clothes on, let me know. Jared already asked about double dating. He said he's been hanging out with one of Marnie's bridesmaids."

"Leah," Autumn said. "Marnie asked him to pick her up in his plane so she wouldn't have to drive from Marengo. I guess they hit it off. That's great, then. We'll figure something out. Now, about the blog. How long have you worked here . . . ?"

He answered her questions between sips coffee and bites of French toast. He had a long day of work around the resort, and it would be several hours until lunch. As he answered questions, Callie slowly worked his shirt's hem out of the waistband of jeans and pressed her hand to the scarring on his right side.

Her touch made him hard, hard and . . . grateful . . . she could stand to touch him at all. No one had to tell him gratitude was the last thing he should be feeling.

A woman's touch shouldn't make him indebted. All that did was put her feelings above his, whether it was intentional or not.

He'd need to work on his self-esteem if he and Callie had a hope of taking their relationship somewhere. They had to be equals, and they couldn't be if all he felt was damaged.

He answered Autumn's question about the funniest thing that had happened to him since he started working at the resort. It hadn't been funny then, but he recounted a time he had to strip to his skivvies and jump into the lake after a kid who floated too far away from the beach on a giant blow-up frog. He hadn't understood why none of the adults on the beach had been willing to go after the boy until he hauled the kid back to shore and his toes were blue when he stepped onto the sand.

No one thanked him, but he didn't tell Autumn that. Without a shirt, he'd been even more of a freak, something to stare at. He'd quickly pulled his Rocky Point Resort t-shirt over his head, tugged his jeans back on, and hightailed it to his room.

That was when Desiree established the free meal policy he enjoyed. She said if he was going to be saving people's lives, he might as well get something out of it since everyone thought themselves above saying a simple thanks.

Later, he thought those people on the beach probably accused him of trying to make up for not saving the girls on the bus. Ivy said he was paranoid and not everything came back around to the accident. After a few days, he forgot about it, but he wondered, again, now.

"I think that's it," Autumn said, detaching the small keyboard from her iPad. "I'm doing Desiree's interview now, since I'm here, and after I finish Stacy's, Ivy's, and Carmen's, if she'll talk to me, I'll post them together. Kind of a series within a series. I know you don't want to feel singled out, and this way it will look like I profiled the resort employees and you happened to be included."

"I appreciate that."

"It's not a big deal. When I talked to Callie about it, I told her I wanted people to start thinking about you as a person who's been hurting just as much as the girls' families. It was horrible what Ed did to you guys at the game. I wanted to write an article on basic kindness and respect for tourists, since Callie's from Decatur. How can we keep this town afloat if we treat people like that? But my editor shot it down. He said it'd be too hot a topic since everyone was already talking about you. It didn't help that after Jared caught wind of it, he fired Ed. The old coot deserved it, as far as I'm concerned. The arena's a public place, and you weren't doing anything."

Except breathing, but he kept that to himself, too.

"Anyway," Autumn continued, shoving her iPad into her bag, "thanks for talking to me. Callie, I'll see you tonight?"

"Yeah, maybe."

"Okay. Have a good day, you two. Thanks, again."

"Thanks for breakfast," Callie said.

Autumn walked away, waving to accept Callie's thanks, and he asked, "You don't want to go?"

"Maybe. For a little bit. Are you starting your day, then?"

"Actually, I was going to ask you for a ride. I need to pick up my truck. They're done painting it."

"Sure. I can do that."

"Thanks."

"Right now?"

He pulled his phone out of the back pocket of his work jeans. "If you can. They just opened."

"Yeah, I just need to grab my purse and jacket out of my room. Do you want to come with me?"

"No. I'll wait for you in the lobby."

"Okay. Be right back."

Her ass twitched as she hurried down the hallway, and she trotted quickly up the stairs. If he would have followed her to her room, they'd be on their way to bed. He wouldn't even have made it to the bed. He'd have pushed her jeans down and bent her over the desk. Something about Callie brought out the desire, the need to take, because she was so willing to give.

It scared him, how quickly she'd consumed him.

Like the fire that ate the bus before he could save those girls.

He stepped outside under the stone canopy and breathed in the crisp air. There were a few people on the lake ice fishing, but on a Monday morning, almost everyone was at work.

The automatic doors chugged open, fighting the cold, and Callie stepped through them. "Are you ready?"

"Yeah."

"I think the interview went well," she said, driving away from the resort. "You'll need to tell me where the car place is."

"I'll show you where to turn. It was okay. Autumn's nice, but it's not the interview that worries me, it's how it'll go over. It was a good idea to group my interview with the others. I hope it doesn't cause problems."

"Me too. If it does, I'll feel like it's my fault, like the game. I still feel terrible I forced you to go."

"Don't feel bad, sweetheart. You had good intentions, and that's all that matters." The endearment stuck on his tongue like glue. When was the last time he called a woman that?

She smiled, and he was glad he tried. Every experience with Callie was going to be new because she would appreciate everything he did.

He directed her to a small dealership on the opposite side of town from the resort, and she stopped in front of the doors, letting the engine idle.

"Are you going to be okay without me today?" he asked.

Wrinkling her nose, she said, "Yeah, sure. I need to work out. You're a bad influence."

"Is that right? And here I thought you were the one who made me miss mine. 'Stay in bed,' she said, blinking her big brown eyes. How can I say no?"

She laughed. "Don't tell me that. Now I'll bat my eyes every time I want something."

He leaned over and rested his hand on the back of her neck. "You don't have to bat your eyes. Anything you want, I'll give you, if it's within my power. Callie—" He swallowed. "I—"

"Don't say it. Don't say it now," she said, pressing her fingers to his lips. "If you say it now, you'll regret it. You wanted to go slow, and if you say it, you can't take it back."

His stomach quivered, and he almost lost his breakfast, right in her lap. He would have told her he loved her, and she stopped him, holy Jesus, she stopped him.

"Okay. I . . . I'll catch up with you later. Callie—"

"I know, Mitch. I *know*. But it's only been a few days, and you're right about going slow, and your parents don't like me, and there's something—" Her eyes filled with tears.

"What? What something?"

She shook her head. "Nothing. Not now. Okay?"

It wasn't okay, he wanted to know what she was going to say, but this wasn't the place and he said, "Okay. Be careful driving. If anything happens to you—" He had to stop because fear clogged his throat.

"I'll be okay," she said, wiping her cheeks. "Do you want me to wait?"

"No. Go work out. I'll catch up with you later."

"Okay. Bye."

He slammed the door and watched her turn into traffic. He should've asked her to text him when she made it back to the resort, but he wouldn't be far behind and he'd check on her later. If she really wanted him to, he'd go to the pool party tonight. No one said he couldn't keep his t-shirt on, and in swim trunks, he'd show about as much skin as he did every summer.

Breathing shallowly through his mouth, hoping to calm his stomach, he waited for the technician to process his paperwork. For the past seven years his insides have been twisted up, stress and guilt eating at him, and even though this was different, Callie was different, he wished he didn't have to worry about anything at all.

"We drove your truck around front," the man said, smirking. "That's going to be six-hundred fifty-four dollars and ninety-eight cents."

He shoved his credit card into the slot, bristling at the guy's attitude. It wasn't the same man he dealt with when he dropped his truck off, and though he'd grown used to being treated like trash, tension crackled even more since he tried to go to the hockey game.

He signed the small slip of paper, shoved his wallet into the back of pocket of his jeans, and yanked on his gloves.

Halfway through the door, he stopped, anger coiling in his belly.

The words weren't on his truck anymore, but they weren't painted over with plain black like he asked.

No, bright pink rectangles flashed on his doors and tail-gate, and it wouldn't take a genius to figure out that he was hiding the nasty insults someone had sprayed on his truck.

Instinct told him to keep walking—he'd never win this fight—but pride told him to defend himself.

"I didn't ask for this," Mitch said, holding the door open with his shoulder, the cold air keeping him from exploding in a hot rage.

"Got a service order here that says you did," the jerk said, waving a paper in the air. "Right here. Cover the graffiti on a black, 2015 Dodge Ram truck. I think we did that."

"This isn't what I meant. Bud knew that. I spoke to him when I dropped it off."

"Bud ain't here today. In fact, he's visiting his wife's family in Wisconsin for Christmas until the end of the month. You'll have to come back and take it up with him . . . or go someplace else and have it painted again."

He wasn't going to pay another six hundred dollars to have his truck repainted. He'd never get his money back from this goddamned place if he did.

"I'll be back," he said, tired of arguing. Bud could've told the guys in his shop to do whatever they wanted to his truck. Just because the shop manager had treated him with decency didn't mean Bud gave a flying fuck what happened after he walked out the door.

"Merry Christmas," the asshole said, rubbing his middle finger over his nose.

He scoffed, a "Fuck you" on the tip of his tongue.

He didn't need to open the door to hear the heavy metal music blasting out of the speakers. Sitting behind the wheel, he turned the radio off and let moisture gather behind his eyelids.

He'd told himself a long time ago that crying over the way people treated him wouldn't change anything, and he deserved what they did because it was nothing compared to what Crystal and Allyson's family went through every day they had to live without their daughters.

But things went on for too long, and fatigue weighed heavy on his heart.

All those years ago, the hospital had been right to put him on suicide watch. He promised his mother if he ever felt like that again he'd find help.

He didn't need a therapist. All he needed was Callie wrapping her arms around him and telling him everything would be all right.

Even if he didn't believe her.

He drove to the resort, fuming. He could have sworn everyone was looking at him and the huge, hot pink rectangles. If his truck advertised a flower shop or a ladies' clothing boutique, the bright color would have fit right in. Had his mother still sold cosmetics, he could have added her name and number and pretended he'd wanted the pink paint on his truck all along.

Desiree texted him as he turned into the staff parking

lot. A Monday morning, vehicles filled all the spaces and he had to park a few hundred feet from the staff entrance.

The snowy, empty trail beckoned him. He'd love to sit, watch the deer, and take a breath, but Desiree had summoned him, and by the tone of the text, she hadn't had enough coffee for him to want to face her.

In his room, he took off his jacket and gloves and grabbed his toolbox since he needed to start his shift right after the meeting. He'd try to fit in another cup of coffee somewhere. The breakfast he ate with Autumn and Callie seemed long ago.

He also wanted to steal a couple minutes to swing by the fitness center after talking to Desiree and say a quick hello to Callie if she was still working out. He missed her, and he tried not to let what she didn't tell him at the dealership bother him. It would come out like everything did, and they'd either get through it or they wouldn't.

"Good morning," Desiree said, grimacing when he accidentally slammed his toolbox against the doorframe.

"Sorry," he mumbled, closing the door. He set the toolbox on the floor and sat in one of the two chairs in front of the resort manager's desk.

Desiree had styled her hair in her usual updo, and she wore one of her business suits and her Rocky Point Resort nametag.

She didn't look like she was in a good mood, and he wished harder for that cup of coffee.

"Mitch." Desiree folded her hands on her immaculate blotter. She hadn't started her Monday morning yet, and coffee steamed in her mug, the rim free of lipstick. "You had a busy weekend."

Unease prickled his skin. "What do you mean?"

She softened, sighed, and picked up her mug. She blew

on the hot liquid, but then set it down again without taking a sip. "I know you went to the hockey game Friday night. I also heard Ed Dunlop, that ornery old man, kicked you out of the arena. You were with one of our guests."

"Yeah." There wasn't anything else he could say.

"The police department contacted me Saturday afternoon asking for the security footage from the cameras that overlook the staff parking lot."

"My truck—"

"I know."

A thick blanket of silence hung over them.

"Did you take care of it?"

"Yeah." Technically, he had. The words weren't on his truck anymore, at least. But he wasn't going to explain what, exactly, the body shop had done. He'd talk to Bud on his own, after the holidays, and see what the manager could do. Bud needed to run his shop on the up and up or the dealership could get rid of him, as easily as Desiree could cut him loose.

"The police are looking over the footage to find out who did it. I haven't heard if they've been successful. If they can pin down who vandalized your truck, the resort will press charges for trespassing."

"Okay. Desiree, we were going to—"

"I'm not done," she said sharply, interrupting him.

Fear rolled in his stomach. God, he needed this job. If she fired him over this shit, he'd have to move to find work.

"Callista Carter was sitting at one of the ice houses sponsored by the resort Saturday morning when she was involved in an altercation."

He opened his mouth to defend Callie, but she lifted a finger, silencing him.

"I know she was protecting you. I know she gave you a

ride this morning to pick up your truck." She sipped her coffee, put her mug down, and carefully rubbed her eyes, avoiding smearing her mascara.

"I can explain," he started, shifting in his chair.

She stood and stared out her office window. It faced the lake where ice houses sat in the distance, grouped together like a little village. There were a few that sat away from the others, like outcasts or kids on a playground who didn't have friends. He related more to the ice houses alone on the lake than he did to real people.

"And Autumn told me she interviewed you for her blog this morning in the dining room."

"It was before my shift—"

She glared. "Mitch. In my years as the manager of this resort, it has pained me to watch the kind of life you've lived since the accident. I wasn't here when it happened, but every day since I hired you, I've seen what you put up with. As a woman, as a human being, that has hurt me." She leaned against the window.

"I should get to work," he said, gripping the armrests until his fingers ached. He didn't want to have this conversation.

Ignoring him, she said, "When we moved to Rocky Point, my son and me, I worried where I'd find work. I took the chance moving here because my son wanted to go to college and we needed the basketball scholarship RPCC awarded him. Even if it meant I'd be cleaning these rooms," she said, gesturing around her office, "I'd do it for my son. That's what parents do for their kids. You might be thinking this doesn't have anything to do with you, but it does. Being a Black single mother in a predominately white town, I feel different. Just, as I imagine, you do because of your scarring. When the owners of this resort needed a manager, and not only did they interview me, but *hired* me? Mitch, you have no idea what a blessing that was. To make a living wage, more than a living wage. To afford the mortgage to buy a small house for my son and me. I could contribute to this community where he goes to school. It was a gift they saw past my color to the skills I have to be able to do the job, and do it well. I'm not stupid, and neither are you."

He never thought about Desiree being Black or how she felt living in Rocky Point. There were a few Black families in town. Rocky Point's previous mayor was Black, but they moved to Decatur two years ago when he didn't win re-election.

"I'm not comparing the color of my skin to your scars. They're different, and I'm not going to insult either of us by doing that. But we both struggle, and that is something I *can* say. We struggle to be accepted, and I recognized that in you when you applied for this job. I haven't regretted it. You've been a good worker. But this woman comes to town—"

"Callie—"

"You've got feelings for her. That much is evident by the way you respond to her name. And she has feelings for you, too. She was defending you out there on the ice," she said, tilting her head toward the window, "and she's probably the first to do so in a long time."

He started at his jeans. They were becoming worn at the knees.

"When you feel like it's you against the world, sometimes when someone says, 'I'm with you, I believe in you,' it's such a relief to know you're not alone. Callie does that for you, and I'm happy for you. But I have my job to protect, and I can't have what's happening come back to the resort."

He knew this would happen. "I can tell Autumn not to post that interview. She can leave me out."

She pressed her lips together and sank into her chair. "I think, for now, that will be okay." She sighed. "You deserve a life. You should be allowed to attend hockey games, and date, and run errands without being harassed, and worse. I don't want to tell you to stop seeing her, especially if she turns out to be the one."

He looked up and met her eyes.

"I'm still a romantic at heart. Living a hard life hasn't beat that out of me. I loved DeShawn's father very much. I . . . we may be looking at you finding other housing arrangements."

"To stop things from happening on resort property," he muttered. It made sense, of course it did, and he'd go along with it if it meant he could keep his job.

"You're paid a good salary, Mitch. I spoke to Stacy before I called you into my office, and she told me you met the requirements for another pay increase. We'll continue your meal plan. But I think, moving forward—" She sighed. "Look. Callie will be going back to Decatur after Marnie's wedding. Perhaps things will calm down then."

"You mean when I go back into hiding the way I was before I met her."

She spread her hands over her desk, palms up. "If you want to put it that way. You were . . . okay with the status quo before she came to town."

"No, I wasn't, but I lived with it because I didn't care about changing it."

"And now you do?"

"Maybe."

"I'll support you how I can, but the resort and the safety of my staff and guests will remain a top priority. Callie should have reported being hassled. She was with Ivy, and she should have reported it, as well, yet I heard about it through gossip. That isn't how I want to run this resort. For every position that happens to open here, Stacy has over fifty applicants needing work."

The sick feeling in Mitch's stomach grew. "Please don't fire Ivy for this."

"I don't plan to. She's a good worker and I know the situation she has at home. I'm not heartless, but you probably think I am, after this." She stood and stepped from behind her desk. Picking up a briefcase, she said, "I have a meeting I need to attend at the chamber of commerce. We'll revisit your lodging situation after the Zimmerman/Fox wedding."

"Okay." It wasn't, but it would have to be.

"I want to help you, Mitch, I really do, but you have to understand that this isn't only about you. It's about me, it's about my son who's still young and his baby girl he asked me to help raise. I don't mean to sound hard, but family should come first. I heard your parents' house saw some trouble, too. Think about it."

She left him sitting in her office.

The coffee in her mug grew cold as he sat and ran through every possible scenario. No one would ever forgive him for what he'd done.

Why should they? Two little girls lost their lives, and it was his fault. He'd destroyed that family like he'd destroyed his own life. He didn't deserve to have an ounce of happiness.

He'd tell her. Tonight. He'd tell Callie he couldn't see her anymore. Then he'd ask Desiree to let him stay at the resort, and he'd try to go back to the way things were.

Even if he hadn't been happy, his parents had been safe

from ridicule, from harm. He couldn't risk his mother's health again.

His father warned him about this, but he'd been too swept up to listen.

He would listen now, before it was too late.

CHAPTER EIGHT

He'd had a firm resolve to break things off, but after his shift, he went to Callie's room and she opened the door wearing her robe. After such a shitty day, he fell into her arms and let her lead him to the bed where she kissed all the strain away.

She opened for him, in every possible way, and as he sank, welcome, inside her, he thought again of how different his life would be if he'd been able to save those girls. The scars wouldn't have mattered had he been a hero. They would have been a badge of honor. Now they were a mark of shame, and the only person who could see past them was Callie.

When he emptied inside her, he mourned the family he wouldn't be able to make, with anyone. Why should he have the privilege of having a family when his cowardice had ripped one apart?

He rolled onto his back, needing the space, but she followed, kissing a trail from his belly button to his lips. "What's wrong?" she asked, nuzzling his mouth with hers. "Did you have a bad day?"

"Desiree talked to me this morning. The shit that happened over the weekend didn't make her happy."

"I know. She talked to me this morning, too. She can't see that none of this is your fault. It's this stupid town that can't let things go."

He tamped down a surge of anger.

She didn't get it.

Brushing a hand over her hair, he said, "Callie, two little girls died. In a fire. I can't think of a more horrific way to go. Being burned to death."

She sat up and licked her lips. "They didn't die being burned to death. They died from heat exposure and smoke inhalation. Did you hear them screaming?"

"Yes." And he wished with everything he possessed he could block those screams out of his mind for the rest of his life.

"They were screaming out of fear, not pain. They were dead before the fire got to them, Mitch."

He shook his head. "Do you know they found their bodies wrapped around each other? They tried to protect one another. I tried to get in there. I tried to pull them out."

"And think. When you went back, when you tried to push through the fire to reach them, they weren't screaming anymore, were they? They didn't burn to death. If you can take *any* comfort in that, do it. No, it's not a pleasant way to go, but you're picturing them being burnt, like witches tied to a stake in the middle of a bonfire, and that's not the way it happened."

It didn't help. Not really. The girls were still gone.

"How do you know? You sound like you know a lot about it."

She tore her damp brown eyes away from his and snuggled into his side. "I . . . my brothers are firefighters. Zach has almost twenty years in the department in Decatur. Brandon, he's . . . in rehab right now. He was trapped in a burning building and almost died. His partner went back and pulled him out. Our father doesn't understand."

Despite the topic, God knew he was tired of thinking about fire and death, his cock hardened as she absently traced his nipple with her fingernail. She straddled his leg and touched the tip of her tongue where her finger had been. If he moved a little, he could slide inside her, but he wanted to hear about her family.

"He's the kind of man where if you fall off your horse, he tells you dust your ass off and climb back on. Immediately. That's not Brandon's way, and he drank to forget. One day he went to work buzzed, and his captain put him on leave. He checked himself into rehab, and he's been living in an inpatient facility for the past month, trying to figure out his life away from firefighting. Away from our father."

She shifted, lining up their bodies, her soft folds cradling his cock.

He couldn't take it anymore, and gripping her ass, he guided his cock inside her. He closed his eyes, leaning his head against the headboard.

She began to move back and forth, her hands on his shoulders, her knees digging into the mattress on either side of his ribcage.

"What do you do again?" he mumbled.

"This and that. I don't really know. I'm just as confused as Brandon is," she said, tilting her hips and adjusting, taking him in all the way. "Let's not talk about it anymore."

Lost in her, lost in the way she could make him *feel*, he asked, "Talk about what?"

Callie rocked against him and guided his hand to where their bodies joined, encouraged him to whisper his fingers over her clit to help her come.

She needed only a second, and she settled onto his sweaty chest, their bodies still joined.

Thank God men were so easily distracted.

Ever since her talk with Brandon, his warning bounced around inside her head. She took a chance and told Mitch about her brothers and he didn't seem to mind either way, or that could have been the sex.

She wouldn't say using sex to change the subject was the right thing to do, but it hadn't been the right time to tell him about her career choice, such as it was. If she listened to her brother, no time would be the right time, but she'd been able to put Mitch off for this long. If she could avoid talking about it for a few more days . . . though she didn't know what she'd do with the extra time.

Desiree's warning spooked her, and it made her scared for Mitch.

She couldn't stop the town from going after him with pitchforks and torches, but it wasn't right that he be punished for those girls for the rest of his life.

The sad, defeated look in his eyes frightened her as much as her conversation with Desiree. She'd hinted that if trouble kept coming, she'd fire Mitch. It wasn't his fault someone vandalized his truck, and it wasn't her fault those jerks on the ice threatened her. She wasn't going to let herself be a target because she was in love with Mitch.

She *did* love him, but she had to figure out how in the

hell they could make it work because what they were doing now wouldn't last.

She'd do better to leave him alone until after the wedding, and then they could talk about dating. The three hours that separated Decatur and Rocky Point were manageable. They'd be able to see each other when she wasn't bone-tired from putting out fires. Real ones.

Oh. Her job.

Dammit.

Her arms tightened around him.

She couldn't lose him.

"Hey, are you okay?" he asked, pressing his lips to the top of her head.

She blinked at him and forced a smile to her mouth. "Yeah. Has anyone told you, you are simply amazing, Mr. Sinclair?"

He chuckled. "Well, maybe once or twice."

She rolled onto her back, tugging him on top of her. "Maybe we should start a fan club."

He scoffed. "I'm sure people would love to sign up."

She met his eyes and let her gaze travel down the puckered skin along his right side. She'd never had a problem with his appearance, and whenever she looked at him now, she didn't see the scars unless she deliberately focused on them.

Mitch needed a place to blend in, a place where even if someone knew his history, they could see past it to the man living in the present.

He'd never find that in Rocky Point.

But in Decatur . . .

"Have you ever thought about moving?" she asked.

"I'll have to, if Desiree fires me," he said, a hard look coming into his eyes. "I don't blame you, Callie, but that's why I came to your room. I wanted to ask that we take it easy."

She tried to act like his request didn't hurt, but it did. A little. That she had the same thought soothed some of the sting. A little. "I understand. As Marnie's wedding gets closer, I'll be busy anyway."

"That was easy," he said, yanking away. He sat on the edge of the bed, leaned over, and dug through their pile of clothes.

She sat up and wrapped the sheet around her. "What do you want me to say? Our relationship's giving you trouble. Desiree's talk with me hit that home, real nice. I'm giving you what you want, and I'm the bad guy?"

"I thought maybe you'd fight a little. 'Boy, Mitch, I'd miss you if we stop seeing each other.' 'Mitch, I really care about you. Are you sure this is what you want?'" He mimicked her voice as he shoved his legs into his briefs.

"I'm not the one who should be fighting," she said, clenching the sheet in her fists. "I'm not the one who's been hiding, who's been taking the easy way out. The town may not forgive or forget, but when they kick you when you're down, you roll over and take it."

That's exactly what she did, whenever her father ordered her to do something. She rolled over and asked for more. Just like Mitch.

The anger burning in her chest died, and she pursed her lips against the tears that threatened to claw their way up her throat. "It's fine. Go."

He buttoned his shirt, leaving it untucked. "I have to protect my parents. I can't live in Rocky Point if Desiree fires me, and I need to be here to look out for them."

Lifting her chin, she said, "I realize that. I also realize that sometimes the right people meet at the wrong time.

Maybe we're those people. A different time, a different place, maybe then love would have been enough."

"Is that what this is? Love? Do you love me, Callie? Can you look at me, see my scars, know what I did, and you can still say you love me? That even in a different town, I'd be stared at, whispered about in public? You'd stand by my side and take it? Because you love me?"

"Yes, and you know why? Because I'd expect the same from you. You don't know me. You don't know my flaws or secrets. Yet this morning, you were going to tell me you loved me. You have no fucking idea who I am, and you were going to tell me anyway. You were going to say it, and I stopped you because I knew you weren't ready. Count your blessings that I did because now you have nothing to take back. Go. It's better for both of us."

"I'm sorry. Enjoy the rest of your stay." Quietly, he walked out of her room and out of her life.

She sat in the middle of the bed, numb.

She wanted to be angry, God, did she want to be angry, but she understood he was scared and was running away. Didn't agree with it, but she understood it.

Now her secrets could remain just that. Secret. Better he end their relationship in the guise of protecting his parents. Better he did it for that, than, pardon the pun, their relationship go up in a puff of smoke when he found out she fought fires for a living.

She could love him, scars and all, but the past was the past, and Mitch's future, though not bright, would be quiet and steady without her in it.

She wasn't giving him much credit, but, well, if he wasn't going to fight for himself, why would he fight for her?

He didn't know the first thing about fighting, and God, she was too tired to show him.

She sank into the bed, their lovemaking scenting the pillow and sheets.

Tears dribbled down her cheeks.

She'd join Marnie and the others at the pool party tonight.

Right after a good cry.

Mitch rarely saw his parents during the week, the Saturday morning visit enough to keep in touch and make sure things were going well for them, but when he turned onto their street, he could finally breathe. He'd let his mother fuss, let Luna beg him to rub her belly, and talk football with this father.

Remember what he was doing all this for.

"There's chili leftover," his mother said, fluttering around the kitchen to dish him up dinner. "How's Callie?"

He sank onto a kitchen chair and popped the top off a bottle of beer his mother set at his elbow to go along with the chili.

"We broke up."

Chip turned away from the sports highlights the six o'clock news ended with, the Vikings taking Friday night's game.

Luna whined.

"Why?" she asked.

He searched her tone for remorse and sympathy and heard none. "Because our relationship was causing trouble. Desiree threatened to fire me if I didn't get it under control, and the only way I can do that is to not see her anymore. Being with her drew attention to me and reminded people I exist. As long as I'm the maintenance man at the resort keeping to myself, people will look through me again and things will go back to normal."

A normal he tolerated because it was safe.

"She agreed to that?"

Too easily. It still rankled she let him walk away. "Yeah. She's not stupid, Ma. We were thrown out of the game and she knows what happened to my truck, to the house. Someone threatened her when she was ice fishing with Ivy. Desiree talked to her, too, and we decided it was the best thing to do."

Even though he was starving, the chili turned to ash in his mouth. Sometimes it was nice to eat a home-cooked meal, even though the resort boasted some of the best food in the upper Midwest, but tonight he couldn't appreciate his mother's cooking.

She sat at the table, a hand towel twisted in her lap. "I hate to say it, but she wanted too much. From you, from the town. She's never lived here. She doesn't know how bad things were, how nasty and cruel people can be. I think it's for the best, too."

His mother's agreement should have made him feel better. He'd let Callie go because he was afraid for his parents. But it didn't.

He held his mother's hand. "It'll be okay. Things will settle down after the wedding."

"I know things weren't perfect, but we had a quiet life and it's more than what some people get after a tragedy. Let me get you some cornbread." She breathed a sigh.

Scooping up more chili, he kept quiet. He didn't want cornbread.

Dropping his spoon, he pushed his bowl away.

It had been a mistake to come here.

"I need to go."

"But you just got here," his mother cried in dismay. "You never visit during the week, and I was so happy to see you park your truck outside."

"I need some time alone."

He scraped his leftovers into the trash, shoved his bowl into the dishwasher, and hurried to the mudroom and put on his boots and jacket.

"Let him go," Chip told Ruby, and he thanked his dad under his breath.

"Son," his dad said as he slammed out of the garage and into the cold air.

He stopped and let his father catch up to him.

Luna started sniffing around a tree.

"Your mother means well," Chip said, zipping his jacket, "but this stuff scares her."

"I know. And you don't know how sorry I am that you have to live with it."

Chip studied Mitch's truck and ran his hand over a pink rectangle. "Not what I had in mind when you said you were getting your truck painted."

"Not mine, either."

"Mitch."

"Yeah?"

"When I said 'this stuff,' I didn't mean the vandalism or the threats. I meant Callie. You're her only son, her only child. We had to fight to have you, too, but you know that. No woman is going to be good enough for you . . . or for her. But one day we're going to be gone and I don't want you to be alone because you coddled your mother's fears."

"I'm not—"

"I know you're not, because they're your fears, too. You're thirty-six years old and it's time you settled down.

You've been wasting time waiting, waiting for something that's not going to happen. This town will never forget the accident, and they'll never forgive you. Callie's from Decatur, didn't you say? Pretty big city." Chip shoved the toe of his boot into the snow, nudged it as a quiet fell between them. An understanding. "A city where they'd leave a man alone to live his life with his family. Where if they found out about what happened here, well, they wouldn't give a damn."

"I won't leave you two behind, if Callie and I . . . if what I said to her today doesn't . . . I mean . . ."

"If you didn't fuck it up," Chip said, smiling faintly.

"I won't leave you here."

"Who said we'd stay? Your mom, she may not want to give you up, but Callie's young and I don't figure it'd take you long to have a baby. I think your mother would set aside any misgivings if you put a grandchild in her arms. Decatur isn't a bad place to live. You can buy a house on the outskirts of town and still live a quiet life."

"I didn't know you felt that way."

"I didn't know I did, but I felt bad after Callie left. Out of fear, we weren't kind, and I'm sorry for that. If you ask her to come around and she agrees, we'll apologize."

"We need the break, Dad, to give things time to cool down. In a few days I'll see how she's feeling toward me."

"And I'll talk to your mother. A change would be good for all of us, and maybe it's something we should have thought about a long time ago."

"I have, but I always thought leaving would be like running away."

"Well, like I said before, knowing when you can't win and running because you're a coward are two different things. The accident was years ago and you've been struggling ever since. I think it's time to realize things aren't going to change and there's no point to keep trying, is there?"

"No." He paused. "I'm glad I stopped by."

"Me too. And son, I don't want you to feel like you have to force a relationship with Callie because she's the first person since the accident who treats you like a person. If it truly doesn't work out, it doesn't work out, but that doesn't mean we can't still move. Make a fresh start in Decatur, maybe a different city. You'd have a better chance at meeting someone else, at least. And your mom wouldn't have any complaints if she had regular access to Macy's."

"I get what you're saying. We have options."

"We have options. Get some sleep. Things are going to come to a head, and the New Year is going to bring some changes. Some we like, some we don't, but we have each other and that's what matters. Callie, too."

"Thanks, Dad."

He started his truck, imagined his mother holding her grandchild.

Callie would be a good mother. She'd teach their children to fight for what was right, to defend themselves against the hate in the world. And he'd teach them to recognize when enough was enough, that it wasn't weak to know when to quit. He and Callie balanced each other out.

Give her a couple of days, then he'd talk to her. Ask her what she thought about maybe getting married someday. Because that's where all this was headed wasn't it? All this talk about moving, having babies. People didn't uproot their lives for someone they didn't want to marry.

He'd tell her he loved her.

And this time he wouldn't let her stop him.

After her cry, Callie met Marnie and Autumn in the pool area. Other guests had started to go back to their rooms, but Marnie was in the partying mood and didn't mind she was late. Drinking wine, they sat in the hot tub and Marnie filled her in on some wedding gossip, including a few interesting things about Leah and Jared, and Jared's ex-wife, Rita.

It seemed that she and Mitch weren't the only newly acquainted couple hooking up, and having a hard time of it, too.

Autumn left soon after the gossip, pleased she had several interviews to transcribe.

She wondered if Mitch would try to get out of his now that they were broken up, but she didn't ask Autumn if he contacted her to retract his interview.

She'd been able to hide her feelings from her friends, but she sniffled on the way to her room, shivering despite having a towel wrapped around her.

Marnie had been thrilled to see her, and that's all that mattered. She was visiting Rocky Point to be in the wedding, to stand up with her friend, and she had to remember that.

Her cell phone was ringing when she let herself into her room, and she scooped it up to answer it.

"Hey, I hope you weren't waiting for too long," she said in a rush the moment she pressed Accept.

"I've been trying to call you for the past fifteen minutes. I was starting to worry," Brandon said.

"I was at a pool party. I didn't bring my phone because

with my luck, I'd drop it in the water and this town doesn't have a store where I can replace it."

"It sounds like you're having fun," he said, and she was grateful to hear shades of the man he used to be in his voice.

"Well, not that much. Mitch and I broke up."

"You told him you were a firefighter then, huh? I'm sorry. I knew that would happen."

"I didn't, actually. Our relationship stirred up a hornet's nest, and he thinks it's better if we back off."

"He doesn't know you very well, does he?"

"What do you mean?"

"You've never been a quitter. You're not going to let him walk away over a little drama."

"Yes, I am, because you're right. The minute he finds out I'm a firefighter, he'll dump me. He should still be in therapy. He hasn't had much, and the accident haunts him. We know what that's like. I tried to tell him the girls didn't suffer, but he didn't believe it. So, we're done. It's fine."

"I'm sorry. When you told me who you met, I didn't think it would work. Now what are you going to do?"

"Enjoy my vacation the best I can. Dad called the fire chief here and told him I'd visit their department. I'd look like an ass if I skipped. I guess I'll do that tomorrow, get it out of the way. Then, I don't know. How are you? Have you made any progress with your nurse?"

"She and I might go for coffee once I decide to skip outta here. I haven't talked to Mom and Dad. All I know is I can't be a firefighter anymore. Dad will think it's because I'm scared, but—"

"You know what, Brandon? There's something Mitch taught me in the few days we were together, and it's this. It's okay to be scared. In fact, it's more than okay. It's necessary. It's real, and it's a part of life. Fuck Dad if he can't see that.

You're no less of a man in my eyes if that's why you don't want to be a firefighter anymore. It costs me every time I run into a burning building, and I'm going to have to decide for myself one day soon how much more I want to pay."

Brandon's strangled breath whined over the line, and she sucked in her own while she waited for Brandon's response. He could take it the way she meant it, with love and respect, or he could get his back up because he'd been dealing with their dad for so long it was a natural response.

"Thank you for that," he finally whispered. "My therapist said the same thing, but I guess I needed to hear it from someone in the family. I *am* scared, and I can't go back on the job."

"Then we'll tell Dad. When I get back to Decatur, we'll confront him together. I'll stand with you, and Mom will have our backs. She goes along to keep the peace, but you know when push comes to shove, she'll be there for us."

"Yeah, I know. I have to get going. It's lights out pretty soon. Thanks for answering your phone, little sister. You've been a big help. And I'm sorry about Mitch, but don't hound him, okay? There's only so much we can take."

"I know. He made it pretty clear what he wanted. Goodnight. Talk soon."

Shivering, her hair dripping cold water down her back, she stood in her dark room, her heart aching.

There was no coming back from the way she felt about Mitch and what he'd done to her.

She'd have to soothe the burn the best she could.

Because that's what happened when she played with fire.

Exhausted, Callie dragged herself into the shower after a crappy night's sleep full of nightmares and tears. She dried her hair, dressed, and ate a quick breakfast in the dining room. Marnie hadn't mentioned plans for the day, and she drove to the fire department, annoyed her father volunteered her time.

She didn't have a fascination with other departments like her father did. His interest came from making sure they were being run correctly, and he would expect her to report back like some kind of firefighting spy.

Due to budget cuts, she found most departments lacking in manpower, but not much could be done about it.

The situation at the Rocky Point Fire Department was the same, and the chief let her know early on.

"We have a firefighter out on maternity leave, and one who just retired. Rick's out with a broken leg he sustained during one of our training events. We're lucky we don't see much activity in the wintertime," Fire Chief Mike Bakersfield said as he led her on a tour of the small firehouse. "We service the farmland around here and some of the smaller towns. I don't suppose you'd be surprised at how fast a barn can burn because a stupid teenager decided to steal a smoke. A bakery went up in Pinnacle, about twenty minutes from here, but by the time we got there, there wasn't much left. Some of these towns, they have a barebones volunteer department, and when things get too hot, it's better if they sit back and let it go."

"I met Mitch Sinclair," she said, poking her head into the department's small kitchen. Two men were washing breakfast dishes, and one looked over at her when she mentioned Mitch's name.

"Damn shame what happened there," Chief Bakersfield said, glaring at the firefighter in warning.

She missed nothing.

There was a lot of animosity in the department toward Mitch.

"Negligence," one of the men mumbled.

"Stupidity," muttered the other.

"That'll be enough," Chief said, gesturing at her to follow him.

The rows of regulation-made bunks looked the same in every station and she ignored them, uninterested.

"No one takes too kindly to Mitch Sinclair," Chief said, leading her into the garage where two firetrucks were parked and ready to go. "Lots of people blame him for what happened. I did too, for a while, but the fact is, bus drivers aren't trained to handle something like that. In that damned blizzard, no one should have been on the road. The school district didn't want to take responsibility for not calling a snow day. The department store chain didn't take responsibility for their driver being on the road in those conditions, though he walked away without a scratch. Doesn't drive truck anymore, I made sure of that."

"The town hasn't forgiven him. He lives a hard life."

The chief nodded, his navy blue RPFD t-shirt straining across his broad shoulders. "I heard about you two getting escorted out of the Bears game, to say it politely. That's small town living. A teenager drowned twelve years ago, and people still whisper about it while drinking their morning coffee and poking at their eggs. Jared Hollister's wife left him and their little girl to strike it rich in New York City and people cluck over that and wonder how she's doing while they squeeze tomatoes in the grocery store. I've been hearing things about some woman sprucing up the Supply Company. No one has anything to do around here except freeze their asses off and gossip. Marnie Zimmerman's wedding has given people plenty to talk about, and Autumn Bennett's blog posts add fuel to the fire. I've heard a few things about you, Miss Carter."

"Callie. She's a pretty one," she said, brushing her fingers over the firetruck's red paint. "She looks new."

"She is. After the bakery fire in Pinnacle, the city board finally approved funds to replace what we had. Too bad it has to take a tragedy for people to see there needs to be change."

"That's usually the way it works," she agreed.

"You've been in some sticky spots yourself," the chief commented, pulling a handkerchief out of his pocket and rubbing her fingerprints off the immaculate bright red engine.

"I don't think you can be a firefighter and avoid them." She didn't particularly want to talk about her sticky situations, since that seemed to be a euphemism for the times when she'd narrowly missed being severely injured.

Or when it happened to someone else while she was on the job.

"I'm only saying, you must feel a kinship toward Mitch Sinclair. Not everyone knows what it's like to lose a life on their watch."

She studied Chief Bakersfield. Was he insulting her? Yes, she'd fought fires where loss of life occurred, and she always felt the cost, deep in her bones. Always wondered if there was more she could have done. Had she been stronger, smarter.

Braver.

She narrowed her eyes and weighed her next words. "Are you accusing me of something?"

"No, ma'am. Simply stating that maybe you were meant to come here, meant to meet Mitch. Talk him down."

"Mitch doesn't need me to do that. What he needs is for this town to get off his back. People blame him for something that wasn't his fault. You said as much. Just because I know how it feels doesn't make me different from anyone else, or any more like him. I do my best on every job. If you've lived here all your life and only fought fires that were small enough, or were caught quickly enough, that no one was hurt or killed, I'd count my blessings."

"I was on shift when we were called out to that barn. I can still hear the cows screaming."

"Have you ever talked to Mitch? Reached out to him?"

The chief sighed and turned away. "I can't say that I have."

"Why not? Don't want to be seen with him? Don't want to show the people of Rocky Point you might have a little empathy, a little sympathy, toward the man?" She sucked in a breath to calm down. "You hear cows. He hears children. I should go."

Just as she took a step away from the truck, the fire alarm went off.

"Looks like we got something special for you," the chief said. "Wanna tag along? Nancy's gear will fit you."

No, she didn't want to tag along. She was on vacation. This was supposed to be her time to rest, physically and emotionally. But he stared at her like he dared her to say no.

"Do you have room for me?" The question was useless. Of course they would.

"Could always use another pair of hands."

"Yeah."

Climbing into the gear that was kept maintained and ready, she watched the company work together like a well-oiled machine. All fire departments responded to a call like this, a choreographed dance where everyone knew their part and no one faltered.

She fit in as naturally as breathing, the team making space for her as a valuable member, someone who would be an asset, and she sat in the truck, the driver racing through town to a residential section.

She tamped down a feeling of unease as the houses flew by, the truck's siren wailing. Residential fires were horrible. Even if everyone made it out, so many memories were lost. So much time documented in photos, so much laughter echoing in the rooms, gone, as fire ate its way through the hallways.

Two police cruisers were parked on the opposite side of the street, and uniformed officers kept people a safe distance away.

Black smoke plumed from the roof . . . of the Sinclair's house.

"What's the status?" the chief barked at a cop, and she stood frozen in place, her gaze landing on Mitch's parents.

"Owners are over there." He pointed to where Ruby stood in Chip's arms, sobbing.

"They said they have a dog, but it's unaccounted for."

Firefighters raced around her, securing the hoses to the nearest fire hydrant.

The cold, crisp air did nothing to alleviate the choking odor of smoke.

Luna was inside.

She stepped forward, her boots crunching over the snow, the gear weighing her down. Lightheaded, her feet moving of their own volition, she thought through a haze she should have eaten a bigger breakfast.

"Hey! What do you think you're doing?" Chief Bakersfield jerked on her arm.

"Luna's in there," she said, shaking him off.

Misunderstanding her, he said, "There's no one inside."

"No one human, but there's a dog in there, and I'm going to get her."

"You're being stupid, and I won't be held responsible if you get hurt. Your father will have your ass if you go in for some dog."

She turned away before she did something she regretted. She couldn't let Mitch's parents lose their dog. They'd already lost their son to a fire and she wouldn't let them lose Luna, too. Her father would hold a peculiar mixture of pride and anger for his daughter who would risk her life to save a fucking dog.

Every second counted, and she secured her helmet and face mask. The air tank alone weighed several pounds, and the protective gear pulled her down like she was trudging through quicksand.

No one came with her.

CHAPTER NINE

"Your parents' house is on fire!" Ivy yelled, careening into an empty cabin behind the resort.

Mitch had been swallowing back a bitter taste in his mouth all morning. He hadn't heard from Callie, and though he didn't want to speak to her—or he tried to convince himself of that, anyway—he hoped that being the stubborn woman he'd come to know her to be, she'd seek him out and try to talk.

After talking to his dad the night before, he wanted to see her and explain what was going on inside his heart and mind. He struggled to give her the space he forced on them.

Luckily, a problem had come up in one of the cabins, and gratefully, he'd trudged through the snow and quiet woods. He'd have some time to himself while he worked on a chandelier's wiring.

He stood on the ladder, the huge light fixture sitting on the floor. The more he poked, the more he realized the wiring in the entire cabin was shot, and the job would require more than what he was qualified to do. He'd have to tell Desiree they needed to call Rocky Point Electric and have a real electrical technician assess the wiring. They would maybe even need to mark this cabin as out of service because his layman's eyes couldn't estimate the amount of time and work it would take to fix the problem.

Desiree wouldn't be happy, but her main priority was the guests' safety, and it was something he agreed with and took seriously.

"What did you say?" he asked, looking down at Ivy.

She stood huffing in her bartending uniform, her winter jacket hanging off one shoulder, her hair even messier than usual. "Your parents' house. It's on fire. I went to the kitchen to grab some breakfast and it came over Dale's police scanner."

He hurried off the ladder, his right foot missing a step, and he stumbled to the floor, his heart in his throat. "Did you call nine-one-one?" he asked, his mind blanking in panic.

"I didn't need to call, the fire department was already on the way when I started running here. Go, Mitch. What are you doing? Go!"

Ivy's order shook him out of his fog and leaving his jacket behind, he bolted out of the cabin. He ran down the trail, his boots landing hard in the snow, to his truck. He'd never been so grateful he kept in shape.

His hands trembling, he tried to shove the key into his truck's ignition and missed, dropping his keys on the floor near the gas pedal. Scrambling, he picked them up and started his truck, the engine growling against the cold. His agitated breaths came out in white puffs as he backed out of his space and shot down the hill toward town.

Black smoke marred the bright blue sky, and swearing

under his breath, he recognized the area of town was exactly where his parents lived. He'd been hoping, though he couldn't have described it then, that Ivy was wrong. That she'd gotten the address of his parents' house mixed up. Though he wouldn't wish this tragedy on anyone, he'd let a little seed of hope settle in his heart that it truly hadn't been his childhood home.

He blew through a yellow light, made a California Roll at all the intersections, and slid to a stop in front of his parents' house ten minutes after racing out of the resort's parking lot.

His parents were standing on the sidewalk, his mother crying against his father's chest. They looked small and defeated wearing their slippers and pajamas. Someone had draped blankets over their shaking shoulders, and Chip watched the flames with an anxious look on his face, his chin resting on his wife's head.

He stared at the fire, the flames licking at the walls and the roof he and his dad re-shingled two summers ago, the firefighters trying to drown the flames. This was all his fault. Somehow, some way, this fire would lead back to him and his audacity to meet and fall in love with a woman.

Things hadn't been good, but they'd been okay before Callie came into his life.

And now the very thing he feared had come true.

Exhausted, so fucking tired of the way his life had been since the accident, he dragged himself out of the truck.

"Ma. Dad."

He stood at the edge of the front yard he used to play in as a child while his mother sat on the porch. He'd grown up in this house, his bedroom the same as the day he left it. His mother hadn't wanted to change a thing, and it brought into clarity what his father said last night. About his mother not being able to let him go.

Chip's throat worked. "Luna's in there."

"Fuck." Knowing there wasn't a damned thing he could do, he stepped forward.

Chip grabbed his shoulder. "A fireman's looking for her. He had words with Mike Bakersfield before going inside."

"Pets aren't a priority," he said.

"Someone cared enough about a dog," Chip said, tears dripping down his cheeks. "But it's been too long."

Firefighters sprayed water on the roof and drenched the neighboring houses to stop the flames from jumping and spreading.

Crowds gathered on the road and sidewalks, and uniformed police officers were keeping them back.

People took pictures or videos with their cell phones, and he gritted his teeth against the pure hate that burned in his heart. Why would anyone want to record such heartbreak?

Part of the roof caved in, the impact shaking the ground, and the crowd gasped. Fire crackled and snapped.

Bakersfield paced.

Sick with worry for a firefighter he didn't know, icy sweat slid down his back.

His stomach heaved.

Applause and cheers cut through his living nightmare, and Chip whispered, "Thank you, sweet Jesus."

A figure wearing firefighting gear trudged around the corner of the house, Luna clutched in his arms, gratitude in the dog's eyes he could see even from this distance.

He fought back tears of relief. He and his parents had lost so much because of fire, at least God saw fit to save their dog. "I want to know what happened. Why our house? Why now? I don't believe this was a coincidence."

Chip's arms tightened around his wife. "All I know is we were talking about moving, and Fate forced our hand. There's no reason to stay in this godforsaken town."

There was a time when he would have argued, but as the firefighter handed Luna to a paramedic, there was nothing he could do but agree.

Inside the house, as the fire sparkled and bit with white-hot teeth, beautiful in its own destructive way, Callie feared she'd have to leave Luna behind after all.

The fire had started in back of the house, in the kitchen, but it was spreading quickly and when she rushed in through the front door, black smoke and heat hit her in the face.

She had a few precious moments to look for the dog, but she had to search the house by feel and the German shepherd hid in fear. The fire spread through the living room, licking at the ceiling and eating at the curtains and a pile of newspapers sitting on the floor next to Chip's reclining chair.

While she searched a spare bedroom that Ruby had turned into a sewing room, she tried to block out her visit to the house only a few short days ago. She hadn't expected to be invited back, and this certainly wasn't the way she thought she'd see their house again.

"Come on, Luna," she whispered, wiggling to stand after looking under Ruby and Chip's king-sized bed. "Where are you?"

She checked their closet and found Luna cowering in the corner behind a laundry hamper and a rack of hanging dresses. "Come on, sweetheart. I got you."

Luna fought her, growling in the back of her throat and baring her teeth until Callie carried her into the sun streaming in from a window. Through her mask, the dog recognized her face and stilled in her arms. "There we go. You know I'm helping. You're a good girl."

She stepped into the hallway and swore.

Flames spread along the ceiling above her head, consuming the spare room she searched only moments before.

She stood frozen, her heart pounding. She couldn't make it out the way she came in. Her training kicked in and she forced herself to remain calm and think. She remembered the layout of the house and the door in the mudroom that opened into the garage. Remembered the stories Mitch told her about his time helping his dad put together birdhouses and squirrel boxes, and later, learning how to change the oil and spark plugs in his truck.

Her only choice was to cut through what was left of the living room to the mudroom and the last remaining exit she could still use to get to the outside.

Hefting a trembling Luna in her arms, she carried her into the living room. Fire and ash fell from the ceiling, the wood screaming. The roof would go soon. She knew the signs. She curled her body over Luna's hoping to protect her from the sparks.

The mudroom was painted white and blue, the floor laid with matching linoleum. A washing machine and dryer set were positioned against one wall, Luna's crate and a box of dog toys in the corner. She focused on the door that would save their lives.

Thankful, she carried Luna through the garage and into the backyard, giving the burning house as wide a berth as she could manage in the small, fenced-in yard. Part of the roof caved in, just like she knew it would, and she fell to her knees in the snow, the cracking and shrieking knocking her off her feet.

Some of the other firefighters clapped when they saw her, hooting in relief.

Mitch and his parents stood huddled near the street.

He wasn't wearing a jacket, and he was probably in too much shock to realize it. Her heart broke for him and his family.

At least she'd been able to save Luna.

She gave her to a first responder who carried oxygen masks for animals. Luna whimpered as Callie walked away, but it was part of the job to see if the other firefighters needed her.

Chief Bakersfield scowled but gave her a thumbs up and waved her toward the truck.

She took the hint gratefully. She desperately wanted a drink of water and a moment to control her racing heart.

"Thank you for rescuing my parents' dog. I know pets aren't a priority."

The words came from behind her, and she stiffened.

Mitch. Shit.

This wasn't the way she wanted him to find out.

Well, they were already broken up. It didn't matter now.

She pulled off her helmet, loosened her mask, and turned around. Someone had given him a blanket.

He stepped back, gripping the fleece. "What the hell are you going here?"

"Hey. I was on a tour of the department when the call

came in, and the chief asked if I wanted to help. I didn't know the address was your house."

He gaped, his lips parted. "You're a firefighter?"

She nodded. "Yeah. We all are. My brothers. My dad."

"You went in after Luna? Why would you do that?"

"By the time we got here, your parents were already out, but one of the cops said Luna was still inside. I couldn't leave her in there. I found her hiding in a closet. I'm sorry. About your house. I'm not an expert, but it looks like the structure won't be too badly damaged. Maybe it can be saved."

"We have no interest in that," he said, never taking his eyes off her. "Just like I have no interest in whatever the fuck I thought we had. You lied to me. You lied to me because you knew every time I looked at you I would see those dead girls."

She flinched. "I wasn't the one who thought of it. My brother, Brandon, said telling you would be the end of us. After he said it, I knew it made sense. In your mind I would always represent fire. The one thing you hate. The one thing you fear most. When you broke up with me because of other things, I let you walk."

"Good. And I'm going to keep walking. Thank you for Luna. You saved my father from a broken heart. At least that's one of us."

He walked away, his shoulders stiff, his spine straight, the blanket's hem tangling around his legs.

She let him go because there wasn't anything else she could do.

She rode back to the station, tended to Nancy's equipment, and helped prepare the truck for the next emergency.

Whispers of arson traveled from one person to the next, and standing outside the chief's office, she eavesdropped on him calling the arson investigator to set up a time to go out to the site.

She grimaced. The Sinclair's house was more than a site. It used to be a home where a family had lived and loved, where two older people had tried to find refuge in a storm.

"Do you really think someone set fire to that house?" she asked, leaning against the doorjamb, her arms crossed over her chest.

The chief slid the cheaters off his face and rubbed his eyes. "I'd be remiss if I didn't consider it, if I didn't let the investigator know the history of the people living in that house. The Sinclairs have been a target of vandalism before, but never this bad. How we'll catch them is another matter. You did good, with the dog. Though you know well enough pets aren't worth the risk."

"Luna knows me. I thought if anyone had a chance of rescuing her, it would be me."

Chief Bakersfield fixed his steely eyes onto hers, and she resisted shrinking away. Holding her ground, she lifted her chin.

"How do you know the Sinclair's dog? How did you know the layout of that house?"

"Mitch invited me to have lunch one day. His mother showed me around."

"It all comes back to you, somehow, doesn't it? Do you know who would want to hurt the Sinclairs this badly?"

"The way I hear it, only most of the town," she said.

He leaned back in his chair and it squeaked under his

weight. "You're not wrong. Which makes things even more difficult. It might answer the why, but unless we get lucky, the who may never come to light."

"I appreciate you letting me come along."

"You do good work. If you ever move to Rocky Point, there would be a place for you in the department."

"Thanks, but I'm not sure if I'm cut out to be a firefighter anymore."

"It's hard work, but the good we do can't be matched. Pardon the pun."

"You sound like my dad."

"I met Ace a few years back. I was pleased when he said you were in town. He runs a tight ship in Decatur, has the highest track record of saved lives and buildings in the state of Minnesota."

"It's a lot to live up to."

"It is, and from what I can see, you're doing fine."

"It hurts," she admitted, her voice hitching, suddenly exhausted. "My dad doesn't understand how much it hurts."

"Your father understands more than you give him credit for. He might be gruff and ornery, but he's still human. Get out of here, now. They can finish up without you. You're supposed to be on vacation."

"Will you let me know about the investigation?"

"I'll keep you in the loop."

"Thanks."

Despite the chief's permission to go, she stayed and finished cleaning, and afterward, drank a cup of coffee and talked with the other firefighters about the Sinclair house. She added her information to the report, took responsibility for saving a pet.

The sun had gone down, and the stars sparkled when she stepped out of the firehouse.

She felt like she could sleep for a week, but rather than go to her room, she sat in the lounge and asked Ivy to pour her a glass of wine.

"This is all your fault," Ivy said, setting a long-stemmed glass of red wine down on the bar with so much force Callie was surprised the stem didn't snap in two.

Anger glittered in Ivy's eyes, her jaw set in accusation.

"I know," she murmured, her fingers twisted together in her lap. "The chief suspects it's arson too, and they're going to start an investigation."

"None of this would've happened if you hadn't come along and upset everything." Ivy viciously swiped her rag at a stain on the bar's wood.

"Do you really believe Mitch deserves the way he's been treated? All I've done is encourage him to stand up for himself."

Ivy deflated. "No, I don't. I hate the way people treat him, but I wish there was a way things could've been better for him without it coming to this."

"'This' meaning the violence, or 'this' meaning me?"

"What do you expect him to do? You're not going to make people change their minds. You blow into town like a tornado, fuck everything up, then after the wedding, you'll disappear, leaving a mess behind that Mitch will have to clean up."

"It wouldn't have been like that if we'd stayed together. I would've stood by him. Through anything." She gulped her wine but it didn't help her relax. A tension headache pounded through her skull, stress stiffening her neck and shoulders.

Ivy blinked at her. "You broke up?"

"If you can call it that. A relationship isn't made in four days."

"I— Why?"

"Because I'm a firefighter and he said he couldn't look at me without thinking about the accident. And he's right. Every time I worked my shift he'd think about that bus fire and he'd always worry if I'm all right. Spouses who *don't* have tragedy behind them have it tough being married to firefighters. I couldn't imagine what Mitch would go through day after day, and I wouldn't ask him to. Getting involved was a big mistake. I didn't know his history, but by the time I did, it was too late."

"You're a fireman?" Ivy asked, squinting her eyes, her head tilted.

"What? You don't think I can be a firefighter? Which is the gender-correct term, if you want to get picky about it. But, yeah, that's how he found out. I went in after Luna, and he thanked me for rescuing her."

"He dumped you because of that? I know I haven't been supportive of his relationship with you, but . . ."

"I get it, and it's fine," she said, sliding her fingertip over the base of the wineglass. "I don't have time for a family. It'd be hard to have children and still keep my head clear enough to do my job. I don't blame Mitch for not wanting to get mixed up in that."

"That's why you didn't freak out when you met him," Ivy said.

She lifted a shoulder. "I'm not a stranger to what fire can do."

"You're probably the only person he's ever met who can understand what happened."

"That didn't work in my favor." She drained her glass.

"What are you going to do now? Let him go?" Ivy asked.

She refilled Callie's wineglass, and Callie didn't stop her. What the hell. She was on vacation, a working vacation, apparently.

"Yeah. There's nothing I can do to change his mind. I'm going to pretend we never met."

Misery flooded her. She couldn't think about leaving Mitch behind after the wedding, but Ivy's description of the mess she'd made was too accurate to ignore. She'd driven into town and started causing trouble practically since the minute she checked in. Mitch might lose his job and his parents were victims of arson, possibly because of what she'd done.

All she wanted was to make him happy. She was such a fool.

He detested her now. The look on his face at his parents' house that afternoon made that very clear. Even if she could convince her father to let her do something else, whenever he looked at her, he'd be reminded of his childhood home gone in a pile of ash.

It was too much to ask of him.

"Can you really do that?" Ivy worried her bottom lip between her teeth.

"You can't keep someone if they don't want to stay."

Blinking back tears, Ivy said, "I know."

"Then you know nothing I say will do anything." She finished her wine and pushed two twenties toward the mousy woman who claimed she and Mitch were only friends. "I was jealous of you, you know."

"Me? Why?"

"Because you're a better match for Mitch than me. I'm loud and aggressive and mouthy, and he doesn't need that. You're calm, thoughtful. Soothing. He'd be lucky to have you."

"We're only friends."

"He needs a good one. Maybe one day he'll find something more in you. There's a reason why people say they're marrying their best friend."

Ivy sniffed a laugh. "Thanks. I guess I'll take that as a compliment, but I don't want Mitch, and he doesn't want me like that, either. I've never seen him do so much for someone, just to make them happy. He'd move mountains for you, Callie, if you ask."

"That's the whole problem, though, isn't it? I've asked him for way more than he could give."

"Maybe if you talk to him—"

She shook her head. "No. In fact, I'll be avoiding him as much as I can. Is he here? At the resort, I mean."

Ivy sucked in a breath. "You didn't hear?"

"No. What is it?" Her heart sank.

"Ruby's in the hospital. Her heart started acting up and Mitch drove her to the ER. I talked to him earlier and he's worried because if she's discharged tomorrow, she and Chip have nowhere to go. They'll be able to find something in Marengo, but he wants to be close in case she needs something."

"That's terrible. He must be devastated." Because of the wedding and other things going on in town, there wasn't an available room anywhere. Their homeowner's insurance would pay for their accommodations, but they were facing the same situation as James's aunt.

"They'll have no choice but to stay in Marengo. It'll worry him they're that far away, but he has to stay here and work."

"I should be the one to go. I've made enough of a mess," she said, sliding off the barstool. "They can have my room. It won't be enough to make up for what I did, but it's the best I can do."

"Callie—"

She lifted her purse hanging off the back of the barstool. "What?"

"He loves you."

"I love him, too, but I am what I am and he's gone through what he's gone through. There's no way we can make that work."

"Then you're going to give up."

She stepped away from the bar. She wanted to pack her things and talk to Marnie as soon as she could. She didn't want Mitch to have to worry a second longer about what would happen tomorrow morning.

"Haven't you ever given up, Ivy? I'm tired. Tired of all of it."

"I've given up, but I was never sure if it was the right thing to do."

"In this situation, I know it is. All I've done is hurt Mitch and his family. The harder I pushed, the more harm I caused. Now Ruby's in the hospital and their house is gone. All because I couldn't leave well enough alone. Mitch warned me, but I was stupid and didn't listen. Leaving is the best thing."

She'd go back to Decatur and drive up for the wedding. It would be a long day, but she'd do it to give Mitch's parents a place to stay.

"You're a good person, Callie. And I'm sorry for the way I treated you when we first met."

"It's okay. You were right all along."

In the lobby, she paused and texted Marnie. The bride-to-be invited her to the dining room where she was eating dessert with her mother and going over last-minute wedding details.

"I'm going to check out," she said, sinking into a chair on Marnie's side of the table.

"Why? Because of the fire?" Marnie asked, pouring steaming coffee into a mug. She nudged it in her direction. "Drink this. I'm going to order you some food. You're white as a sheet."

She hadn't eaten since breakfast, and gratefully, she let Marnie order her a bowl of soup and a cheeseburger.

"Yeah, kind of. I talked to Ivy in the bar a few minutes ago and she said Ruby's having heart problems. She's in the hospital now, but she and her husband won't have anywhere to go when she's discharged. They could probably find a room in Marengo, but they should stay in town in case the police or the fire department needs to talk to them. The fire chief opened an arson investigation."

"Good Lord," Gail Zimmerman muttered, a mug of coffee close to her lips and a piece of half-eaten cheesecake in front of her. "I hope she's going to be okay. Is it serious?"

Famished, she breathed in the scent of vegetable soup the server set in front of her and forced herself not to grab a fistful of fries off her plate and shove them into her mouth. The adrenaline pumping through her veins leftover from the fire was wearing off, and her hands shook. She wrapped them around her hot mug to steady them. "Ivy didn't say. All I know is she has a weak heart." She pressed her lips together to push back her tears.

"What will you do about the wedding?" Marnie asked, a worried frown on her face.

She knew Marnie wasn't so self-centered she cared more about the ceremony than Mitch's parents, but the selfish question made her grit her teeth. "I'll still be in it, but

I'll drive from Decatur that day and drive back after the reception. It'll be okay. Not ideal, but Ruby and Chip didn't ask for their house to burn down, either. It's the least I can do."

"Don't go back to Decatur unless you want to," Gail said, patting her hand. "Stay with Hugh and me. We have a spare room I use for scrapbooking that has a futon in it. You'll have plenty of privacy. I'd offer you Marnie's old bedroom, but Hugh's mother is staying with us. It might not be the most comfortable, but there are a few things we need to start doing for the wedding, and I'm sure you'd like to know what comes of the fire."

It wouldn't be any of her business what the investigators found, but yeah, she definitely wanted to stick around to keep an eye on Mitch.

"Thank you. I will, if you don't mind." She spooned up some of her soup. Hunger churned her stomach, but it made her queasy, too.

"Of course not. We offered the room to James's aunt, but she's too good to sleep on a futon." Gail laughed. "Her loss is our gain. I met her at Marnie and James's engagement party, the wretched woman."

She finished her food, and her stomach settled as she walked to her room, Gail and Hugh's address saved in her phone. She'd pack her bags and bring her room key to Mitch at the hospital.

She didn't like the way they left things at the house, and she would tell him a proper goodbye. She wanted to tell him how sorry she was, that there were no hard feelings. It might be too little too late, but she wanted to wish him the best.

Mitch shifted in an uncomfortable chair next to his mother. Ruby laid in bed, dozing, the heart monitor recording the steady beat of her heart.

She'd scared him, after the fire was put out. Standing on the cold sidewalk, a stranger's blanket wrapped around her shoulders, it sank in they had nowhere to go and her heart began fluttering. It brought him back to the fire seven years ago. This time, at least, he could stay by his mother's side, and he hadn't left her room since she was admitted. After his father spoke to the arson investigator, Chip went to the cafeteria to eat, leaving Mitch alone with her.

Slouching in the chair, he mulled over Callie's involvement in the fire.

He didn't want to blame her. She wasn't responsible for the way people acted or the grudges they held on to, but even the investigator raised an eyebrow when he told her everything that had happened since he and Callie started their love affair.

Having the insurance company's approval, Chip made reservations at a hotel in Marengo. Mitch hated the idea of his parents being so far away, but taking time off to be with them would put Desiree in a bind and he was already walking on thin ice.

His mother shifted in the bed, and he reached over to hold her hand.

"I'm surprised Callie isn't here," Chip whispered, treading lightly into the room and passing him a disposable cup of coffee. "She doesn't seem like the type not to care about something like this. Did you tell her your mother's in the hospital?"

"No. She was at the fire . . . Dad, she was the one who rescued Luna."

Chip sank into the chair next to him. "I don't understand."

"She's a firefighter. I wanted to thank the guy for rescuing Luna, and it was her. She said she was visiting the fire department when the call came in." He stared out the window. Rocky Point's hospital was small, only two stories, and Ruby's room looked into the back of the building where the hospital's staff parked their cars. "Pretty ironic she helped put out the fire she started, huh?"

"You can't know this wouldn't have come down the pike sooner or later," Chip said mildly, his voice rising in volume when his wife didn't stir. "Some way, somehow, you would've met another woman. Humans aren't made to be alone, we're hardwired to belong to someone. Pinning this on Callie isn't fair."

"It might not be fair, but that doesn't make it any less true. She should've been honest with me from the start. I could never be with a firefighter. She told me a little about her family, and her brothers and her dad are firefighters, too. I should have put two and two together when she told me that, but she never said she was. I guess she knew I wouldn't take it very well."

"It's a dangerous line of work."

"Yeah, it is. One of her brothers was trapped in a building and he's in rehab now."

"You were broken up before you knew."

"Yeah, and this is just another reason why we don't belong together. I want life to go back to normal."

Chip sipped his coffee. "Mitch, you should know by

now there's not going to be a normal, not for you. The things other people take for granted every day are things you live without. Friends, acceptance in a community, a partner. You have none of that. How do you think going back to normal would do you any good? I think if you're going to fight your way upstream, you might as well do it with a woman by your side. A woman who knows just what, exactly, you went through when that bus went up in flames."

"She lied to me. We were talking about her family when we were in bed. She . . . distracted me when I asked what she did." His cheeks flamed with realization and shame. Why did the conversations he had with his dad about Callie always involve sex?

"She's an intelligent woman," Chip said, shrugging. "College-educated. Strong under pressure. She probably knew you'd act like this. If she loves you, she'd want to avoid that, don't you think?"

"That doesn't make it okay to lie. Even if it was a lie of omission."

"You're looking for excuses not to be with her, and I want to know why. Are you scared, son?"

He set his coffee on the ledge of the window and held his head in his hands. "I don't deserve what she's offering me."

"If you really believe that, then there's nothing I can say," Chip murmured. "I can tell you that it was God's plan, or that things happen for a reason, or that you did your best. There was a lot going on that morning. The weather, that semi being where he wasn't supposed to be. All these years you've been punishing yourself for those two girls, but you saved more lives than were lost that day, and it's a damn shame you can't see that."

He stared at the floor.

"Has Callie lost any lives?"

He jerked his head toward his father. "What?"

"Has Callie lost any lives?" Chip huffed a laugh. "I make her sound like a damned cat. When you work a job like that, you're bound to see death. Paramedics, policemen. Doctors. Helping people is a gift, but you can't save everyone. What does Callie carry around with her?"

"I don't know."

"Then maybe you should ask. Because the way I see it, you two are kindred souls. It's why you were pulled together so quickly. She could see you, and you saw yourself in her. No one's done that for you, Mitch, and God, if you can find it, why push it away?"

"I couldn't live with it. Every time she went on a call I'd worry, no, obsess, about her safety, about her coming back to me. I've tried to shut fire out of my life, and being with her, I'd have to deal with it twenty-four hours a day. And these babies you keep telling me to have with her, how would we raise them? Teach them to expect Mom to never come home every time she went to work? I can't live like that. I'd rather be alone."

Chip rose and stood by the side of his wife's bed. He leaned over and pressed his lips to her forehead. "Be careful what you wish for, son. God might see fit to give it to you."

Callie shoved her suitcase into the backseat of her car. The temperatures plummeted when the sun set, and the engine groaned, cursing her for wanting to go somewhere. The bright stars looked sharp against the black sky, brittle, like they would shatter if she touched them.

She'd spoken with the front desk about transferring her room to the Sinclairs, and a timid boy at the counter—his nametag said his name was Sean—called Desiree, at home, no less, to ask if that was okay. There was a waitlist, he explained, and if someone checked out ahead of schedule, the party at the top of the list had first priority.

Desiree asked to talk to her personally, and she explained what happened and why she wanted to help.

Sounding none too happy, Desiree said, "Let the reservation desk know if they decline your offer. If you decide to keep your room, we need add your credit card back to your profile. If they decide to stay at the resort, ask them to please check in. The records need to be updated with current information."

"Thank you. I will. I'm sorry if this has caused an inconvenience," she said, smiling slightly at Sean to reassure him things were okay.

Desiree sighed. "I'm sorry that the Sinclairs are dealing with this. You're being very kind."

"It's what anyone would do. Goodbye, and thanks."

She handed the receiver to Sean who put the phone to his ear, listened briefly, and hung up a moment later.

At least Desiree had been okay with it. She'd be happy to tell Mitch that side of things was settled.

She entered the hospital's address into her phone's GPS. At this time of night, the streets were empty and she parked in a small side lot only a few minutes later. The dinner she ate rolled in her stomach. There were things she needed to say to Mitch, and she wasn't looking forward to it. Because this really would be their last goodbye.

No one sat behind the information desk, but she found

a nurse's station and a tired nurse pointed her in the right direction.

In a waiting area near Ruby's room, Mitch's dad stood in front of a Keurig machine watching the coffee drip into a disposable cup, and she hesitated. She wanted to see Mitch, but maybe this was better. A blessing in disguise, she could say what needed to be said to Chip.

"Mr. Sinclair," she said, her boots squeaking against the freshly waxed floor as she walked down the hallway toward the older man.

Moving slowly, as if strain and exhaustion were weighing him down, he turned toward her. "Callie. Are you here to see Mitch?"

Touching his arm, she encouraged him to sit. She sank into a cushioned chair next to him, dug into her purse, and pulled out the key attached to the Rocky Point Resort keychain. "No. Well, I . . . no. I wanted to let him know, or you know, that I'm checking out of the resort. Desiree said it was okay if I gave you and Mrs. Sinclair my room. I heard she might be discharged in the morning and you don't have anywhere to go. So, here." She thrust the key at the man who only blinked at her.

"You're driving back to Decatur? Tonight?"

She considered her options. What were the chances of she and Mitch bumping into each other if she lied? It'd be possible, since he worked at the resort and she'd be spending a lot of time there, and if Ivy saw her, she would tell Mitch Callie was still in town, but it wasn't any of Mitch's business what she did. She decided on a half-truth. "I'm staying at Marnie's mom's house tonight. But then, yes, I'll be driving back and forth between here and Decatur until the wedding."

Tears filled his eyes and they sparkled behind his

glasses. "I appreciate that, Callie. Especially since I haven't gotten a chance to apologize for the way we treated you when Mitch brought you to lunch. Ruby . . . she's had him all to herself, and it scared her, I think, the thought of sharing him."

A small smile lifted her lips. "We can be honest. It's more than that. Mitch was doing okay, alone, before we met."

"I hope you don't believe that. You've shown him what a good relationship can be like, what a good *life* can be like, but it's hard for him. Ever since the accident, his main priority has been protecting us, though I've tried like hell to get him to live for himself. Guilt has chewed away at that boy."

"It's difficult to stop feeling like that." She paused. "How's Luna?"

"She's okay. The vet's going to board her until we can figure things out. Mitch said . . . thank you . . ." Chip cleared his throat. "He told me he doesn't think much of you being a firefighter, but we're grateful for what you did."

She jiggled the key Mitch's father had yet to take from her hand.

He wrapped his fingers around the keychain, and she stood, ready to put this horrible mess behind her.

"You're welcome, but it doesn't make up for what I've done or who I am. I'm nothing good for Mitch, or your family, and I'm so sorry for everything that's happened. Tell Mrs. Sinclair I wish her a speedy recovery, if she wants to hear it from me. Take care."

She hurried down the hallway.

In the parking lot, she sucked in a deep breath of cold air. Gail said she'd have the futon made up by the time she came back from the hospital. Maybe she *would* go back to

Decatur, whether there were wedding things to do or not. She could even skip it entirely. All she would do is make the wedding party numbers even. Marnie wouldn't miss her. Not once all the activities started.

She didn't feel like partying anymore.

What she needed was her family.

She pulled her cell phone out of her purse and selected the number for Brandon's rehab facility. He'd understand what was going on. His advice had been good so far, and maybe he could help her through the rest.

The line rang, and she threw her purse into the backseat next to her suitcase and slammed the door shut.

"Look, the little girl who thought she could kick our asses."

Three men stood in front of her car, dressed in leather jackets, glee spread across their faces. With a pit growing in her stomach, she recognized them from the morning she sat with Ivy on the ice. She'd forgotten all about the jerks who called Mitch names.

She moved the phone away from her ear and lifted her chin. "And I can do it again, too."

The one she shoved on his ass laughed. "Grab her."

She whipped around to get into her car, but they were faster.

His two buddies gripped her arms, and she dropped her phone in the snow. Scared, her heart slamming against her ribs, she bucked, lifting her feet off the ground and kicking at the air, but they were alone now, bold without witnesses, and the asshole's friends didn't stay in the background like they had on the ice.

The prick she'd tripped snarled in her face, his breath hot and putrid on her skin. "Not so brave in the dark, huh?" He gripped her face, his fingertips digging into her cheek and jaw. "Take her around the corner. Let's see what she's been giving up to burn boy."

Sweat dripped down her back, and she struggled against the two holding her. One shoved his hand in her hair and yanked. Heat seared her scalp. "Assholes," she hissed. "You're never going to get away with this. You're so tough, three men against a woman. Your mothers would be so proud of you."

"Shut up, bitch."

She had to get away, but as they dragged her through the empty parking lot, she searched for someone who could help her.

There was no one around to save her.

CHAPTER TEN

"You're ruining your chance of being with a good woman," Chip said, walking into Ruby's room. Coming up on midnight, Mitch had been dozing, his chin anchored in his palm, his elbow digging into his knee.

"Huh? What?"

"Callie stopped by. Said she checked out and offered your mother and me her room. She had it okayed with your boss and everything."

He tried to work his way through the fog. It had been such a long day, and fatigue and worry punched him down. He hadn't thought to talk to Desiree and let her know what happened. "Callie was here? She talked to Desiree?"

"She just left. She didn't want to make the drive to Decatur this late, and she's spending the night at Marnie's mother's. She's leaving in the morning, then she'll be back for the wedding. Mitch, I don't think I need to tell you that if you let her walk away, you're going to regret it for the rest of your life."

"It wouldn't work, Dad."

Chip groaned in frustration. "No one's saying you have

to marry her tomorrow. Can't you date? Get to know her? There's more to a person than their occupation. You're more than a maintenance man at a resort. She's more than a woman who fights fires. If that's all we were, then I'd be in trouble because all I'd be is an old man retired from a paper mill with nothing left to say. Your mother and I have coddled you since the fire and it hasn't done you a bit of good. Go talk to her. Buy her a cup of coffee and tell her you're sorry, and if you decide after that it's really over, at least you can say you broke it off with your wits about you."

He thought about what his dad said. He could tell her good luck, that he didn't blame her for the fire. All she wanted was for him to live a better life. It wasn't her fault she didn't understand that he couldn't. That no one in Rocky Point would let him.

Give her a kiss. One last kiss on the lips that hadn't minded gliding over his scars, that had set his body on a different kind of fire.

He sighed. "That was nice of her. I didn't want you driving to Marengo in the morning. You're too tired and worried to be behind the wheel."

"You're tired and worried, too. After you talk to her, go back to your room. Your mom's sleeping and there's no reason to be up all night. Maybe if things work out, Callie can sleep with you instead of at Gail's."

"Dad."

"Just go. Before she drives away. You can still catch her if she gives her car a chance to warm up."

"Okay. But I'll check on you before heading to the resort."

"Good luck, son. Prove to me we didn't raise a fool."

"That'd be hard to do," he said, grabbing his jacket, "because I'm beginning to suspect that you did."

Mitch jogged down the empty hallway. He paused in the spacious lobby, choices running through his head. He could either go out the main doors or the side door. If Callie was like him, she'd gone through the main doors, since visitor parking was located in front of the hospital, but there were parking spots closer to the building along the side. Everyone parked as close as they could when it was this cold outside.

He took a chance and bolted through the side door, the cold smacking him in the face as if he'd run into a sheet of ice.

Her car still sat in a parking space, and he sighed in relief. He hadn't missed her. But her car wasn't running, and quiet blanketed the lot. No one was venturing out this late, not in sub-zero temperatures.

He cupped his hands around his eyes and peered into her car. Her purse was laying in the backseat next to her suitcase.

She could have gotten a ride. Marnie could've picked her up and taken her downtown to have a drink. He overheard talk of everyone meeting at the Viking a time or two. Not that he'd ever been invited. Not that he'd ever go if he was.

He scanned the lot, but nothing seemed out of place. A squirrel ran up one of the trees that separated the hospital's parking lot from the city's sidewalk.

Something glittered on the ground in the milky blue light drifting down from the light poles, and he almost stepped on it as he turned to go up to his mom's room and tell his dad goodbye.

His dad would be disappointed he missed Callie, but she would come back to town for the wedding and being separated for a few days so they could breathe wouldn't be a bad thing. It didn't matter he already missed her with a fierceness he couldn't describe, and she hadn't even left yet. The thought of her slipping away gave him an ache comparable to what he felt whenever he thought about those little girls.

Stunned, he stopped. He hadn't thought about Crystal and Allyson since the fire. He'd been too wrapped up in what was happening with Callie and his parents.

He waited for the guilt to come, but it wasn't the guilt and shame that usually bore down on him when he thought about that family. An acceptance of sorts wiggled its way into his grief.

Whether the residents of Rocky Point believed it or not, he'd done the best he could.

A chime tinkled in the air, and he picked up the object half covered in the snow.

Callie's phone.

"Brandon's Rehab Center" glowed white against black, and before the call went to voicemail, he pressed the Accept button. "Hello?"

"This is Brandon, Callie's brother. Can I talk to her?"

"She's not here. She must have dropped her phone and didn't realize it. I'll make sure she gets it back."

"What do you mean she dropped it? She called a minute ago but when I got to the phone, she wasn't there. Where the fuck is she?"

"She came to—" It would take too much time to explain what Callie was doing at the hospital, and a note of agitation had already crept into Brandon's voice. "I'll find her. I'll have her call you back."

"Who is this?" Brandon demanded.

"This is Mitch Sinclair," he said. "I'm . . . in love with your sister. I'll have her call you as soon as she can."

Over Brandon's objections, he disconnected the call.

If Callie had been in the middle of calling her brother, she hadn't dropped her phone without knowing.

His truck.

His parents' house.

Now the woman he loved.

"Callie!" he yelled, his panicked voice echoing over the parking lot. "Callie!"

He clung to the idea she'd gotten a ride, though in his heart he knew that wasn't what happened. Not at all.

"Think, dammit!" he growled to himself. "Callie!" he shouted again.

He stood panting, clutching her cell phone, and over the rush in his ears, he almost missed the soft, thin, whimper that whined from around the corner of the hospital.

"Callie!" he shouted, taking off at a run.

He used her phone to dial nine-one-one.

"Nine-one-one. Do you need police, fire, or ambulance?" a calm, female voice asked.

"Police. I'm at the Good Samaritan Hospital, in the lot adjacent to Minnetonka Boulevard. There's an assault taking place. Hurry!"

He disconnected and shoved Callie's phone into his coat pocket.

The phone call wasted precious seconds, but he wanted whoever was hurting Callie to pay. He'd never stood up for himself, but he would for her.

Rounding the corner, he searched the shadows, and fury sparked in his veins.

Two men had her pinned against the building, hiding

near an enormous dumpster, and a third man stood in front of her, laughing as she struggled, her legs kicking against the men holding her back. He touched her cheek, smoothing the hair away from her face. The meagre light revealed his touch was anything but kind.

He was still too far away to stop what he knew was coming, but he yelled, "Don't!" his voice raspy with dread.

The bastard gave no indication he heard Mitch at all, and he slapped her, the sharp crack bouncing off the walls.

He raced toward them, his teeth bared. "You son of a bitch. Let her go."

The asshole looked over his shoulder and smirked. "Hey, burn boy, coming to the rescue. Just the man we wanted to see."

"Mitch!" Callie struggled against the two scrawny men holding her. One looked like a rat, his beady eyes assessing him with wild excitement, and the other, his face pockmarked from a bad case of acne that hadn't totally abated, glared at him with an expression of complete hate.

"I said let her go."

"Or what? What are you gonna do?" The man tilted his head and stared at him, narrowing his eyes. "You couldn't save those girls. Couldn't save your dog. Oh, is that it? You can do something about this—" he waved his hand between himself and Mitch— "because there's no fire? That it? Fire make you a coward, you pussy?"

"Leave him alone," Callie said, surging forward. "You have no fucking clue what you're talking about."

"No, he doesn't. You know how I know I can do something about this?" he asked.

"Come on. Tell me." Laughing and bouncing on the balls of his feet, the jerk wiggled his fingers, motioning him closer.

His asshole friends held Callie, gripping her arms, and her breath streamed out her mouth as she fought, trying to escape their grasp.

He wanted to pay the bastard back for putting his hands on her, and calmly, he lifted his arm and punched the smug fucker right in the middle of his face. Cartilage snapped.

The son of a bitch dropped to his knees, howling. Blood gushed out of his nose, down his chin, and saturated the front of his jacket.

"Didn't think I'd do it, did you? Didn't think I had the guts. But you know what? I'm smarter than you are, I'm stronger than you are, and I don't need to hit anyone to prove it. Consider yourself lucky I didn't do more because you deserve it, you prick."

In the distance, sirens wailed, and the two holding Callie let her go and ran, leaving their bleeding friend behind. Their boots crunching over the snow, they disappeared through the trees and onto the dark street.

Callie staggered toward him and crumpled in his arms, and he held her tightly, closing his eyes against a rush of tears.

A police cruiser slid to a stop near the dumpster, and an officer flew out of the car, a hand on his weapon.

"They went that way," he said, pointing over Callie's shoulder. "They took off when they heard the sirens."

"I'll call it in." The cop spoke into a radio mic attached to the front of his jacket, then said to Mitch, "What happened to him?"

The lights of the police car strobed red and blue over his body, and he poked the guy's leg with his boot. "I think I broke his nose."

"Miss? Are you all right?" the officer asked, bending

over the bleeding man curled in a fetal position. Blood turned the snow bright red.

She stepped out of his embrace, but he didn't let her go far. If he had his way, she'd never leave his sight again.

"I'm fine. He hit me, but I'm okay. If Mitch wouldn't have . . . I don't know what they would've done."

He knew. If he'd wasted any more time bullshitting with his dad or trying to convince Brandon someone had picked Callie up, they would have gotten away with it.

The cop helped the moaning man to his feet. The bleeding had subsided but blood still trickled over his mouth and down his chin.

"Busted nose for sure," the cop said, nudging him toward the cruiser. "Let's go to the station and sort it out over some coffee."

"You're not going to arrest him?" He tried to keep the disbelief out of his voice.

The cop's eyes hardened.

He flinched, and Callie rested a hand on his arm.

He'd forgotten who he was, whom he was dealing with, and thought, by chance, someone would listen. The cop wasn't familiar, but general dislike for him had traveled through the small town's police department.

"I'll take your statements at the station. Maybe we can chalk this up to a misunderstanding and no one will need to press charges."

Callie slipped her hand into his. "It's okay," she murmured.

No, it's not, he thought, but he had no choice but to agree.

The officer pushed Callie's attacker into the backseat of the squad car, one hand on the top of the asshole's head. The cop glanced at them, climbed behind the wheel, turned the lights off, and slowly drove out of the hospital's parking lot, leaving them alone in the cold.

No one would care if he and Callie didn't show up at the station. They'd be glad to sweep it under the rug. It's what the department always did whenever he had a complaint. Like his truck, or the vandalism to his parents' house.

Because of who he was and what he'd done.

He brushed his finger lightly over her cheek. "Are you hurt?" he asked, his face numb. Past midnight, the cop had the right idea, he had to admit. He wouldn't be surprised if the temperature registered ten below or colder.

"I'll be feeling it tomorrow," she said, leaning away. "But not as bad as that guy. I had no idea you would do something like that."

He huffed. "Sometimes you have no choice, whether you want to or not. I wasn't going to let him get away with hurting you, Callie."

"It was my fault he wanted to. That was the guy I took down on the lake the other day. Wanted revenge for wounding his pride, I guess."

"Son of a bitch."

"I should have left well enough alone." She trudged over the packed snow and headed toward her car.

"You were only defending me."

She looked at him out of the corners of her eyes. Even in the thin security lights of the parking lot, he could see her cheek and lip were already starting to puff up.

"If I would've known how little you cared, I wouldn't have wasted my energy."

He didn't want to argue. Instead, he pulled her phone out of his pocket. "Here. I found this in the snow. If you hadn't dropped it, I would've thought you'd gone with Marnie or Autumn for drinks or something."

Callie took her phone and woke it up. "I was going to talk to my brother. I better give him a call on the way to the station. He's probably going crazy. Thanks."

He tried to smile. "I answered when he called back. I think by now he's pretty worried."

"You talked to Brandon?"

"Yeah. I'm sorry."

"No. It's . . . okay. I'll see you at the station."

"Right."

He stood in front of her car as she slipped into the driver's seat and started the engine. He motioned for her to lock her doors, and after hearing the locks click into place, walked to his truck parked in front of the hospital.

He should've insisted on giving her a ride, but more than likely they'd go their separate ways after leaving the police station. He had no idea when he'd see her next.

Because of him, someone assaulted her.

He'd be lucky if she talked to him ever again.

Tight from stress and cold, he rolled his tense shoulders and started his truck.

When Callie saw how little help the police would be because he was involved, maybe she'd finally understand what he'd been tolerating all this time and why it wasn't worth it to defend himself.

It caused nothing but more trouble.

Callie called her brother's rehab center as soon as Mitch turned his back. She hoped she wasn't causing Brandon any grief with his staff. They had a strict schedule, and it was past Brandon's lights out.

He answered after only one ring, and though he tried to keep the tears out of his voice, she heard them when he answered.

"Hello?"

"Brandon. It's Callie. Why are you answering the phone?"

"Jesus." He paused and blew out a breath in a burst of static. "I told the director what happened. I knew you'd call me back and he let me wait. Mitch said you dropped your phone."

"I did. Just not the way he thought. A couple of goons caught me outside the hospital—"

"The hospital? Jesus Christ. Do I have to check myself out and drive up there?"

"No! Listen to me." She eased to the curb in the middle of a residential section. She should have ridden with Mitch. She had no idea where the police department was located. "I defended Mitch a couple of days ago and I dumped a guy on his ass. Tonight he and two of his friends caught me outside the hospital. By chance, Mitch was right behind me and stopped them before anything happened."

"Are you hurt? You're beating guys up? Callie, you're supposed to be having tea parties and watching strippers. What the fuck?"

"I'm not hurt and Marnie's bachelorette party isn't until next week. I can't stand the thought of people treating Mitch this way. You know they call him burn boy? It makes me sick."

"For God's sake. I thought you two broke up."

"We did. But someone set his parents' house on fire and I checked out of the resort to give them a place to stay."

"Someone burned down their house? Holy fucking Christ. Does Dad know?"

"Probably. I was doing that stupid tour of the RPFD and the chief invited me to go on the call. I think he was testing me, and he chewed me out for going in after the dog—"

"I'm going up there. You keep opening your mouth and bullshit keeps spilling out."

"It was *not* my fault I happened to be there. I wouldn't have given the stupid fire department a single thought if it hadn't been for Dad. I'm on *fucking vacation,* and all I get is shit."

She started crying then. She choked on her sobs, trying to regain her control, but the harder she tried to stop, the harder she cried.

"Are you gonna be okay?" Brandon whispered.

Sniffling, she said, "Yeah. There's a lot going on and I don't know how to deal with it, but I'll be okay."

"You said you checked out of the resort? Are you driving home tonight?"

"No. I'm staying at Marnie's mom's. I should text Marnie and let her know what happened."

"Okay. You have a place to sleep at least. What are you doing now?"

"I have to go to the police station. Mitch is already there. Then going to Gail's to get some sleep. They want me to stay and help with wedding stuff, but at this point, I only want to go home."

Brandon was silent, then said, "How would Mitch take that?"

"He won't care, Brandon. He's got a lot on his plate with his parents' house and his mother's health. I was at the hospital because I was giving Mitch's dad the key to my room. His mother has a weak heart and she was admitted after the fire for observation. Mitch's mind is on other things."

Other things like running from his problems. Turning his back on the things that mattered, like the way people treated him.

One thing she did learn through this whole mess was that she couldn't fight other people's battles.

She was tired, and she was done.

"I don't think that's true. Why did he go after you tonight?"

"I don't know. Because he wanted to say no hard feelings? Thank me for giving his parents my room? Tell me goodbye because I told his dad I was leaving town until the wedding? It could have been anything."

"Because he wanted to see you?"

"He told me how he really felt this afternoon when he found out I was a firefighter. He caught up with me to thank me for saving Luna, only, I had my gear on and he didn't know it was me. If that makes sense."

"It does, but you've been on enough calls to know that during emergencies people say things they don't mean. I talked to him when I called you back. He answered your phone."

"Yeah, I know. He told me."

"Yeah, well, he told *me* that he loves you. He knew who he was talking to, Callie. You don't tell a family member that unless you mean it. Unless there's a commitment behind it."

"He . . . said that to you? He hasn't even told me that." She laughed, the sound watery and sad.

"Yeah. He did. And I know you love him too, or you

wouldn't be going through this bullshit. But the real question is, what are you going to do about it?"

"There's nothing I *can* do. You were right all along. He hates that I'm a firefighter."

"Work it out. It's not like you want to be one anymore. You were thinking about quitting before you met him. God, you act like giving up the department would be a fate worse than death." He sucked in a breath. "Shit."

"It's not that. It's Dad."

"Fuck Dad. Isn't that what you told me? Fuck him and his firetruck."

The absurdity of the statement made her laugh. Really laugh.

Brandon joined her and the tension drifted away.

She wiped her nose with the back of her hand. "I need to go. Mitch is probably wondering where I am."

"Don't let those bastards get away with it. If they hurt you, make 'em pay."

"I plan on it. Goodnight, Brandon. I hope I didn't mess things up with you and your staff."

"You didn't. I'm in rehab, not prison. They expect a level of propriety, and it makes me feel better, to be honest."

"Good. And please, don't come up here. Focus on your health."

"Okay. Goodnight, Callie, and for God's sake, start being careful. You ride into town and all hell breaks loose."

"This town needed some mixing up."

"*Pffft.* Not sure you had to be the one to do it, but okay. Let me know how things go."

"I will. I promise. Goodnight."

Brandon hung up the rehab center's landline, the old-fashioned receiver dropping into the cradle.

She tossed her phone onto the seat and drove into the empty street.

She'd text Marnie once she made it to the station.

Mitch told Brandon he loved her.

A smile pulled at her mouth, and she winced.

Maybe this would work out after all.

"That didn't go very well."

"I didn't think it would."

Callie stood on the front steps of the police department, a sleek building compared to the old courthouse sitting next door.

"What are you going to do now? Dad said you checked out of the resort. Thank you for that."

She shivered. Sore, tired, she needed some ibuprofen and ten hours of sleep. "It wasn't a big deal. I'm staying at Marnie's mom and dad's. I texted her to let her know what happened, and she's at their house waiting for me."

"Then you're going back to Decatur?"

"Yeah," she said, looking away. "There are things I could be doing with my time off."

"Do you think, before you leave, we could get a cup of coffee or something?"

She rubbed her eyes. "What for? I know how you feel about me and what I do. It's my fault someone targeted your parents' house, it's my fault those guys cornered me tonight. The cop even said so."

Mitch swore.

"Not in so many words, but he did. And you knew it was going to turn out this way, didn't you?"

He jerked a shoulder. "Yeah. I've lived like this for a long time."

"Well, maybe you shouldn't have. I need to get going. I'm tired, and I hurt." In more ways than one, but she wouldn't tell him that. "And it's colder than hell out here."

"Will you text me when you make it to Marnie's place?"

"No. It's none of your business what I do. We broke up, remember? I hope your mom's okay. Goodnight."

She stomped to her car, got in, and slammed her door shut. She couldn't let him straddle the fence. He either loved all of her or he didn't. Relationships required compromise and he threw her away before they could find one.

Fighting with the town was useless. She understood that now. Autumn was wrong. Maybe way back the town had been split between those who believed Mitch had done all he could and those who blamed him for not saving those little girls, but no more.

He could take the blame for that. For hiding, for appearing guilty because he'd *felt* guilty. For taking responsibility when there wasn't any to be taken.

Autumn was wrong, and she'd been wrong, too. After all the years that had gone by, there was no way he was going to redeem himself now. It didn't matter how hard he fought.

Her realization had come too late.

Sluggish because she hadn't given it time to warm up, her car heaved in reluctance as she drove to Marnie's childhood home.

The front porch light shined in welcome. She parked on the street and grabbed her suitcase and purse out of the backseat.

Marnie was watching for her and greeted her wearing

pajamas. "I wanted to make sure you were okay," she said, holding the storm door open.

"Just tired."

"You look more than tired, and you have a fat lip," Marnie said, motioning her into the house.

"It's what got me into this mess," she said, trying to find a little humor.

"Did they catch the jerks who did that to you?"

She kicked off her boots and followed Marnie into a basement room that had a card table, storage shelves, and a brand-new futon squeezed together against the walls. Blankets and pillows were piled at the end of the futon, and tears of relief and gratitude welled in her eyes.

She sank onto the fluffy cushion and rested her head on a pillow that smelled of fabric softener. "Yeah. Two of them ran away but they were picked up a couple of blocks from the hospital. The guy Mitch hit said he only wanted to scare me a little. I think he would've done more than that, but it's my word against his."

"Your face didn't say otherwise?" Marnie lifted a finger. "Hold that thought. Why don't you change into your pajamas? I made coffee, and I'll bring you a mug and some painkiller."

"Thank you. I don't mean to cause so much trouble."

"Stop it. It's no trouble."

She changed into sweatpants that had DECATUR FIRE DEPARTMENT stamped down one leg and a matching t-shirt. She kept her thick socks on and wrapped a blanket around herself. Sitting on the futon, she began to shake.

She hadn't thanked Mitch for stopping them. The cop hadn't mentioned charging him with battery, and hopefully, he'd be let off with self-defense and a slap on the wrist.

She'd be pressing charges, though. Even if the cops didn't want her to because, in their words, she'd started the whole thing that morning on the ice, she wanted those assholes to pay for what they'd done. Through stiff lips, she'd pointed out if those men hadn't approached her and Ivy in the first place none of this would have happened.

Marnie walked in holding a steaming cup of coffee and three ibuprofen, and she sighed in relief. As she sipped the coffee that Marnie laced with brandy, she filled in her friend.

"You love him, huh?" Marnie asked, rubbing Callie's back.

"Yeah. I really do," she said. "But when he looks at me now, he's going to see a woman who whipped the town into such a frenzy someone burned his parents' house down. He sees a firefighter. He sees the accident."

"Did the fire department say they thought it was arson?"

"They opened an investigation, but how could it not be? It's too big of a coincidence."

"Mitch's dad didn't blame you when you went up there to give them your key, did he?"

She set her empty mug on a small table near the futon. "No. I don't think so. Maybe. It feels so long ago, I can't remember. He was worried about his wife."

"You and Mitch love each other, and by the sound of things, a lot. It's amazing what people can overcome when they love each other that much. Why don't you get some sleep? I'm going snowmobiling with James, Jared, and Leah tomorrow, unless you want me to stay here."

"No, you should go. I don't want to stop you from hanging out with your friends. Leah came a long way for the wedding, and she's spending time with Jared, I hear."

Marnie's eyes crinkled. "I think they've got something going. It's hard on Leah, though. She doesn't come from a stable family, and her ex-husband is a total asshole. It's difficult for her to trust, but Jared's a solid guy. Leah won't find anyone better."

"I'm happy for her."

"Me, too. Now, if Autumn could find someone, I'd be thrilled. I want to see all my friends settled with good men." She yawned. "Do you need anything else? I told Mom I'd stay here tonight. She was worried about me driving across town in the middle of the night."

"Won't James miss you?"

Marnie grinned. "He might, but it'll be good for him. Goodnight, Callie. I'm glad you weren't hurt."

"Thanks. Have fun tomorrow."

"We will. If you need anything, I'll be in the living room sleeping on the couch."

With her head swimming from exhaustion and the doctored coffee, Callie made up the futon and snuggled into the soft blankets and down pillows. As far as sleeping on a futon went, she could have been stuck on the floor and she was thankful for the thick cushion.

If Mitch went back to the hospital tonight to sit with his mom, maybe his dad would sleep at the resort. She hoped so. Chip had looked worried and tired, and he needed to take care of himself because the next few weeks would be hard on all of them.

She'd helped people clean out their houses, finding things to salvage, picking through memories still intact enough to keep.

Digging through the ash could be physically, as well as emotionally, draining. Not to mention heartbreaking.

In the morning, she'd visit Ruby and bring her some

flowers. The woman didn't like her and Callie couldn't blame her, but she would apologize.

Maybe Mitch would look for her, after all this was said and done. Maybe he'd look for her, and she'd let him buy her a cup of coffee.

They could hold hands and talk.

And they could start over.

The way they were meant to be.

Her phone woke her out of a dead sleep, the chiming near her cheek rousing her from a vivid dream. She'd been rescuing Luna, but in the dream Luna wasn't a dog, she was a huge pink pig.

The scents of coffee, eggs, and bacon floated through the air, and she inhaled. No wonder she was dreaming about pigs.

Her phone chimed again, and in the semi-darkness, she groped for it. The blinds hidden by lace curtains kept out a good portion of the blinding sunlight. Thank God.

She grabbed her cell, her body stiff. She needed coffee and a hot shower, maybe more ibuprofen, though wiggling her jaw, her face didn't feel as bad as she thought it would.

Her dad's number glowed on her cell phone's screen and she groaned. She wanted to ignore it.

The call went to voicemail before she could force her fingers to press Accept. She'd already missed five of her father's calls this morning. This morning? What time was it? Good Lord, it was almost noon.

Her phone chimed again.

"Hello?" she croaked, her throat dry. She didn't need coffee. She needed a glass of water.

"Callie. I've been trying to call you all morning." Her father's gruff voice held a note of concern, and she struggled to sit up.

Her stomach heaved against the remnants of spiked coffee and little else. She rested her head against the back of the futon and willed her nausea to go away.

"I'm sorry. I just woke up."

"Chief Bakersfield called. He told me about the fire."

She wasn't awake enough to have this conversation. "Ah-huh."

"He said you did a good job."

"Okay."

She couldn't keep her eyes open. If her father hung up now, she could fall back asleep.

"We had breakfast with your brother this morning."

"How's Zach doing?" she mumbled.

"Not Zach. Brandon. Are you listening to me?"

Brandon? That was news. "I am. I'm trying. I didn't get in until late."

"That's why I'm calling. Brandon told us what happened. You couldn't let us know you're okay?"

"Yesterday was a long day, and I'm fine."

"I called the police station and talked to the captain. You aren't fine, and I gave him an earful. What kind of town is he in charge of, I want to know. Blaming you for attempted rape."

"That wasn't—"

"Don't tell me that wasn't what was going to happen."

Her stomach heaved again.

She deliberately hadn't brought up the R word. Didn't want to think about it. Didn't want to admit that if Mitch hadn't been there to help her, with three against one, she would've had zero chance of defending herself against anything they did.

"I told him if he let those men off with only a warning, I was going to sue the police department and the entire town for damages."

"Dad—"

"And this guy, this Mitch Sinclair, I want to thank him for intervening."

"He was nice about the whole thing."

"Brandon said he's in love with you. I did some checking, and he's that bus driver from a few years ago."

"Yeah. Dad, why did you call?"

"I'm telling you why I called. Because I want to meet the man who's going to marry my daughter."

"Dad! We're not getting married. We're not even dating. His parents' house caught fire yesterday and he's got other things on his mind besides courting me."

"I know about the house, and I know you rescued their dog. Bakersfield told me the whole story, damn near went back seven years and ended with the arson investigator looking at the site this morning."

Her eyes flew open. "He did? That was fast."

"Intent is serious," Ace Carter said, tapping what sounded like a pen against paper.

"What did he find out?"

"She. Jillian Frost."

"Jillian looked at the Sinclair's house? How did she drive up here so fast?"

"Bakersfield called her the minute the fire was put out. With all the tension surrounding the Sinclairs, he knew something wasn't right."

"I was still at the station and overheard him call someone, but I had a feeling he thought the Sinclairs brought it upon themselves."

"His opinions don't matter, and you know that."

"What did she find out?" she asked, swallowing past the lump in her throat.

"She found the site of origin the minute she stepped into what was left of the kitchen. It was classic gasoline accelerant. The arsonist didn't care too much about getting caught, threw the gas can in the neighbor's backyard. There won't be any prints—I don't think anyone is that stupid—but he didn't even try to cover up the evidence."

"I wonder why Mitch's parents didn't hear it. Usually arsonists wait until nighttime to set fires."

"Jillian will be questioning everyone involved. Even you. Tell her hello from me when you see her."

"I will. Thanks for letting me know."

He paused, and she waited.

"Brandon's looking good," he finally said.

"He . . . sounded good when I talked to him last night," she said hesitantly.

"He's not going back to firefighting." Her father sighed.

"You knew that, Dad. The minute he checked himself into rehab."

"I never meant for you kids to think I wouldn't love you if you weren't firefighters."

"He said that?"

"Didn't have to. The shame in his eyes when he told me said enough."

"I'm sorry."

"There's nothing to be sorry for. My path isn't his . . . or yours. If you didn't want to do this anymore, why didn't you say so?"

She scoffed. "So you could tell me how disappointed

you were? So you could belittle me and tell me that I was born to serve? To pull my big-girl panties up? That's all it was with you, you know? How to help, our call to duty. Our family's legacy. Brandon was driven to drink and had to check himself into rehab before you would listen. Zach spends all his time at the station while his poor wife worries if he'll come home from a call. Haven't you noticed how hard he's become? How tired and brittle?"

"It's hard work."

"I know it is. And you never miss a chance to tell us how weak we are when we try to tell you we can't handle it."

"I didn't mean to sound that way."

"Well, you do."

"What do you want to do, Callie?"

"I don't know. I have savings. I have time to think about it."

"Then I accept your resignation. Effective immediately."

"Dad—"

"I'm not angry. I want to be, but I don't have the right. It's your life, and you should live it how you like, but I hope your mother and I raised you to still want to do good in this world. Somehow."

"I do, but I don't know how or what yet."

"Will you stop by the house when you're back in town? Your mother and I would like to see you. Bring Mitch."

"He doesn't want anything to do with me. I'm the reason his parents were targeted in the first place."

"Bakersfield told me about what's going on, and Brandon told me what little he knew. Talk to me. Let's figure this out."

She curled around her pillow and explained everything that had happened since she'd driven to Rocky Point. Her plugged drain and falling for Mitch almost from the minute she met him. Her outlet and their first kiss, the hockey game, kicking that jerk's ass on the ice. Her father interrupted her then to praise her, and she smiled into the phone. The animosity and hatred she'd stirred up insisting Mitch should be left alone to live a normal life despite his inability to save all the children that day, and then to the fire.

"I don't want you to feel responsible for it," Ace said.

"How can I not?"

"Because you're not, and anyone with a lick of sense will know that, too. Including Mitch and his parents. Are they going to rebuild?"

"I don't think so. Mitch said they had no interest in it, but he didn't say what else they were going to do."

"I started a collection online. I don't know what their situation is, but a little extra never hurts. Fires make people tear up. Bakersfield sent me some pictures."

"Thanks, Dad. They'll appreciate it."

"Brandon said you gave up your room. I'm proud of you, Callie." He cleared his throat. "You're my daughter, and no matter what you do, or choose to do, I'll be proud of you. You're a sweet, caring, intelligent young woman, and if Mitch can't see that, I'll knock him alongside his head."

She laughed. "I think you'll have to stand in line. Brandon said the exact same thing."

"After the wedding, can we . . . it's been a long time since we've sat down as a family. Brandon . . . he looks better, sounds better, but he's far from being back to a hundred percent. What he's carrying around, maybe he never will be, but, if we can have a meal once in a while, I promise to behave."

"He's scared, Dad. So am I." Her hand was starting to

ache and she desperately needed to go to the bathroom, but she didn't want the conversation to end.

"I'm sorry. When you were kids, I did everything I could to protect you. You're still my children, but that protectiveness got lost along the way and I need to find it again. When you get back, we'll talk more. Try to have a good time, and good luck with Mitch. I read the accident report. He wasn't to blame."

"He wasn't, but the town can't let it go. He's scared, too, in his own way."

"Then maybe you need to do a little protecting yourself."

"I have, but it doesn't seem to have helped much."

"It has. Probably more than you know. Keep it up because it sounds like no one needs it more than Mitch."

"Yeah. Thanks, Dad. I love you."

"I love you, too."

She disconnected the call and raced to the bathroom. While her bladder emptied, she smiled at her lap. She'd never felt so light.

She was no longer a firefighter.

She could do what she wanted, and, unfortunately, she wanted Mitch.

Mitch woke up to his father poking him on the shoulder. He'd spent the night in his mom's room after giving his statement at the police station.

Callie hadn't texted him to let him know she'd made it to the Zimmerman's, though he'd hoped and checked his phone every five seconds until he drifted off. He'd forced his dad to go to the resort and sleep, and finally Chip left, looking more tired and sad than he'd seen him in a long time.

Defeated.

How he felt.

All these years, all that struggle, for nothing.

In the end, Rocky Point's residents successfully chased him and his parents out of town. There was no reason to stay.

He showered in his little room at the resort. Whether he felt like it or not, he had to report for work. He waited in Desiree's office, grateful she pushed it back to the lunch hour. As always, his toolbox sat at his feet.

From the start, the day had seemed different somehow,

an ugly foreboding thrumming through his bones. More bad things were going to happen, but he'd quietly gone about his work, kept to himself, and waited. He expected Desiree to breeze in holding her coffee mug and a termination letter, but she didn't.

"I'm sorry about your house." Desiree set her briefcase near her desk, hung her purse and jacket on the coat rack by the window, and sat in her chair. "Are your parents okay?"

"Yeah. Mom spent the night in the hospital, but she was released this morning and she's doing all right. Dad slept here. Callie—"

"I know. I okayed it. If there's anything more I can do, let me know."

He cleared his throat in annoyance. "What happened to me bringing bad things to the resort?"

She ignored him, changing the subject. "I read about Callie's attack."

He blinked. "You did?"

"It's on the front page of the *Rocky Point Daily Journal*. You didn't see it? Someone gave Autumn Bennett the full scoop, right after it happened, too, to squeak past the deadline like that, and the editor-in-chief let her run with it. Her byline is above the fold."

"I . . . had no idea."

"She described you and Callie as a couple and said how we're treating our own is horrendous when, as a close-knit community, we should be looking out for each other. I agree. I have to admit though, after I heard about the fire, I thought about letting you go, but Autumn played the article just right. If I fired you now, I'd look like the biggest bitch this side of the Canadian border."

He scoffed. "I'll have to thank Autumn for being my PR manager."

She lifted her hands and spread her fingers. "Do you want me to apologize for protecting a job that pays my bills, for protecting the people who work at this resort? There's no denying that they, whoever 'they' are, lashed out at your parents to get to you. Would you want the staff and guests of this resort to be hurt if they had decided to target you and your room instead?"

"Of course not, but I shouldn't have to pay for people being idiots. I've paid enough, and I've done nothing wrong." He clamped his mouth shut.

She lifted her eyebrows. "Also, a collections campaign popped up online early this morning. Half of a fifty-thousand dollar goal has already been donated."

"I'm sorry?"

"I don't know who started it, the creator's anonymous, but it's been circulating on social media all morning and it showed up on my feeds several times while I was in my meeting. It wouldn't surprise me if, by the end of the day, the goal is met."

"I can't believe it." The first person he thought of was Callie. She was the only person who cared about him and his parents enough to do something like that.

"Believe it. It'll give your parents a nice chunk of money to help rebuild their house beyond what their insurance will pay out. They'll have a beautiful home at the end of all this mess."

"They have no interest in rebuilding. We're moving."

Her eyes widened. "You are?"

"They're moving to Decatur. And I'm . . . going with them," Mitch said, his heart pounding.

"Then you're putting in your notice?"

"I'll give you a month, maybe two, but I've always

looked after my parents and I won't let them move without me."

"Okay." She blew out a breath. "I appreciate that. It might very well take me that long to find someone to replace you. Not everyone is a jack-of-all-trades like you are, Mitch. I'll be sorry to see you go."

"This is a good job, and I appreciate you taking a chance on me all those years ago, but Callie, with all her pushing and attitude, is right. I should never have put up with the way I've been treated here. I did my best when that bus caught fire, and after trying to save those girls, I've suffered in more ways than one. But you know what? Even murderers are let out on parole, are offered a second chance. I deserve one, too."

She sprang out of her chair and gripped him in a tight hug. "You have no idea how happy I am to hear you say that. No idea. I'm so glad Callie came along and was able to show you that. How is she?"

He jerked his shoulder and stared at the floor. "I don't know. We said our goodbyes at the police station last night. She stayed at Marnie's mom and dad's, and she's going back to Decatur until the wedding."

"But Autumn's article implied you two are together."

"We were, but we . . . stopped seeing each other. She's a firefighter, and I thought I couldn't live with that, but then I saw her trying to fight off those assholes, excuse me, and I'm all mixed up. When I see her, I see fire, but I also see a woman I could spend the rest of my life with. The woman I *want* to spend the rest of my life with, but I've been alone for a long time."

"Are you afraid she won't give you the space you need to adjust?"

He frowned. "What do you mean?"

"Mitch," she said, laughing, "out of anybody in the whole world, she would be the one to know how you feel. What you tried to do that morning, she does on the job every single day. You don't think she hurts? You think she fights fires to have fun?"

He sighed. It's what his dad was trying to get him to understand at the hospital. He watched her carry Luna across his parents' yard. How difficult had it been for Callie to decide to go in after her in the first place? How brave she was to risk her safety for a dog, simply because she knew his dad loved her.

"I can see by your blank stare you didn't *think* at all. Maybe if you stopped throwing yourself a pity party, you'd realize that she needs a little empathy, too. I can't imagine what trouble she sees in a city as big as Decatur. She'll give you space and time if you ask. If you push her away out of fear, she may never take you back when you're ready."

A half an hour later, he stumbled out of Desiree's office. He needed to find Callie and explain some of the hard truths he'd come to figure out with his dad's and Desiree's help.

He prayed she was still in town.

Callie called the hospital and confirmed Ruby's release, and she found a small flower shop and purchased a basket of wildflowers. They looked a little rough, but December in Minnesota wasn't the best time of year to buy flowers.

Chip answered when she knocked on the door, and suddenly she was in his arms, being hugged so tightly she could barely breathe.

"Thank you again, for Luna," he said, his voice rough with tears. "It didn't sink in yesterday, what you did. No one else would have gone in after her. I stood right there on that sidewalk watching my house burn, and I know no one else would have tried. You have no idea how much it hurts to think about my girl being trapped in that hell."

Gently, she stepped out of his embrace. "I might have some idea."

Chip colored. "Of course you do. How stupid of me."

"It's okay. I called the hospital and they told me Mrs. Sinclair had been released. I brought her some flowers."

"She'd love a visitor. They told her to take it easy, and she's been resting. Thank you, for the room. It'll make things a lot easier."

"I'm glad I could help. I've assisted other families who have gone through this, and I know how hard the next few months will be."

"The house was full of things, and losing what was inside will hurt, but they're only things. My family's safe, and that's what matters most." He cleared his throat. "I'm going to take a look around. I've lived in this town all my life but I've only been in the resort a handful of times."

She paused. "If you see Mitch, will you tell him I'm okay?"

"Sure. You don't want to tell him yourself?"

She looked down at the flowers. "We aren't on speaking terms at the moment."

"I see. I'll let him know if I bump into him. Have a nice visit." He stepped into the hallway and closed the door behind him, leaving her standing in front of the bathroom.

Memories of meeting Mitch flooded her heart, and tears filled her eyes. How gentle he'd been when he held her while she sat on the vanity. How his hands trembled when he'd touched her.

"Are you going to stand there all day?" Ruby called from the bed.

She laughed and started forward. "I'm sorry. I . . . met Mitch in this room, and I was remembering the first time I —"

"Saw him?" Ruby asked, her eyes twinkling. She sat on top of the bedspread dressed in black leggings and a pink sweatshirt that looked new, two pillows propping her against the headboard. A copy of a newspaper laid next to her.

She blushed. "Yes, exactly."

"Those are gorgeous," Ruby said, tilting her head at the flowers.

"Um, not much selection this time of year." She set the brown wicker basket on the dresser next to the TV.

"We don't get much of anything when it's this cold. Sit down, if you'd like to stay for a minute. I read the paper. Assholes. That's what they are."

"The paper?" she asked, dragging a small, cushioned chair closer to the bed.

"Autumn Bennett wrote the front page story about the fire and your attack."

"I wouldn't quite call it an attack," she said, taking the copy of the *Rocky Point Daily Journal* Ruby handed her. The photo of the Sinclair's house brought more tears to her eyes, and through watery vision, she scanned the article. She appreciated Autumn's sympathetic tone toward Mitch and her and the disgust aimed at the people who lived in town.

"Even Mayor Wilson called Chip this morning and said they'd be prosecuting to the fullest extent of the law.

Whoever set the fire, and those sons of bitches who went after you. They got off lucky, when Mitch saw them hurting you."

"He saved me from a bad situation."

"You saved him, too, Callie." Ruby sighed. "I wasn't very nice when Mitch brought you by. I was scared. Please believe that. It wasn't because I don't like you."

"You were right to be afraid of me. I brought you and Mr. Sinclair nothing but trouble." She played with the zipper of her jacket unable to meet the woman's eyes.

"Come here, honey," Ruby said, scooting over on the mattress.

She tugged off her boots and laid on the bed, and Ruby wrapped her arms around her.

The woman's gentle embrace set loose the floodgates, and she cried into Ruby's shoulder while the older woman smoothed her hair.

"I'm sorry," she sniffled, trying to stop crying. "The fire was my fault." This brought on another round of tears.

"Shh, shh, it's okay. It's going to be okay. We convinced ourselves it was okay to go along with how things were, but that was wrong. We were afraid to rock the boat, and when you came along . . . well, you did more than rock our stable little boat. You capsized that sucker, and we couldn't be more grateful."

Blinking away the tears, she looked at Mitch's mother. Ruby's cheeks were rosy and her eyes glittered with . . . maybe not health, she still looked tired, but with possibilities.

"You gave Mitch a reason to fight. You gave him something to fight *for*. When I met you, I saw a woman who was going to take my son away and hurt him more than he already has been, but that's what Chip made me realize.

Mitch could only hurt more if he didn't have you. Nothing matters without love."

"I do love him, Mrs. Sinclair."

"I know you do, and it scared me. It still does, and when you have children, you'll see for yourself one day. The people your kids meet and fall in love with, they don't take your children away, they add to your family. I'm not losing my son, I'm gaining a daughter. Isn't that how the saying goes?"

She sat up and wiped her cheeks. "Thank you, but Mitch is . . . well. He dumped me. We're not together."

"And I believe that like I believe there's a bridge for sale. The way Mitch talks about you, the way his eyes light up. You two aren't over. Not by a long shot. I know it's only been a few days, and if you're inclined to take a little advice, I say, have some fun. Enjoy each other. He needs that. You're the first woman since the accident who can look at him, who can . . . well, I'm not blind. I know when two people have been fooling around. You may take that for granted, but Mitch doesn't. You willing to be intimate while he looks the way he does . . ." Ruby blushed. "He'd get after me something awful if he knew what we were talking about."

Callie held her hand. "I know what you're saying. We talked a little bit about our past relationships, and the women he's dated treated him just as terribly as the people in this town. I can't promise I'll never hurt him because I've already done that, but I'll try my best to be there for him. To give him what he needs. Even if that means time apart, like now."

Ruby laughed. "Time apart? When was the last time you saw him?"

"I'm not sure," she said, frowning. "Twelve hours or so?"

"That doesn't sound like much time apart, if you ask me."

"Well—"

"I know my son," Ruby said, nudging her off the bed.

She slid off the mattress and stood by the chair.

Ruby followed and pulled the hem of her sweatshirt over her hips.

"Mrs. Sinclair, shouldn't you be—"

"I'm not on bed rest. I know my son," Ruby repeated, "and no offense, dear, but I know him better than you do. He'll come around, and sooner than you think. While we wait, we should eat a late lunch in the dining room. I'll text Chip, and he can meet us there."

"Oh, but I should—"

Ruby raised her eyebrows, and she laughed. "—Really eat lunch with you and Mr. Sinclair."

"That's a good choice, though I'm only allowed decaf coffee."

A ball of tension untangled in her chest and she blew out a breath. "We're going to get along, aren't we?"

"It's my fault you didn't think we would, but the truth is, I already love you like a daughter," Ruby said, catching her hand.

She didn't know what to say. To be included in Mitch's family meant more than she could put into words. "Thank you, but I don't feel like I deserve it. I've made a mess of everything."

"Nothing worth having comes easy," Ruby said, wiggling her feet into a pair of new tennis shoes. "Our lives are going to be different, and different doesn't have to mean bad. I think things are finally going to get better."

She shoved on her boots and walked with Ruby down

the empty hallway. It wasn't only Ruby's life, and Mitch's, and Chip's, Ruby was talking about. It was her life, too.

Her life would be different.

It would be better.

Ruby invited Callie to watch a movie in their room while they waited for Mitch to finish his shift, but dark shadows smudged beneath the woman's eyes and Callie declined, suggesting she get some rest instead. Chip gratefully agreed, told her a quick goodbye, and herded his wife down the hallway toward the stairs.

She stood in the lobby smiling in bewildered amusement.

Her smile faded as she thought about what to do for the rest of the day. She was welcome at Gail and Hugh's, but coming and going felt strange, and rather than driving to Marnie's parents' house, she drove to the *Rocky Point Daily Journal*'s offices.

She met Autumn outside the newspaper's building, digging through her purse, her hair hanging in her face. Callie had never seen her looking so disheveled.

"Autumn, I was just coming to see you."

She smiled, but it faded as her gaze darted past Callie's shoulder.

Callie frowned in concern. "Are you okay?" she asked, turning around.

A man stood across the street glaring, his hands tucked into the pockets of a worn work jacket.

He would've been attractive if he hadn't looked so mean.

"Who's that?" she asked, inching toward Autumn in a gesture of protection.

"My ex. Ignore him. I was going out to grab a bite to eat, but I changed my mind. Let's go back inside."

She made eye contact with the man and committed his dark blond hair and narrowed stare to memory. He watched them scurry into the lobby, a vicious snarl twisting his lips.

Autumn didn't slow, even when the receptionist threw them a puzzled look.

"Do I need to kick his ass?" she asked as they walked through the bullpen.

"No. Stay away from him."

"What's he doing here?"

Autumn took off her coat and hung it on the back of her chair. "In Rocky Point, you mean?"

"I guess so."

"He wants me to give him another chance. I don't want to."

"Does Cole know?" she asked, taking off her jacket too.

Autumn's head snapped up. "What does Cole have to do with anything?"

"Oh. I thought . . ."

"Don't think." Moaning, Autumn sank into her webbed chair, and with her foot, pushed the other toward Callie. "Sit. I hope you're not hungry. My appetite disappeared."

She sat in the chair, the murmur of voices and the clicking of fingers tapping on keyboards surrounding her. "No. I had lunch with Mitch's parents."

"How's Mrs. Sinclair doing?"

"Good. She looked good. She's a strong woman."

"She has to be, to put with all the shit these past few years have flung at her," Autumn said. "What can I help you with?"

"Nothing. I just wanted to thank you for the article that ran today. I think it will help."

"You're welcome, but you don't have to thank me. I think it will help, too, and I was happy to do it."

"How did you know about . . .?"

"What happened in the hospital parking lot? I have a source at the station. She called me when you and Mitch were giving your statements. Are you doing okay? Shaken up?" Autumn winced. "You're probably tired of people asking you that."

"It's nice so many people care," she said, hiding her hands in her sleeves and tucking them between her knees. "My dad started a collection campaign—"

"That was your dad? Excellent! Since you're here, can I interview you for the blog? I can get an article out of it, if you don't mind."

"I don't, as long as it will benefit Mitch and his family. But if you can, please keep my dad's name out of it. Maybe more people will donate if there isn't someone attached to the campaign."

"I completely understand, and it's no problem. The blog will get more eyes on it, and I sent Cole to the house yesterday to take a few pictures of what was left after the fire. We'll add them, too, and news about Luna. Is she okay?"

"Yeah. Mr. Sinclair thanked me for going in after her, and she's going to be fine."

They chatted for a while, the voice recorder Autumn used unnerving her, but after a few minutes she forgot about it and they were visiting freely by the time she ran out of things to say.

After being ambushed outside the hospital, a bad taste lingered in her mouth, and hugging Autumn goodbye, she said, "Be careful with that guy hanging around. If you need anything, and I mean *anything*, I'm staying at Marnie's mom and dad's."

"Thanks, but I'll be fine. Eventually he'll get tired of it and stop. Are you going to the dinner and dance Marnie and James are hosting at the resort? I need to look at the activities sheet, but I think it's coming up in a couple of days. She wants an excuse to get dressed up, and the open bar doesn't hurt."

"I'll be there. It sounds like fun, and I need to start being a better bridesmaid."

"Ask Mitch to go. It'd be nice if he started doing things again."

She shrugged. "Maybe I will. Talk to you later."

As she wove through the bullpen to reach the lobby, she ran into Cole. She nudged him aside and asked, "Did you know some weirdo is watching Autumn?"

Cole clenched his jaw. "He comes and goes. He's back, huh?"

"He was standing outside earlier. She was going to go eat lunch, but she changed her mind when she saw him. Will you bring her somewhere?"

Cole rubbed the back of his neck. "Well—"

"That was an hour ago," she said. "She's probably starving by now."

"Okay, yeah, I'll ask her. Catch ya later, Callie."

Cole stopped to chat with someone on the way to Autumn's desk, and waiting impatiently, she shifted from foot to foot.

He finally moved on, and Autumn glanced at him with an expression that looked like hope . . . but Cole said something and she shook her head.

Shit. Maybe they weren't as close as she thought.

Cole touched Autumn's shoulder, but she didn't yank away, not like an angry woman would. Instead, she picked up her jacket and purse.

Callie spun and hurried out of the building before they discovered her spying. To her relief, the man who'd been loitering near the street was gone.

Mitch texted Callie after his shift asking her to meet him at the resort. He had to catch her before she left town, and he hoped he wasn't too late. He'd counted on her sleeping in, packing her things, and saying goodbye to her friends. Maybe Marnie would convince her to stay. Part of his meeting with Desiree had included discussing a few activities Marnie and James were having at the resort, and he was sure Marnie would want her entire wedding party to attend them.

He was going to sit in the bar with Ivy while he waited for Callie to answer, but Jared Hollister stepped through the sliding glass doors and into the lobby, and Mitch paused, wondering what he was doing at the resort. Stomping the snow off his boots, Jared saw Mitch and lifted his chin in greeting.

"Are you here to see Leah?" he asked, then pursed his lips. He'd approached Jared like they were old friends, and even though Jared had invited him out, it could have been a generic courtesy.

But Jared didn't seem to think anything of it, only shook his head and jerked his thumb at a small conversational area near the shining floor-to-ceiling windows that looked over the lake. He didn't speak until he was perched on the edge of a white leather chair, his ball cap in his hands. "I need to talk to you for a second."

Mitch sat in an identical chair next to him, a table that was covered in local magazines positioned in front of them. "I'm sorry about the comment—"

"Don't worry about it. Leah and I *are* seeing each other. Don't know where that's headed, since she's from New York, but anyway. I took her snowmobiling with Marnie and James earlier today and I stopped by the arena after we got back, checked to see if anything happened while I was gone."

"Okay?"

Jared rolled his shoulders. "One of my maintenance guys was fixing a locker in the boys' locker room, and a group of high school kids came in after hockey practice. They were bullshitting like kids do. Girls, a weekend party, but then a couple of them started talking about the fire."

"The fire at my parents' house?" Mitch asked, confused.

"Yeah. One of the boys was a Dunlop. Ed's grandson. He was bragging about his grandpa teaching you a lesson for thinking this town had forgotten about what happened. Doesn't help that the girls would be in high school now. Ed's grandson was probably in elementary school with them."

He swallowed. "Ed Dunlop set the fire? We need to—"

"I already told the cops what Luke overhead. They said they'd look into it."

"I appreciate it," he said. "The police and the fire department haven't given us much information. I figured they don't care who did it."

"It's not a problem. Luke happened to be in the right place at the right time. You know those kids don't care about poor slobs like us, talked around him like he was invisible.

But I thought you should know. I hope it pans out for your mom and dad."

"Thanks. I can't imagine Ed being that angry because I was trying to go to a Bears game."

Jared shifted in his seat and looked down at the floor. "That's part of the reason I'm here. He was pretty pissed I fired him for kicking you and Callie out of the arena. He probably blamed you for losing his job, and I'm really sorry about that. If I would've known he'd do something so fucked up—"

"No. Don't think like that. I'm grateful that you did. It's more than what anyone else has done in a long time. You couldn't have known Ed would do something that, and, well, don't feel guilty if you're glad it wasn't your house. If Briar—that's your daughter's name, isn't it?—if Briar had been inside or . . ."

Blood drained from Jared's face. "I never thought about Ed targeting me like that. I've worked with him for so long that was the last thing that crossed my mind."

"No one wants to think that about another person, but it made us see things need to change. We're being pushed out. Once the news comes out it was Ed, there are people who'll side with him and won't be scared to tell us, either. It would've been easier if we'd jumped, as the saying goes, but at this point, it doesn't matter."

"I read Autumn's article in the *Journal* this morning. I'm sorry about what happened to Callie."

"She's tough. She'll be okay." He paused. "You and Leah all right?"

Jared laughed. "Nope. She's going to turn my life upside down. Already has in a lot of ways. Things will get worse before they get better. Anyway, I'll let you get back to your night. Meeting Callie?"

"I'm hoping. I have a few things I want to tell her. Things I should have told her a long time ago."

Jared slapped him on the shoulder. "Good luck, then. I'll catch you later."

"Yeah. Thanks again. Appreciate it."

He checked his phone. Callie still hadn't responded. He'd give her a little more time, then he'd hunt her down. Even if that meant driving to Decatur tonight to see her. He had some things he needed to say, and he wouldn't wait any longer.

A beer would calm his nerves, and he trudged into the bar to wait.

Ivy drew him a glass of his favorite beer they kept on tap. "How's it going? I haven't talked to you in a while."

Her willingness to pick their friendship up right where he let it fade off shamed him. "I'm sorry. Things have been busy."

"I know. I don't talk to anyone but you, and it's been a quiet week. For me, at least. I'm sorry. I'm being really selfish right now. How are your parents?"

"They're doing okay. In Callie's room, watching TV, I think. You're not being selfish, you just need more friends."

"It's tough to have friends when you're working all the time."

"Things still the same?"

She smiled ruefully. "Things will always be how they are."

"I hope not, for your sake." He sipped his beer.

"You're leaving, aren't you? One of the housekeepers heard you and Desiree talking and started spreading it around." She blinked back tears.

"Yeah. I gave her a couple months' notice. I'm going to

help my parents start the new year in Decatur, and I'll be moving there, too."

"So you can be with Callie?"

"No. Because I should have listened to what everyone was telling me. People don't want me here. They've held on to the resentment, the anger. The hate. They'll never let me forget what I did because *they* can't forget. My parents could have died. I'm not taking any more chances."

She dabbed her cheeks with a cocktail napkin. "But this is about Callie, too, isn't it?"

"Yeah. I love her, and I've been telling everyone but her. I texted her s little bit ago, and I'm hoping she'll text me back. I want to see her and put all this behind us."

"I hope you can."

"Thanks. Me too."

"What will you do for work?"

"I don't know. I'm hoping people will see past how I look, and there's a better chance in a big city that if they've heard about the accident, they won't care, or take it personally, at least. Mom and Dad are definitely looking forward to it. They've put up with a lot to stand by me."

"No one deserves a fresh start more than you. I'll be right back." Ivy walked down to the end of the bar and served a man wearing a suit who looked to be on a business trip, a black briefcase sitting on the floor near his stool.

He checked his phone, but Callie still hadn't messaged him.

More than likely she was on the road. He waited too long to contact her. He'd have to chase her down, then. After all his resistance and objections, it would take more than a six-hour round trip to convince her that he changed his mind and that he wanted her whether she was a firefighter or not. That would be a hurdle he'd have to jump over from time to time, but he wouldn't let her job keep him from loving her.

"Let me give you a hug goodbye," Ivy said, wiping her hands on a white rag.

"I'm not leaving for a while yet."

"I know," she said, coming out from behind the bar, "but you're going to be busy helping your mom and dad, and when you and Callie make up, you'll be spending all your free time with her. Don't feel bad about it, either. I'm happy you found her."

He drained his beer and slid off the barstool. He'd miss Ivy. They shared a commonality in being outcasts, being misfits in Rocky Point. Her for completely different reasons than him, but they'd bonded over having no one else.

It would be difficult to leave her behind.

Someone had already done that to her once.

"We'll always be friends, Ivy."

"I know, but it won't be the same." She stepped into his embrace and wrapped her arms around his waist. It would have been simple if he could have felt something for her. It would have been easy to move beyond friendship, if only his heart had played along.

He sighed. "Yeah. I know." He kissed the top of her head and closed his eyes.

When he opened them, Callie stood in the entry of the lounge. She backed slowly away and then turned and started running down the hallway toward the lobby.

CHAPTER TWELVE

In her mind, she knew that Mitch and Ivy were only friends. They'd told her that enough times Callie believed it for the truth it was.

But it didn't stop her heart from cracking, just a little bit, to see the thin, disheveled woman wrapped in Mitch's arms, his lips pressed to the top of her head and his eyes closed like there was nowhere else in the world he'd rather be.

"Callie! Callie, wait," Mitch shouted behind her.

She stopped but didn't turn around. "I didn't mean to interrupt."

"You didn't. I was telling her goodbye."

Dread balled in her stomach, and she whipped around in the middle of the lobby. "Where are you going?"

"I'm moving. We're moving. Can we talk? Somewhere more private than this?"

Standing behind the reservation counter, Sophia curiously looked at them, as did the couple checking in.

Nodding, she said, "Okay."

She followed him to his room, and when he shut the

door, she leaned against it, her hands shoved into the pockets of her jacket. She wanted to hold him and never let go.

Mitch took his time unbuttoning his work shirt, hanging it in a narrow closet. Wearing a white t-shirt and jeans, he sat on his bed and untied his boots. He pushed them out of the way with his foot. "How are you? Were you able to sleep okay?"

"Yeah, I slept fine. I didn't have nightmares, if that's what you're asking."

"Are you sore? He slapped you so hard."

The words brought back the crack of the asshole's palm meeting the side of her face, and she gritted her teeth, the shock of it traveling down her spine. "No, I've been taking ibuprofen."

Mitch stared at the floor. "I should have gotten there sooner."

She shook it off. She was safe in Mitch's room now. "You did what you could. I never . . . thanked you. For helping me. They would have done a lot worse if you hadn't shown up."

He met her eyes, and the amount of pain in his stole her breath.

"How are *you* doing?" she asked.

Standing from the bed, he asked her, "Do you remember when you called me to your room to check that outlet by the sink?"

She let herself smile. "How could I forget?"

He stood in front of her and slowly unzipped her jacket, the metal teeth rasping in the quiet. "You sat on that vanity in your little robe and watched me fuck around. I was rock hard, and I prayed to God you wouldn't notice."

"When you touched me, I didn't want you to stop." Her pulse quickened and her nipples hardened.

"Your skin is so soft, and you let me kiss you. I thought, Jesus Christ, what in the hell did I do to deserve this beautiful angel? Because that's what these seven years have felt like. Hell." He paused. "What did you see when you first looked at me, Callie?"

"A man who'd been hurt in a fire," she whispered.

He pushed her jacket off her shoulders, and her heart pounded so loudly she wouldn't have been surprised if he could hear it. She looked at him now, scar tissue marring the right side of his face, slippery and mottled pink and brown. The blaze puckered the skin down his neck, scars rippling under his shirt. He reached out to touch her hair, and the light glimmered against the scars on his arm, scar tissue stretched across his hand and knuckles.

She caught his fingers and pressed her lips to his palm.

"But you didn't change your opinion of me after you found out about the accident."

"No, I didn't."

"Why? Why didn't you feel the way people in town feel? Why didn't you hate me? Why weren't you disgusted I couldn't do my job to save all the kids on that bus?"

His voice was fire and smoke, and she stared into his shadowed eyes, hypnotized. He stood so close to her. She could kiss him, if she moved only an inch.

"Because I know what it's like."

"Because you know what it's like. Because you know what *what's* like, Callie?"

Tears dripped down her cheeks. "Because I know what it's like to lose someone."

"How many people have you lost on the job?"

She jerked away. "Why are we talking about this? I

already know how you feel about me and what I do. Do you want to rub it in I've lost lives? Do you want to hold it against me? Will it make you feel better?"

He recoiled. "No, of course not."

"I've lost three people. I've been a firefighter for eight years and I've lost three people. I wasn't fast enough. Wasn't strong enough. I couldn't find them in the smoke. When something like that happens, you have to make the choice. Keep looking and risk your own life, or be smart. In those circumstances, I had to save myself. There's no point in trying to do the impossible. All you end up doing is killing yourself."

"It's why you didn't give up on me, isn't it?"

"We all do the best we can. You did your best when you tried to reach those little girls. I do my best. When it's not good enough, it's no one's fault."

"I didn't believe that. I didn't believe it wasn't my fault."

She stepped into his arms and pressed her cheek against his hard chest. His shirt smelled of detergent and sweat. "It's not, but there isn't anything else I can say to convince you. You have to believe it for yourself."

"Do you?"

He brushed a hand down her hair, and she melted. It'd been too long since he'd touched her, and she missed him.

"It took me a long time to accept it, lots of therapy after every fire, but yeah, I do."

"I'm getting there, but I need you to be patient."

"I will, but you need help, too. There's no shame in getting help." She turned her head and rubbed her lips against his shirt. "I've missed you, so much. How you touch me, the way you're so gentle, like I could break any second." Abruptly, she stepped back. "But you made it clear how you feel about me and my job. If you asked me to meet you to tell me that there's no chance you could ever change your mind, then say it. I have my suitcase in the car and I'm ready to head out the minute we're done." It was a lie, but she wasn't going to stand here and let him drag this out because he wanted her but didn't want all of her. All of her flaws. All of her mistakes.

"No. That's not what I wanted to tell you. I wanted to say that I believe we were meant to be together. Because of what you do, you understand me in a way almost no one else on this earth can. You can call it whatever you want, but when I stepped into your room for the first time, when you looked at me and saw *me*, not my scars, not my vulnerabilities, not my weaknesses, that was Fate. Someone, or something, sent you to me, and instead of fighting it, instead of pushing you away, I need to hang on for dear life. Because you saved me, Callie, and I love you."

The words came out of his mouth slow and thick, but sweet. He stepped toward her and when she didn't move away, he skimmed his fingers over her damp cheek, down to her mouth where her lip was still puffy. "Don't go back to Decatur. Not without me."

She let out a sob and launched herself into his arms.

He caught her and hugged her, tangling his fingers in her hair. "Stay with me," he said, and she nodded against his shoulder.

"Yeah, I will," she said, her voice muffled.

He turned off the light, but the glow from the stove's bulb in his kitchenette kept them from standing in complete darkness. His room didn't have a window and he'd never minded until now—Callie deserved starshine and moonlight—but the dim light would be enough. He smoothed his hands down her arms and pulled her sweater over her head.

She wore a tank top under her sweater, and he pulled that off too, revealing a lacy bra. "Does this mean we aren't broken up anymore?" he asked, cuddling her against his chest. He nuzzled her neck with his lips.

"We were never broken up. Not really."

He chuckled. She was right. He never felt like they were broken up because no matter how much he denied it, he knew he could never live without her. "You're a wise woman."

"Ah, your mom pointed that out when we had lunch this afternoon."

"Let's not talk about my mom now," he said, tugging on her hand and leading her through the shadows to his bed. "I do have some news about that, but right now, all I can think about is getting you out of your panties."

"Mitch Sinclair, that's not very romantic," she said, laughing, playfully pushing him away as he reached for the zipper of her jeans.

"I'm romantic. I'm super romantic." He kissed her belly, eased the denim over her hips, and said a humbled prayer of thanks when she ran her fingers through his hair, nudging him closer.

He'd been stupid, blind and stupid, but she wouldn't hold that against him.

She would accept his apology, would accept him and all that he was, and from now on, they would only think about the future.

He unclasped her bra, tossed it onto the floor, and pulled back his bedding. She kicked off her boots and her jeans, and wiggled out of her panties, throwing them in the general direction of the rest of her clothes.

She slipped into his double bed, the largest his room would allow, and watched him undress. He didn't feel any apprehension taking off his clothes, didn't worry she'd flinch at what she saw. This woman loved all of him, and he would never take it for granted.

He slid between the sheets, and she curled her body around his. It wasn't any time at all before her hands discovered how much he wanted her. He closed his eyes and let her play, her fingertips brushing over his cock and the pre-cum gathering at the tip, and enjoyed being with her, sinking into her warm kiss.

"I'm sorry," he murmured against her lips.

"Me too," she said, wiggling farther up his chest.

He rolled, reversing their positions, and wrapped his arms around her. Tenderly, he pushed inside her, and she lifted her hips, asking for all of him, like he knew she always would. They were as close as two people could be, and it didn't feel like it would ever be enough.

He reached between their bodies and circled his finger around her clit. She gasped, arching her back. "Please," she cried, gripping his biceps. Mitch felt the second she was about to come, her muscles hugging his cock, and her body pulsed around him as the orgasm quivered through her body. Unable to keep control, he followed a second later, his body rigid with a pleasure he didn't think he'd ever experience again. When he was finished, he collapsed on top of her, hot and sweaty. He tried to move off her to give her room to breathe, but she didn't let him go, panting and giggling into his neck.

He laughed. "I'm too heavy for you."

"Just for a minute." She kissed him, slipping her tongue into his mouth.

"You're insatiable," he said, amused, resting his forehead against hers.

"Hardly. You're still inside me. I think you're the one who can't get enough."

"I'll never tire of you, Callie." He met her eyes and brushed her hair away from her face. "This may have been too quick, we've known each other barely a week, but I'll never get tired of you and I'll never leave you. You've given me back a piece of myself I lost in the fire. That piece is you, and I'll always feel broken if we aren't together."

"That's sweet," she said, rubbing his scarred cheek, "but we'll take it slow. This has been a week full of terrible things, and I still feel guilty about your parents' house. We both need to have some fun. We need that. A little fun."

"That means a lot to me. I need to learn that I can enjoy life again, that I have a right to be able to enjoy life again, and if my life has you in it, it will be that much easier. Thank you."

"You're welcome."

He slid off her and spooned her lithe body from behind. She wiggled into him and pressed her lips to his hand clasped in hers.

"Jared Hollister stopped by to see me earlier," he said, his chin grazing the top of her head. "His maintenance man at the arena overheard some boys talking in the locker room, and it turns out Ed Dunlop set my parents' house on fire, to get revenge, I guess, for losing his job."

She rolled over to face him. "That's crazy. I'm so sorry."

"At least now we know who did it."

"Is he going to report it?"

"He already did."

"Good." She paused. "I wanted to ask you about that. How did your parents not hear him? Arsonists wait until nighttime to set fires. To cover their tracks, and also because fires attract more attention in the dark. How did your parents not hear Ed in their kitchen? He must have broken something to get inside."

He'd asked his dad that very same question, and while he was a grown man, talking to a woman he'd just made love with, the answer burned his throat.

"Mitch? What were your parents doing? It wasn't that early in the morning. They should have been up and moving around by then."

"Well. You know."

"No. I don't—" She sucked in a breath. "Oh."

"Yeah, apparently they were having a really good time, and they didn't hear anything."

She started laughing.

He sat up. "It's not funny—oh, hell, yes, it is," he said, and he started laughing, too.

Listening to Mitch laugh smoothed over the jagged tears the last few days had ripped into her soul. She sat up and scooted between his legs, and he wrapped his arms around her. "But what about Luna?"

"All I can think is that Ed doesn't live that far from my parents, another reason, I think, he chose my parents' house instead of going after Jared, since he lives on the other side of town."

"Holy shit, I didn't even think of that."

"He didn't either, but he hasn't had a reason to live on

the defensive like I have. Anyway, when my dad would take Luna for walks, they would bump into Ed sometimes. Luna knew him. It's the only explanation I can come up with. Otherwise, she would have torn into whoever tried to get into the house."

"That makes sense."

"I asked Desiree if my parents could keep her in their room. She was reluctant to say yes, but she's not as tough as she wants people to think she is. I'm going to pick her up at the vet's tomorrow."

"That's nice of her, and I'm sure your dad will be relieved. He can't stop thanking me for rescuing her. So," she said, shifting away. She wanted to look him in the face when she told him her news. "You're moving to Decatur."

"Yeah. Mom and Dad are, too. There's too much to deal with here. You were right when you said I shouldn't let people treat me like shit, but sweetheart, no one in town is going to change their mind. I can take the blame for that, if you want me to. I didn't stand up for myself when it mattered, and that was my mistake. But it's too late. No amount of blogging, or any articles Autumn writes, will make anyone think differently. Her article might have swayed some people, but not for the long-term. I can't keep asking my parents to go through this because I'm a stubborn fool who doesn't know when to quit."

"You'd move, then, even if we didn't work out."

"Callie, moving to a city where you live, that's a bonus. Whether I tried to tough it out here, or if my parents and I decided to move to Marengo or somewhere else, it wouldn't matter. I'd make this work wherever we are because I love you. Something you haven't said back to me, if you think I haven't noticed."

She grabbed his hand. Her fingertips bumped over the

ripples of his scars. "Because I need to tell you something, and then you can decide if you still want to hear it."

"You're scaring me a little bit."

"I'm sorry. I don't mean to." She blew out a breath. "I know you have a problem with me being a firefighter—"

"No. That was me being stupid. I told you that because you're a firefighter you're able to accept who I am, and it's a gift. I was wrong to tell you I couldn't handle it. What you do for other people . . . it makes you even more special to me."

"Shit. Really? Because as of this morning, I'm not a firefighter anymore."

"What? Did you quit for me?" he frowned, and she rubbed her fingers against his lips.

"I didn't quit for you. I quit for me. I decided to stay in Rocky Point for the full two weeks Marnie blocked out for her wedding because I was burnt out. Brandon checked himself into rehab, and I was close to doing the same. I was tired. But our dad . . . he's captain of our department and wouldn't even listen to me talk about taking a break. He and my mom had breakfast with Brandon this morning, and he called me afterward. What Brandon told him must have finally gotten through, and he said if I wanted to quit, I should quit. His approval meant a lot to me, more than it should have. I'm rambling." She wouldn't try to fit her and her father's history into this conversation. They'd have plenty of time to talk about that. "He gave me an out without making me feel weak or unloved, and I accepted."

"Sweetheart," he said, hugging her closer, "I'll support whatever you want to do."

"Thanks. That means a lot to me, too. I don't know what I want to do yet. I have some money saved, and I don't need to look for work right away. Maybe I'll go back to school. I can help you and your parents find a place in Decatur. I have a townhouse, but—"

"I should live in my own place for a little while. I'll have a lot of adjusting to do, and I know there will be value in going through some of that alone, in a place where there won't be so much bitterness and resentment."

She smiled, but sniffled, too. "Maybe not *all* alone." She paused. "This is going to work, isn't it?"

"Yeah. I'm going to do whatever it takes, to make sure it does. I put in a two months' notice here. I have a little saved up, too." He held her chin between his finger and thumb and touched his nose to hers. "What do you say we help my parents find a place to live, then we take a vacation. Preferably somewhere warmer than fifteen below?"

"Really?"

"Really. I mean, I can't guarantee my parents won't want to come . . ."

"They can use some of the money from the collection campaign."

"How do you know about that?"

She smothered a laugh. "My dad started it."

"He did?"

"Yeah. Brandon told him a few things about us, and he checked into you and what happened. Autumn's going to add the link to a blog post she's putting together. I talked to her this afternoon and gave her another interview. My dad said he wants to meet the man I'm going to marry."

He cleared his throat. "I'd like to, but I need time."

She snuggled in his embrace and said, "I know. I do, too. Not being a firefighter anymore will be strange. Good, but strange. Let's take it one day at a time."

"You still haven't told me, Callie."

Feigning ignorance, she flopped onto her back and

stretched her arms above her head. "I have no idea what you're talking about. You know all my secrets now."

He slid his fingers between her breasts and down her belly. "This isn't a secret. I want you to tell everyone you know."

"That I love you?"

He laid beside her and propped his head in his hand. "You can get rid of the question mark, if you don't mind."

She laughed. "I love you, Mitch."

He kissed her, and this time she caught the subtle notes of beer.

"Will Ivy be okay without you here?"

"Callie—"

"No, I mean that, really. I've spoken with her a little, and she seems troubled."

"Let's just say, I'm glad I'll be staying here until after Marnie's wedding."

"What's going on?"

"Nothing we need to talk about now."

"Then what should we talk about?"

He pulled the sheet and bedspread over their bodies. "How about we don't talk?"

"That's a good idea."

She tilted her head as he kissed his way from her ear to her shoulder. "Who knew my life would change because I needed the maintenance man?"

"I thought we weren't talking?" he mumbled, his breath whispering over her skin.

"We're not. I'm only thinking aloud. How grateful I am my sink needed fixing."

"I fixed your sink. You fixed me. It was an even trade. Now stop talking."

His lips captured hers, she had no choice.

She wrapped her legs around his waist and succumbed to him and all he had to offer. Her life would change, for the better.

Mitch's would, too.

First, she'd enjoy the rest of her vacation and watch her best friend marry the love of her life.

Now she could stand next to Marnie confident that one day, she would do the same.

Jared and Leah's story is now available! *His Frozen Dreams* is available on Kindle, in Kindle Unlimited, and Paperback.

Do you like billionaire romance? Sign up for my newsletter and receive a free standalone novel, an ugly-duckling billionaire romance, *My Biggest Mistake*. There you'll be the first to know about sales, new releases, and what I'm working on. Don't miss out! Go to www.vmrheault.com/subscribe.

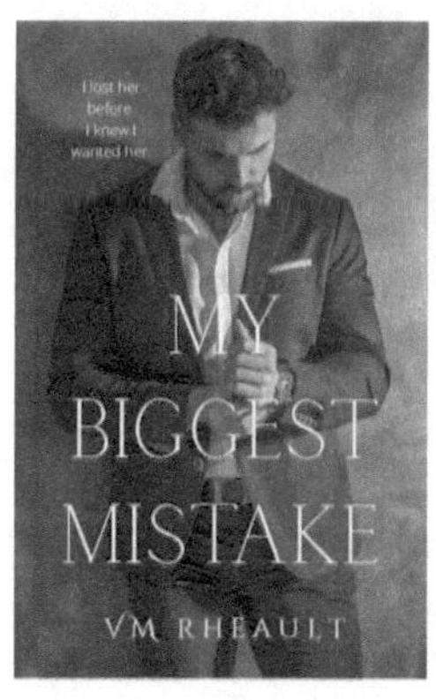

ACKNOWLEDGMENTS

Thank you to Tina Poppler Sather, Chris Smith, and Rob Fish, my high school friends who live in International Falls, MN, (the small town where Rocky Point, MN is loosely based and my hometown) for answering my questions about how things are now. I haven't walked on a frozen Rainy Lake for twenty-five years. And yeah, I just cried a little typing that.

Also thank you to Gareth S. Young for proofing these for me. I appreciate your time.

One last thank you to all my friends who support me, be it in real life or the various Facebook groups I'm a part of. Writing this series was a fun, wild ride, and I couldn't have kept my sanity without you.

(A Steamy Enemies to Lovers Standalone)

His Frozen Heart

(A Rocky Point Wedding Book One)

His Frozen Dreams

(A Rocky Point Wedding Book Two)

Her Frozen Memories

(A Rocky Point Wedding Book Three)

Her Frozen Promises

(A Rocky Point Wedding Book Four)

As VM Rheault

Captivated by Her (Cedar Hill Duet Book One)

Addicted to Her (Cedar Hill Duet Book Two)

Rescue Me

Give & Take (The Lost & Found Trilogy Book One)

Lost & Found (The Lost & Found Trilogy Book Two)

Safe & Sound (The Lost & Found Trilogy Book Three)

Faking Forever

Twisted Alibis (Ghost Town Trilogy Book One)

Twisted Lullabies (Ghost Town Trilogy Book Two)

Twisted Lies (Ghost Town Trilogy Book Three)

A Heartache for Christmas

Cruel Fate (King's Crossing Book One)

Cruel Hearts (King's Crossing Book Two)

Cruel Dreams (King's Crossing Book Three)

Shattered Fate (King's Crossing Book Four)

Shattered Hearts (King's Crossing Book Five)

Shattered Dreams (King's Crossing Book Six)

ABOUT THE AUTHOR

Vania Rheault has lived in Minnesota all her life. In 2003, she graduated with a BA in English with a concentration in creative writing from Minnesota State University, Moorhead. When she's not writing, she's sleeping, working her day job, or going to movie night with her sister. Find her at vmrheault.com